THE TAXIMAN'S GOD

By the same author

FICTION

Dance Under the Pink Hibiscus

Wise Men

NONFICTION

Modern Tithing: Religious Taxation in the Post-Christian Era

Deconstructing Marriage

WITH THE CREATIVE WRITERS PROJECT

Laughing Lions

THE TAXIMAN'S GOD

AND
OTHER STORIES

W. SCOTT NEWMANN JR.

iUniverse, Inc.
New York Lincoln Shanghai

THE TAXIMAN'S GOD
AND OTHER STORIES

iUniverse books may be ordered through booksellers or by contacting:

iUniverse
2021 Pine Lake Road, Suite 100
Lincoln, NE 68512
www.iuniverse.com
1-800-Authors (1-800-288-4677)

ISBN-13: 978-0-595-36736-8 (pbk)
ISBN-13: 978-0-595-81156-4 (ebk)
ISBN-10: 0-595-36736-4 (pbk)
ISBN-10: 0-595-81156-6 (ebk)

Printed in the United States of America

FOR TERRY

Contents

❀

Foreword . . . . *xi*

By Malevolence

The Tryst 3
excerpted from Children of Wrath

By War

The Barricade 13

By Mental Homicide

Sweetie 39
excerpted from Children of Wrath

By Self-Murder

The El 53

By Justice

The Ice Bullet 61

By Indifference

La Guardia's Sin 73

By Infirmity

Delicious Ambiguity 81

By Accident
Dance Under the Pink Hibiscus. 87
        previously published as a novella

By Age
anno domini 135

By Sacrifice
The Exchange. 143

By Design
Surf Sleep 153

By Surprise
The Taximan's God. 157
Afterword. 213

Acknowledgements

I would like to thank Beverly Shay for her careful review of this manuscript and her valuable suggestions as to this work's mechanics. In addition I extend special thanks to the following professionals: to Trudy Fedorko, MD, for her invaluable and specific assistance in regard to medical trauma and to Jeff Shook, MS, LPC, for his striking insight into *emotional death.* I would also like to bless my sister Terry for her candid expressions of fear, hope, pain and joy as she passed from this world into the next, to Beulah Eden for her frank dialogue regarding the spiritual dimensions of suicide, Warren Lunt for his prophetic insight into the mind and heart of our God and, of course, my dear wife, for her untiring support of my many projects. Finally, I fully recognize the debt owed to the consummate, Eternal Father who sits and weeps at the feet of all his children…even me.

Gratias ago vos, Abbas.

—SN

Foreword

"God hath kept the power of death in his own hands, lest any man should bribe death. If man knew the gain of death, the ease of death, he would solicit; he would provoke death to assist him by any hand which he might use.

But, O my God, my God, do I that have this fever need other remembrances of my mortality? Is not mine own hollow voice, voice enough to pronounce that to me?

All mankind is of one author, and is one volume; when one man dies, one chapter is not torn out of the book, but translated into a better language; and every chapter must be so translated; God employs several translators; some pieces are translated by age, some by sickness, some by war, some by justice; but God's hand is in every translation, and his hand shall bind up all our scattered leaves again for that library where every book shall lie open to one another."

—John Donne

BY MALEVOLENCE

"Even at our birth, death does but stand aside a little. And every day he looks towards us and muses somewhat to himself whether that day or the next he will draw nigh."

—Robert Bolt

THE TRYST

He adjusted the mist setting on his wipers to a slower speed to accommodate the fading storm and turned off the Interstate into Alexandria where he had been asked to come. He also changed out the cassette, preferring the sweeter, more romantic tones of Patsy Cline to the guilt-ridden lyrics of Waylon Jennings.

Alexandria had been founded in 1749 by George Washington, or so he had been told, and was, therefore, one of the oldest communities near D.C. General George had actually lived there. As a matter of fact, several other historical figures had lived there including Robert E. Lee. Every time Phil entered a township like this he became sentimental. The tall oaks and willows guarding each pristine home and estate combined to give the weight of historic virility. A lot had happened in towns like this, he thought.

Accelerating through an amber traffic light, he scanned each side streets for any sign of the playing fields Linda had mentioned. What were her words exactly? "Exit off the highway into Alexandria and follow Keene Mill Road until you see some soccer or baseball fields or something. When you pass the fields, turn into the next neighborhood on Argus and just follow till it dead ends. I'll meet you there." This last was punctuated with a desperate "Hurry!"

Linda had always been good at devising secret places for them to meet. Their first liaison following their initial meeting was one Agatha Christi would have admired. He remembered the directions she had given then, too. "Take the Metro to the Mall, stop at Union Station and walk to the Library of Congress. Be there at noon and I'll pick you up. Don't worry about finding me, I'll find you." It was totally insane, but he loved the whole cloak and dagger thing. When he had arrived that day, the weather had just turned cold, the wind picking up and rushing furiously through the ancient maples in front of the Capital across the street. He had done as she had asked and arrived in front of the

Library a few minutes before noon. The traffic had been heavy and the people, bundled against the biting wind, rarely looked up from the pavement. Before he knew it a dirty blue Honda pulled up to the curb and she motioned out the window for him to get in. He obliged and was whisked away to some invisible, Bohemian-like coffee house near Georgetown University. He hadn't frequented places like that in over a decade and felt painfully awkward. He hadn't even been fond of these places back then. But Linda, watching his chagrin, ran an inviting hand across his thigh under the table and leaned over to whisper in his ear.

"You look like a fish out of water," she giggled. Phil just looked into those eyes and nodded. All he wanted to do was go back to her place or a hotel room or something, but it was evident that Linda had other plans. Rising from their tiny round table, pulling his hand behind her, she nodded and smiled at a young, sparsely bearded waiter and led Phil to the back of the tiny room. Phil noticed the waiter return the smile and then gaze wantonly at Linda's behind as she waltzed through the crowd.

Devlyn's was just the one cramped room and most hours was populated by Georgetown coeds, a few professors and many of the 60s throwbacks common to D.C. around that time. Local legend had it that the proprietor came to the east coast decades before from the open cities of Texas in an effort to escape the heat. On her expedition through the major east coast cities she had arrived in Washington and promptly fell passionately in love with a Georgetown law student. Their romance, kindled as it was on a law school campus, flowered in bistros and late-night coffee houses, where their discussions would often endure till dawn. Devlyn decided to stay and, as the story goes, opened a little coffee house near the campus so she could find comfort in the huddled conversations of young hearts. Brother, Phil thought, what BS.

Elbowing his way through the crowd and holding on to Linda like a tow-cable his mind reeled seeing the state to which human beings had fallen. He remembered when he had been in college and the time he had wasted in places like this, but since his eyes had been opened by the business, everything he saw was viewed in the stark light of comparison. The atmosphere of his business was pristine and surgical; he was a winner and so were those with whom he associated. Comparing it to the smoke-filled, tumultuous bistro surrounding him was disastrous and nearly made him want to flee. Yet, as he passed a professor, replete with long, gray ponytail, in an impassioned, philosophical debate with some young students, he felt somehow quickened. At least there was life here. Life, but sadly, no real purpose.

Their journey to the dim back quarters of Devlyn's complete, Linda opened a clapboard door labeled, DISCUSSION. The word was scrawled in purple tempera on the chipped white enamel and decorated with psychedelic flowers and a peace sign. There was no doorknob or latch on the door as far as he could see, just a spring at the top which held it closed. In fact, she opened the door by means of a two-inch round hole cut in the wood where the knob should have been. A small sign dangled on the outside of the door by means of a knotted string passed through the hole and on it was written the word, OPEN. Once on the other side of the portal, they found well-worn stairs leading up to a sunlit unknown, and as they entered Linda reached back and turned the faded, dog-eared paper sign over to read, IN SESSION! Just as the door slapped shut, Phil heard a young male voice call after them, "Hey, Kat, how're you doing?" But she ignored him and climbed the narrow flight.

Phil trailed behind her up the stairs, twice bumping his head on the low ceiling until they emerged in a very tiny garret apartment, with a rusted iron bed in one corner and a small fireplace in the wall next to it. He had barely gotten to the top of the stairs before Linda was undressing him. His surprise and tangible fear of lack of privacy caused him to resist, but she pulled him to the bed tearing at his clothes and hers until he capitulated. They made love till the sun, which poured through the single window, slanted in afternoon orange and the restaurant below quieted with the lull before dinner.

Holding her in his arms afterward, Phil remembered the young man who had called her Kat and asked her what that meant…she only smiled and kissed his neck.

There were several other rendezvous like that and always in unusual and hidden locations. Linda was playful and adventurous and it thrilled him, but always and forever she was a mystery. The questions he had asked about her past she ignored and when he had attempted to tell her about his own situation, she demurred.

"I don't want to know about you, about your wife which you might or might not have, your children if any—I only want to know you inside me." If not an open book, she was undeniably insatiable when it came to sex. And for some reason she had chosen him.

This aspect of Linda he enjoyed. It was as if she could consume him and still not be satisfied. But sometimes her desires crossed boundaries that even Phil had not dared venture over and he found himself, in those moments, exhilarated by her, frightened by her. She was real and she cared for him, but the evidence of her passion told a story that could not be denied—she had a past and wanted a future. Not surprisingly, the one aspect of him that she sought information about was his business. What did he do, how did it work, who was in it with him, could anybody do it, how did the money work? She never tired of asking questions or listening to him talk. And he never tired of giving her answers.

Glancing to his right, Phil noticed the playing fields Linda had mentioned and slowed his car to begin to look for Argus. The clock in the dash read 12:15 p.m.

He was not unaccustomed to driving alone at night, in fact he liked it, and it had become almost a regular event now. Several years earlier when he was working at his J.O.B., it would have been a problem had he come home late. Let's face it, a purchasing agent at J.C. Penney's did not punch out at 11:00 p.m. But Jackie was trained now. Opportunity meetings were held at night, beginning at 8:00 p.m., sharp and ending whenever the last *newbie* left. Even then, they sometimes lasted well into the wee hours of the morning. Over the past two years as he toiled to reach the next level of recognition he conducted more and more meetings, sometimes five or six in one week. It was only in the last few days, with the advent of his relationship with Linda, that he shortened his weekly schedule so he could spend more time with her. Of course Jackie was unaware of this and he fed the illusion by dressing in his suit on evenings when he was to meet Linda, as if he were going off to "draw circles."

There was Argus, he grimaced in satisfaction and turned his Cadillac onto the dark rain swept street. The storm, which had abated earlier, was again flexing its muscle.

Argus was not a long street, in fact, it was only about 10 blocks. Turning his headlights off he tried to follow the curve of the road by the light of two dim street lamps, but with the rain and the slapping of his wipers it was difficult at best. Crawling forward a few feet at a time he found the dead end at last, and not seeing anyone there, turned his car so he would be facing up the street. On his right was one of the largest houses in the neighborhood with a narrow sidewalk separating him from its expansive lawn. He readied himself to drive away if any lights came on. But as he sat there with the rain roaring on the cabriolet top and Patsy Cline crooning in the background, he realized that it would not be easily explained if he were to be discovered here after midnight. Immediately he cursed under his breath his agreement to meet Linda tonight. His mind calculated the risk in dollars while the clock in the dash ran the tab.

If she didn't arrive in a few more minutes he was leaving he decided, checking the electric door locks for the third time. The one thing he didn't need was some nervous homeowner calling the police, or worse yet, a patrol car cruising by *after* Linda was with him. The longer he sat, the more this meeting didn't make sense and had she not been crying when she called, he probably would have already left. Just as he was about to drop the car in gear and drive away, angry with himself for being so foolish, he saw a small, dark figure, head down and hands shoved deeply into raincoat pockets striding toward him on the sidewalk. Turning off the stereo, he held his breath for a second, but as the figure came closer he recognized the long tapered legs and spike heeled shoes. It was Linda.

Punching the electric lock open, he looked on in surprise as Linda opened the car door and plopped onto his leather seats completely soaked and slammed the door. She wore a black plastic raincoat but for some unknown reason she was without a rain hat or even an umbrella. Her hair was a dark and tangled mess, with rivulets of water streaming down her face and all over the seats. The black leggings she wore appeared soaked through and her shoes, as much as he liked them, were probably ruined.

"What in the world happened to you?" he asked in amazement. In all the time he had known Linda he had never seen her out of control. But when she got into the car and the dome light came on, he could see by the mascara running down her cheeks and total lack of concern for her appearance that something was seriously wrong. "Where's your car?"

"You know I don't have a car," she responded staring down at her lap. "Besides, I wanted to walk." That was typical Linda, he thought.

"So why *didn't* you borrow your friend's car? What happened?" The questions he wanted to ask were too many, too soon.

"I had to see you tonight, that's all. Is that all right?" There was rising anger in her voice and he decided to leave it alone. For a moment they just sat together in the dark listening to the rain pelt the car and her breathing as it came in short exasperated bursts. The glow from the instrument panel didn't reveal much except the glistening coat and the total mess of her hair and he was tempted to turn the dome light back on, but the nearness of the "neighbors" prevented him.

"I was glad to get your call tonight," he lied. Nothing. "Why don't we go to that coffee house you like so much, what was it, Devlyn's?" he asked, beginning to put the car into gear.

"No," she said sharply, her hands thrust deeply in her pockets. "I want to stay here. I want to talk."

"OK," he said relaxing. They sat for another second and then he reached out to hold her hand.

"DON'T!" she shrieked, pulling away from him and huddling tighter in the corner.

"What the hell is wrong, Linda?" Phil demanded, worried now. She had not been like this ever, he thought. Jeez, what could've happened to turn her off so hard. "You're going to talk to me, Linda. Right now, do you hear? I want to know what happened. Did somebody hurt you? Did I do something, forget something? I'm sorry, whatever it is, OK? Just talk to me!"

His pleadings seemed to fade away into the darkness and the white sound of the rain falling all around them. She sat and sniffled and he sat and stared at her. Nothing happened.

Finally, she cleared her throat and spoke.

"You could at least offer me a handkerchief," she said sniffling, her hands in her pockets. Phil sighed heavily and straightened his right leg out, leaning to his left so he could reach back to his rear pocket. Taking his eyes from her, he glanced out the drowning windshield at the two street lamps which burned mutely down the street.

Linda watched Phil struggling with the linen, trying to dislodge it from his pocket. For an instant she hesitated, observing how desperate he seemed to please her. In the same instant another scene crossed her mind—him struggling desperately, passionately to meet her needs over the past two weeks. But like all visions, in less than a second it vanished. At that moment, with cold precision and practiced skill, Linda withdrew the .25 caliber pistol from her rain coat pocket, put its black muzzle in the cup of Phil's right ear and pulled the trigger.

Linda felt the air in the car constrict as the concussion of the blast swept around her. She winced in pain as her ears compensated and it seemed, not only was the oxygen compressed in the car, but time as well, compressed and expanded. Her eyes sought Phil's eyes at the instant the silver-tip bullet shattered his brain stem. It was a game she played. He blinked and seemed to make an effort to look in her direction, but the light of his mind drained away before his body could make the trip.

As often as she had done this, she could never get over how time slowed to play out every detail, like a novice magician who enjoys repeating his tricks. She saw with perfect clarity the bullet entering Phil's head and how he stiffened as if to receive it, like children do when being inoculated for tetanus. She also saw the extremity of death as it captured his heart, the weak, uncontrolled shaking as his body died. The muzzle blast had been exceptionally bright, like the flash of a camera, and in its light she had seen the triumphant fountain of blood from the wound.

For a moment she sat still in the car. Phil slumped behind the wheel, his eyes staring vacantly down toward the center console, one hand still in his back pocket. Linda could feel his blood running in her hair, off her face, taste it on her lips—it was now time to go. Grabbing the latch she threw open the door and stepped out onto the sidewalk and into the rain. Still holding the pistol in her left hand she reached an extended right finger down to the power locks and depressed the button. Just as she placed her hand on the door to push it closed she had a thought. Leaning down one last time into the car, she reached out and flicked on the stereo, turning the volume up so country swing once again filled the air. Then straightening up, she bumped the door closed with her hip and walked around the car into the street.

As if on cue, a faded blue Honda slid out of the darkness next to Phil's idling Cadillac. The man behind the wheel glared at Linda, who stood in the street face to the clouds allowing the rain to wash the blood away. After longer than he liked, she dropped her eyes to his then proceeded around the front of the car and to the passenger door where she opened it and got in. Once inside, she let out a deep breath and shook her wet hair. Then, like a doctor after surgery, she grasped the heel of the surgical glove on her left hand and pulled it over and off her fingers. She then repeated the operation with the right hand which still held the .25 caliber pistol. As she drew the glove off her palm the fine elastic stretched and covered the snub-nosed automatic completely. "How'd it go?" the man at the wheel asked as he drove down to the dead end and turned around.

"Like what you'd expect," she answered casually. Nodding with satisfaction, he accelerated past the dark car parked at the curb and headed up Argus to Keene Mill and then to the highway. Linda stared out the front windshield as they passed Phil in his car.

"How do you feel?" the man asked, looking at Linda as she began to restore her makeup with the help of a lighted, vanity mirror.

"I'm hungry," was her only response and the man smiled, picking up a small cellular phone and punching in a long distance number.

"Hi," he said when the line connected, "let me talk to him." He waited for ten minutes with the phone shoved under his chin, negotiating the early morning traffic and cursing under his breath. Linda smirked at his pained expressions, but continued with her makeup.

"Hello? Yeah, it's me…Nah, we're on the road now. Yeah. Yeah, it's done, no sweat." With that the man looked over at Linda and nodded approvingly. She smiled. "What? No, hell, Kat's fine, I told you she was a pro. Nah, she says she's hungry. O.K., I'll tell her. Yeah, no sweat. I'm on a plane tomorrow out to you. Good…" and he terminated the call.

"My employer extends his sincere appreciation for handling everything so…*neatly*," he said, leaning heavily on the last word.

"That's fine," Kat said, having finished with her face and moving on to her hair. "But doesn't your employer have some *tangible* thanks he'd like to give me, say 10,000 more little thank yous?"

"That's why I like working with you, Kat; you're always thinking ahead." Nudging her arm, he gestured to the back seat where a small workout bag lay. Kat held her hair up with her right hand and reached into the back to retrieve the bag. Once it was snuggled in her lap she opened it and began reviewing the contents.

"All headliners, I see," she said holding up a neatly bound bundle of $20 bills.

"You'll find an extra $5000 in there, Kat," the man said with a more serious tone. "There may be another *situation* in our immediate future and I suggested to my boss that we keep you close at hand. Do you see any problem with staying in touch?"

"I don't know. Will this situation involve as final a conclusion as this last situation?"

"I doubt it," he replied turning on to the Washington Street Bridge. "But if we should need some help it will require your…well, your special talents." Tom ran his eyes down the length of Kat's body and smiled.

"That can get expensive," she said noticing his apparent amusement.

"So what else is new? Say, where you wanna eat? You said you were hungry." Kat stared at the Potomac as they passed over the bridge and squeezed together her brightly painted lips, evening their color.

"How about seafood?" she said finally, depressing a window button and watching the glass hum down. Leaning out, her hair streaming. she heaved the latex wrapped pistol far over the bridge's railing and out into the swirling waters of the river.

BY WAR

"Death is patiently making my mask as I sleep. Each morning I awake to discover in the corners of my eyes the small tears of his wax."

—*Philip Dow*

THE BARRICADE

"Of what was the barricade made? Of the ruins of three six-story houses, torn down for the purpose, said some. Of the prodigy of all passions, said others. It had the woeful aspect of all the works of hatred: Ruin. You might say; who built that? You might also say; who destroyed that? It was the improvisation of ebullition. Here! That door! That grating! That shed! That casement! That broken furnace! That cracked pot! Bring all! Throw on all! Push, roll, dig, dismantle, overturn, tear down all! It was the collaboration of the pavement, the pebble, the timber, the iron bar, the ship, the broken square, the stripped chair, the cabbage stump, the scrap, the rag, and the malediction...

"You saw there, in a chaos full of despair, rafters from roofs, patches from garrets, with their wallpaper, window sashes with all their glass planted in the rubbish, awaiting artillery, chimneys torn down, wardrobes, tables, benches, a howling topsy-turvy, and those thousand beggarly things, the refuse even of the mendicant, which contain at once fury and nothingness. One would have said that it was the tatters of a people, tatters of wood, of iron, of bronze, of stone and that the Faubourg Saint Antoine had swept them there to its door by one colossal sweep of the broom, making of its misery its barricade. Logs shaped like chopping blocks, dislocated chains, wooden frames with brackets having the form of gibbets, wheels projecting horizontally from the rubbish amalgamated with this edifice of anarchy the forbidding form of the old tortures suffered by the people. The barricade Saint Antoine made a weapon of everything..."

—*Victor Hugo from Les Miserables*

CALMENTÉ

Calmenté stood in the sun before the officer of police wiping the perspiration from his balding head, stealing a look from time to time at the members of the National Guard loitering in the plaza. The cartridge boxes at their waists bracketed by their bayonet sheaths or the swords of the officers, heaved his already nervous stomach. His wife had told him not to go, insisted that it was a fool's fancy. Even while she put the bread and cheese in his pail and covered it she lamented his arrest that was all but assured. The city was not the place to be now, she urged, the police, the army, they were still arresting rebels, chasing them out of the holes in which they had hidden.

"I've heard when they suspect a man they take him instantly, from his woman or children, arrest and execution!" His wife stood behind him as he harnessed the mule, her voice a pitiful mewl. "Madame Boulis, the youngest sister of Monsieur Diep who owns the boulangerie, she told me in a whisper that the National Guard is under orders to finish all traitors with the bayonet or sword only! Apparently cartridge for their carbines is so dear that they dare not have a firing party. Oh, Monsieur, I tell you it is horrible, horrible!"

Closing a heavy leather buckle and giving the patient beast's neck a few pats of gratitude, he turned and reached for the wooden pail his wife held before her. She was always more handsome when her blood was up, he thought, brushing aside the wisps of hair that had escaped her bonnet. Her flushed, anxious face eased a bit as she remarked a familiar wry smile, a white grin flashing in her husband's darkened features. Having found her gaze he held it briefly and then turned to the wagon.

"Very well, Monsieur," she said in a feeble attempt at indignation, "you needn't heed my warnings. I am only a woman of the country, as you know. Go, go to the city," she flung up at him, her arms folded across her bosom. "So there is work there? So there is, I am sure. Au revoir, Monsieur, *au revoir*!"

The reigns gently slapped the mule's haunches and the wagon started forward in an eruption of rattles and groans. As he rumbled off through their startled chickens and few geese, she turned her head away and blew out a sigh of angry frustration. The reddish sky beyond their tiny home promised another day of sticky, oppressive heat. She would certainly need to keep the children...*Mon Dieu, he has forgotten his hat!* Picking up her skirts she ran through the open door of their cottage and vanished inside. In a moment she was back, her breast heaving beneath her bodice, hair askew, grasping a greasy woolen cap in her hands while her eyes searched the distant half-lit road for the wagon. There, further away than she had hoped and shrouded by the dust from its wheels she saw the wagon, her husband's bent form on the high seat jostled by the roughness of the road. His silhouette in the early morning was so familiar, the limp reigns held loosely in one hand while the other held a clay pipe. On his head was a straw hat, pushed far back the way he liked. *Mon Dieu*, she sighed again.

"Your papers appear in order," the officer said from his campaign chair in the shade. He was seated a good three feet behind a folding table in the more moderate environment provided by a striped canvas awning. The bivouac at the Rue de la Chanvrerie had been hurried into construction only hours following the putting-down of the *emeute* on the sixth of June that fateful year, 1832. The prefecture of police in Paris superseded during the crisis by the officers and commanders of the National Guard had moved quickly to regain their authority establishing checkpoints throughout the ruined streets and plazas of the city. The considerable establishment at the conjunction of the Rue de la Chanvrerie and the Rue Saint Denis faced the massive and terrible barricade of the Faubourg Saint Antoine. Its purpose, beyond a visible declaration of vigilance, if not sanity, was the practical enforcement of the civil code and, if possible, the prevention of summary executions by the National Guard.

Another minor role was the immediate and systematic dismantling of the barricades that choked off the thoroughfares of the city. This enormous task was accomplished as most bureaucracies accomplish anything; by the issuing out of papers, licenses, permits, orders, warrants and—the real fuel that fed the machinery of order—money.

"You will be paid according to this bill," the officer said thrusting a bit of foolscap into Calmenté's hand. The printed half-sheet was smeared and falsely printed, the stuttered image obscuring the words and figures and he stared at it hopelessly. Extending the paper back toward the officer Calmenté shrugged and tried a deprecating smile.

"What, you cannot read? *Merde!*" he snorted and pushed the paper away from him pointing toward the barricade behind them where many other wagons were already being filled. "For each undamaged weapon; musket, carbine, pistol, musketoon, sword, bayonet, dagger, knife, you will receive five sous; for broken or damaged weapons, one sou; for undamaged cartridge you will receive one sou per box, there is no reward for damaged cartridge." Calmenté looked from the officer who was leaning forward and shuffling papers on the folding table toward the barricade and the work. He could see a workman pulling the shattered and bloodied corpse of an insurgent from the debris and his stomach turned over again.

"The rest of the garbage you haul away to the pits to be burned—40 sous per wagon." Calmenté stood silently staring at the mangled body as it was allowed to slip and then tumble to the ground in a heap. The workman wiped his hands on his frock, straightened his cap, then reached back toward the wreckage of the barricade. Calmenté could hear the crows bickering amongst themselves on the eaves of the houses.

Hearing no response to his recital, the officer looked up from his papers. Seeing only Calmenté's back he leaned around and looked beyond to the barricade. "O, *oui*," he nodded. "As you discover the dead, you will please to take the utmost care with those of the National Guard or the army; call for help if you find yourself in need. As for the dead rebels, just put them aside. The knacker will take them out of the city in due order. There will be no compensation for removing the dead." His voice took on an officious air again. "It is a generous service the free citizens of Paris gratefully acknowledge."

Calmenté turned back as the officer finished scratching out his order. He stood for another moment as the officer sprinkled sand on the page and then blew it off. "There," he said, thrusting the bill into his hand. "Keep this with you at all times. You must produce it for any officer or soldier that demands to see your warrant." Calmenté nodded and, after carefully folding the paper and putting it in his tunic, he bowed to the officer, placed his hat back on his head and took his mule in hand. "Peasants," the officer sniffed.

The National Guard stood at various intervals along both sides of the slowly eroding barricade. Most loitered with little interest, pressed against the store fronts seeking what little shade there was, muskets slung over their shoulders or loosely held by their sides. One party seemed to be organizing their dead comrades, each being laid carefully down, a cloth of some type placed over their faces. Another few were gathered in the shattered remains of a café talking loudly amongst themselves, their shakos and muskets scattered along a few benches and on the tops of broken walls.

A score of wagons ranged along the three-story, 700-foot length of the barricade, their owners like ants on the skin of a dead beast, industriously plucking off the detritus to supply their colony. Calmenté walked along leading his mule toward the furthest extremity of the barricade, toward the terminus of the Fauberg where no other wagon sat, near the ruined café where the guards discoursed. Stopping a short distance from the barricade, Calmenté walked around behind his mule, talking softly to the animal while he hobbled him and filled a bag of oats to sling around its neck. Patting the animal affectionately, he pulled on a pair of hide-gloves and approached his day's work.

"O look, another *citizen* to help us," a thick-tongued guard declared loud enough for Calmenté to hear. There was a collective chuckle amongst his comrades and the clink of a bottle somewhere in the shadows of the gutted façade. Calmenté halted a few paces from the massive barricade and stared at the amalgamation of flotsam that was collected there. From the corner of his eye he caught the movement of heavy uniformed figures in the shadows, a few indistinguishable words floated out and then more laughter.

Reaching his hand forward he grasped the leg of a shattered bureau and tugged sending a cloud of dust and debris cascading around him. Small pebbles pattered down amidst the wall of wreckage, a few bouncing off the brim of his hat and landing around his boots. But upon looking down he saw they were not pebbles at all but ball and grape-shot; misshapen, flattened and torqued by their impact upon the substance of the barricade. The fury of the riot made manifest in its smalls, like the droppings of a bird of prey.

"*Citizen*, attend," came the voice from the café. Calmenté drew a breath and straightened from his task. Turning he saw a youngish sergeant moving from the shadows of the destroyed café onto the broken paving stones near at hand. "Your warrant," he demanded, unsteadily throwing his head back in a ludicrous attempt at authority. His complexion, disagreeably dirty and flushed with wine showed unhealthily in the daylight covered in aggravated red pimples on sallow yellow skin. Calmenté pulled the document from his jersey and unfolded it for the sergeant. But it was snatched away before he could finish, torn from his fingers to the hoots of the other soldiers. The sergeant, unbalanced by his effort wavered on his feet and quiet laughter leaked again from the shadows.

"A license to scavenge, eh, *citizen*?" The sergeant leered at him then turned to the shadows for support. "Come to Paris to see the sights and make your fortune, eh? Well this is lucky for you, isn't it *citizen*? We die and you make money fro…" but the sergeant did not finish. A bedlam of stamping boots and clattering buckles accompanied the arrival of the officer as muskets were slung and shakos quickly appeared.

Calmenté watched as the officer quietly but sternly addressed the sergeant and the five soldiers that sullenly appeared, squinting from the café. In a few moments following a brief and vicious harangue, the officer dismissed the soldiers and after watching them tramp awkwardly away he approached Calmenté and returned his warrant.

"My apologies, Monsieur, the last few days have taken a great toll on my men. Many of their friends lay dead in this street." This he said sadly looking up and down the length of the great, jagged wall. "Continue your work, si vous plait." Nodding curtly, the officer strode away in the direction he had sent the others. Calmenté watched him retreat back toward the Rue de la Chanvrerie, then returned to his work. But as he took his place again at the base of the great barricade, his eye caught the glint of something bright on the ground, nestled amidst the scattered balls and other shakings. Squatting down, he picked up the object and rubbed the dirt from it, realizing at last that he held between his fingers a perfectly made leaden grenadier, a toy soldier complete with brilliant red plumed shako, crossed belts and drawn sword. In the brilliance of the sun he could even see the huge, flamboyant mustaches on the tiny face. The workmanship was the finest he had ever seen. Smiling a private smile and thinking of his little son he slipped the grenadier into his pocket, patting it fondly.

THE LEADEN GRENADIER

Phillipe jerked the ends of his neck cloth tightly together and tied them securely, stanching the flow of blood pouring from his lacerated thigh and cutting off, for the moment, the subtle thought forming in his mind that today might indeed be his last day on earth.

"Francois!" he shouted above the clash around him. Looking over his left shoulder, he could just make out his younger friend leaning precariously over the edge of the redoubt aiming his carbine at the retreating Sappers. "*Merde,*" he hissed between his teeth as he stood and swiveled to gain an advantage on the step. Cupping his hands before his mouth, he roared above the sporadic pop of muskets and confused shouting, "*Ass!* You'll be shot, get down, get down *now!*"

Francois looked toward his friend and grinned. Then, with that idiotic cherubic smile stretched across his face, he returned to his carbine sighting carefully, deliberately along its barrel, till at last he pulled the trigger. With a singular bang and flash the carbine discharged its terrible duty and when the powder smoke cleared Francois, was still exposed on top of *la Barricade,* hooting and wagging his head at the retreating soldiers, oblivious to danger.

"*Damn* that boy," Phillipe hissed pulling his throbbing leg behind, over the rim of the firing step toward the promontory where Francois sat casually reloading his carbine. It had always been the same, he thought as he negotiated the sharp bend in the barricade that opened up the furthest point of extension. When he was seven, he had to swim the river, had to rush ahead, leap in without thinking…and who saved his miserable hind?

"*Merde!*" he winced, convulsively grabbing at the torn sleeve where a whistling ball sliced the cloth and scored his skin. "*Ass!*" he shouted again, jerking his body around the bend and once again behind the scantlings of the barricade. *I* saved him, he thought. I saved him.

The smoke had cleared abruptly, parted by a sudden breath of wind and there, seated on the apex of the barricade once again aiming his carbine, Francois sat entirely exposed. Phillipe looked around behind him and saw the sad slaughter of the most recent sortie—at least three dead. Focusing his energy, he lurched forward and stretched a frantic hand above his head toward Francois' extended foot fumbling with protruding beams and debris until he felt the living substance beneath his hand. Convulsively, he grasped the foot and wrenched his friend backwards over the edge of the mount down in a collapse of refuse amidst the whining of spent balls and shouted cursings from the National Guard.

As the dust settled, Phillipe gasped for breath and clutched at his thigh which had been tramped on in the fall, and all the while Francois laughed where he had fallen.

"*Idiot! Ass!*" Phillipe spat, rocking back and forth holding his leg. "You could have been killed. Francois, listen to me, I am in earnest. Those bastards would have cut you down, they had your range."

"Oh, Phillipe," he panted sitting up and brushing filth from his waistcoat. "Those bastards to which you refer couldn't hit the Faubourg itself, much less this worthy citizen. Beside," he said standing and reaching out for his friend, "I have you to protect me."

Phillipe grimaced as he stood and in a paroxysm of rage, savagely grabbed Francois by the shirt, pulling his face close to his own. "Listen to me, you pimp," he growled, "this is not a game, some contest in which to show away. Those soldiers are coming back next time to finish us, to kill us. We need every weapon now, every man. Yes, even an idiot like *you*."

Francois' face lost much of its casual gaiety and he stared into his friend's eyes but did not speak. The sporadic crack of muskets had all but disappeared, and all around the men other defenders were mechanically stacking the weapons of the dead and carrying the wounded who could not walk to shelter. Many were quenching their thirst at a rain barrel by one of the bordering shops, taking huge draughts in their cupped hands or in whatever container offered. A few began to prepare for the assault they all knew must eventually come.

After a moment, the two men visibly relaxed, Phillipe sighing heavily with a wry smile creasing his blackened face. "You…you are intolerable," he said.

"Always," Francois responded.

The two men moved away from the barricade toward a makeshift command post amongst the shattered and stripped dwellings bordering the street. Easing himself onto an overturned trough, Phillipe stifled a moan as he extended his leg and reached gratefully for the bottle of wine Francois offered.

"That looks pretty bad," Francois said indicating the blood-soaked bandage.

"*Bastards…scum*," Phillipe ejaculated between mouthfuls. "I wasn't even armed."

"And you worry about me," Francois scoffed. "You'd better arm yourself next time you go up on *la Barricade*. As you said, this is no game."

"I am aware of the serious nature the day affords. Can you possibly think I would be here otherwise? You forget that I actually helped write our proclamation."

"How can I forget? Tell me, do the dictates of the *emeute* really go as far as wallpaper?"

"You call me a fool," Phillipe said dangling the now empty bottle between his legs. "I wrote that proclamation to legitimize this *emeute*, as you call it. I wrote it to publish the reason for arms."

"The bourgeois know the reason for arms but don't care, my friend. You care as do most of these," he said indicating the milling few in the lowering dusk. "And *he* used to care, but not so much any longer." This last toward a young student who lay limp and pale against a shutter, his blood in a dark pool beneath him. Both men looked at the boy and then turned away.

"And you," Phillipe asked quietly, "do you care?" The younger man stood away from his wounded friend and stretched his back gazing up at the twilight sky. Another defender nearby kindled a small fire from the fragments of a smashed stool and Francois gazing down, stared long into the shuddering flames. After the pause he shook his head and walked away to retrieve his carbine.

"If you don't care then why are you here?"

Francois walked back out of the gloom and sat down next to his friend on the upturned trough. Resting the carbine against his knee, he pulled a leather bag from his pocket then reached out to grasp his friend's hand, extending it palm up. From the bag he pulled a tangle of miniature figures and placed them on the outstretched palm.

"What are you doing?"

"Remember these, Phillipe?" Francois said, reaching into the leather pouch again and withdrawing a bullet mold and spoon. "How many campaigns did they see?" Plucking a particularly elegant lancer from the heap, Francois dropped him into the spoon and held it over the dwarfish fire. In seconds the lead softened and the brilliant colors bubbled and ran, forming a tiny silver pool. With care he removed the spoon from the fire and poured the molten lead into the mold, then set it aside to cool.

"When we were children, Phillipe, we played at war using armies of lead. This battalion is what is left of my army." This time he took a private soldier from the heap and laid him in the spoon, again putting it to the fire. "When I joined the *emeute* I did so not to sacrifice myself on some glorious altar of freedom like you and these others, but to experience the moment—to thrust myself beyond the paleness of my proper education and respectable occupation. To live, Phillipe, that is why I joined you here at *la Barricade.*" Resting the melting spoon in the fire, he opened the mold and tapped out the harlequin colored ball, snipped off the leader and dropped it into his bag.

"You're a fool!"

"O, my friend, you don't know the pleasure I had putting the first of these balls square into the chest of one of those brutes out there. Finally," he laughed, "I have found out the proper use of these martial figures." Another soldier disappeared quietly into the mold and, in turn, another ball dropped into the leather bag. The passionless end they met, consigned as they were to the fire, chilled Phillipe almost as much as the casual brutality boasted by his friend. He did remember the campaigns they had fought as boys, stretched at length on the Turkish carpet in his father's study, framing the lines and squares of battle, bringing up artillery and cavalry, advancing sappers or grenadiers. They had spent hours playing at war, hours in grave counsel as to whether advance or retreat was necessary, but always winning, it seemed, and never cruel.

"There is no honor in that type of gross…brutality."

Francois smiled as was his wont but continued at his forge, casting murderous death into each pawn, removing them singly from his friend's open hand till there were but few remaining. Beyond their conference the sounds of a company of the guard gathering at the extremity of the street echoed along the breastwork and into their enclave. "Come, admit it, Phillipe, there is no better use to be made of these masks of war. Surely, even you can see that."

"You're wrong, Francois," Phillipe said. "These were toys for children, no more. We were boys, and today we are patriots, not monsters!"

"Ah, just one lonely grenadier left. Come little warrior, join your comrades…"

"No," Phillipe said, closing his hand on the tiny soldier. "This one I will keep to remind me of my friend, the one I *used* to know." Staring into Francois' eyes, he softened a bit and smiled thinking of the lad he had pulled sputtering from the river, sputtering but laughing. "Je t'aime, mon ami. Je t'aime beaucoup."

"Oui," Francois muttered, putting his mold and spoon back in its bag, and he walked away toward the barricade with his carbine slung over his shoulder.

Bojeanic

Standing slowly, his hand to the burning pain in his back, Calmenté stared at the extent of the progress he had made and blew out his cheeks in disgust. Six long hours had seen him disengage, load and haul away three full wagons of debris to the pits and still the barricade loomed before him enormous and grim. Of arms for which he would be paid extra, he had delivered to the prefecture of police only a few pistols and a dozen or so broken and bent swords. A chit for 25 sous was folded carefully into his pocket and though his sturdy gloves had protected his hands, he wore a deep gash in his left forearm, a substantial gratuity paid by *la Barricade*, he thought sardonically.

So intent had he been on his work that the large piece of glass fell from a splintered window sash with scarcely a nod of recognition. The searing pain and the bright jet of blood in the sunshine had been his only introduction. And as he reached to jerk out the broad shard, he saw his reflection as clearly as if he were standing before a peer-glass in the Tuileries. His face, there in the glass, was lined and tired, glistening with sweat and flushed with exertion, wretched, overcome with melancholy and singularly despondent. It was time, he decided, to find a place and take his ease.

After he had taken the time to bind his arm and had retrieved his dinner bucket from under the wagon's bench, he retreated from the brilliance of the noontime sun onto a curbstone situated beneath a scrap of tattered awning. There in the shade he removed a damp cloth from atop the bucket and set to the cheese and hard roll his Jeanette had prepared.

Chewing slowly, savoring the grainy fullness of the cheese and the hard crust of the bread, Calmenté gazed out at the other men as they too went to their dinners; some crawling beneath their wagons, others resting in doorways or destroyed façades nearer the barricade. The scores of National Guard that had been haunting the plaza all morning were all but vanished. It was true a few sullen men, their uniforms darkly stained with sweat, still patrolled the perimeter, but with little interest and less enthusiasm. Even the crows were subdued.

Inside the bucket Calmenté found a cup of milk, a rag bound tightly over its mouth. He retrieved it and took a refreshing draft, then wiped his mouth with his right sleeve and leaned carefully back against the wall. He was tired and purposed to take a few minutes to close his eyes. He would be better for the rest, he affirmed pulling his hat over his eyes and relaxing further, better and stronger. As the strain on his body eased a slight breeze fluttered his shirt, and his mind, now cool and complacent, was set adrift.

"Bonjour, mon ami!"

Calmenté started awake, his mind a whirl of confusion, his relaxed frame convulsed into instant response at the booming voice. Before him, with a smile as broad as a boulevard, stood a huge, red-haired man, beaming down upon him.

"Asleep like a cat in the sun," he said in a rich baritone. "Ah, I envy you. When my mind is troubled, I cannot rest even though my body would drop to the ground from fatigue." Calmenté appraised the giant and wondered if there had ever been a time when that physique had been so taxed.

"Rest is truly a thing to be savored," Calmenté remarked, adjusting his hat and sitting back against the wall.

"Truly," the big man responded, plumping his large frame down by Calmenté, kicking his huge feet out in front. The strangeness of the greeting coupled with this man's obvious affability confused Calmenté. Looking over at the big man, he was greeted by the same ingenuous face, the same smile. It was surely a strange moment.

"I am Pierre Bojeanic from Diep." Calmenté grasped the extended hand and winced in his grip. "My mind is disturbed by what I have found in the barricade," the man continued. Calmenté nodded and frowned thinking of the gruesome relics he too had found amongst the rubbish. "Do you read?" asked Bojeanic, and as Calmenté was considering the abruptness of the question, the giant thrust a fragment of a book toward him. "I found this in the hand of a dead man," he said simply. "I must know what is written here."

Calmenté took the proffered pages from Bojeanic, remarking the cloud of sadness that passed over his amiable face. It was indeed strange what a man would cling to in the extremity of death, he thought, having often been puzzled as he sifted the wreckage of this barricade. He had seen many men clinging to their weapons as seemed natural enough, and once he had noticed a man holding fast to a simple flag, their battle standard, he had supposed. But a few held onto other, more personal things; a wine bottle in one case, a few had clutched letters, many their comrades who likewise held them—comfort and familiarity in their final agonies? It was clear to Calmenté that each man, upon seeing the moment of his death, clung to that which gave him the most comfort and eased him through that transition. And this man had held the fragment of a book.

The pages in his hand were the final few of a small pocket volume, its greater part torn by what brutality its owner met in the last few moments. Blood spattered the visible top page and the evidence of great violence clung to its back cover, where it was slightly burned. He held the once finely printed book at a more liberal distance from his eyes in order to focus its elegant characters and Bojeanic crossed his arms over his massive chest taking on the appearance of a child about to be tutored. It was difficult at first, finding the thread of the story, for it was a narrative, as it winded its way to a conclusion amongst the now dull brown spots and smears of blood. Finally, after a false start or two, he found a sentence from which he could put before his singular audience a coherent recital. Holding the few pages against his upraised knee and again resting his head on the broken façade, he began carefully to read.

THE SHATTERED BOOK

The pool of waste in the bottom of the ship lay motionless and oily, black-bodied flies glistening dully on its surface, bloated and frozen like pebbles on a page. Adelle gazed at them sadly, as she had all the events and all the people of these past several months. Henri had admonished her more than once of this habit; "Unworthy of our mission, little one," he would say, then adding quickly, "...*and* your beauty," with a wink and his quick, sly smile.

She had loved Henri's smile and that way he had of always turning her eyes upward to the higher places. As her mind played over his dark smiling face again, she sighed heavily and tried to turn her body. She winced as the rough wood tore open the clotted wounds on her hips and shoulders, freeing her blood to flow once again. She didn't mind so much, she thought, it was a better feeling than the tight stiffness of the crusts anyway.

Panting quietly, she settled her weight and pushed her mind around to think of her village, of *Capentras,* of Henri and his dark good looks, of Father Alain and the little dog that always followed her from the *epicerie* to the edge of the square and never beyond. The weather would be turning now, she decided, noticing the flies stirring on the pool below her. The leaves of the tallest trees would be ending their autumn dance and the villagers would begin fretful preparations for the inevitable *mistrals* of winter. She remembered that tearing, shrieking wind and the shuddering of the roof above her bed. Her stomach suddenly heaved, as her memories were once again invaded by the visions of recent days.

The insane tilt of the ship had sent all of them, all of the children tumbling upon each other in a mass of screaming, terrified bodies. Sickness also came in a rush, vomit pouring upon them, mixed with the filth of the hold and the constant shower of sea water from the open hatchways. Those unable to grasp a wooden beam or support fell free, like pitching stones, colliding with others if they were fortunate. If unfortunate, they pitched into the unyielding beams of the ship, smashing their limbs or their heads. The storms she could remember melted into a haze of disjointed phantoms and disembodied shrieks, always ending the same pitiful way, with shuddering blackness and then the terrible dragging out of the dead under careless, splendid skies of purest blue.

Below her, the black flies had found the bright crimson of her blood dripping onto the feted surface of the pond and were again feeding hungrily, their hairy mouths deep in the flow. Adelle looked away toward the slit of light above her head, toward the harbor where their ship stood at anchor, motionless in the stink of dead fish and rotting garbage. The calm of the bay was so profound that it was like a millpond, the only ripples coming from the black water that slid off the raised oars of the galley below their lee. She could just make out the shimmering water that clung to the wooden oar and at its terminus, the sun-darkened wraith that sat chained to his bench, staring mutely ahead at nothing.

The babble of voices in a strange tongue broke her thoughts again, as did the frantic slap of naked feet and the clump of boots on the deck above her. The din could only mean that men were coming once again. Men were coming below to take more of them away for the price of their foolishness. Would they finally take her this time, she wondered. Again she smiled sadly and thought of Henri.

"Here, take my shirt," he had said suddenly, ripping the bloody garment from his back and shoving it toward her in the darkness. "Put it on quickly and when they stand you up, slouch and cough. Do not look them in the face, mark me, I am in earnest!" Hissing this last, he grabbed a sodden cap from the murky filth of the bilge and thrust it onto her head. "Pull it down low over your hair and do not wipe that off!" he said pushing her hand away. "The worse you look *and* smell the better." Then his stern face softened and he winked. "You look like a dirty boy, little one," he whispered.

And then the men had come down into the hold with their caged flames, their flowing robes and their bright smiles in dark faces. "Pretty, pretty children," they would coo, touching and handling the boys and girls in the dark. Slowly they moved through the children, glancing at this one and then the next, always smiling, always touching. Then, amidst the crying and choking gasps of her friends, the mumble of foreign words and the clinking of coins into greasy hands, their numbers decreased and the hold would grow dark once again.

Closing her eyes as the hatch above her opened to the day, Adelle summoned a last memory of Henri and the splendid hope that had drawn them together and away. Strangely, she could only remember the cross she had stitched onto Henri's neck cloth the night before they boarded the ship bound for Palestine. Its arms were simple and sharply defined, scarlet as all of those she had seen along the way, but especially at the seaside.

The words on the cross were simple, "…suffer the little children." Now, in the dim light of the approaching lamps she could no longer make out the words or the color or even the shape of the cross. It was only a tattered slip of filthy cloth, worn almost away between her worrying fingers.

"Mon Dieu, here is another one," a voice said harshly. Swiftly, strong, gentle arms lifted her from the hiding place where Henri had placed her the last moment she had seen him.

"Stay here, little one," he had said. "Stay here and do not make a sound. I am leaving but you will make it to Palestine, to Jerusalem. Take the banner and never let it leave your hands." And he was gone as all the others had gone, in a jostle of cries and strange, evil voices.

"Oh, little one," the voice said, as its owner carried her from the dark hold onto the deck of the ship. "Oh, little one," he said again, kneeling gently down and placing her on a reed mat under an awning. Adelle's blistered lips curved into a slight smile and her mind settled on Henri's dark sly smile and the dancing leaves of *Capentras* and from her fingers, the tattered cloth slipped away.

"What have you found, Faustin?"

"*Goddamned* monsters," the voice broke. "*Monsters! Mon Dieu*, the gallows is too good for them!"

"Yes, Faustin, the gallows is too good for th…"

Calmenté stared at the interrupted phrase, then turned the torn page. There was nothing beyond the brief account, except a scorched and bloody fragment of cover with the words *Au revoir, Mon Petit Une*—farewell, my little one, etched in discolored gold. He sat for a moment, his mind going over the narrative, and then he looked at Bojeanic. The giant was snoring, sprawled against the broken stone of the façade a foot or so away, his huge shoes thrust into the street, his red hair a mass of tangles and confusion, framing an oblivious but affable face. There was no telling when his audience had lost the thread of the story and passed into dreams, but assuredly, thought Calmenté, he was no longer troubled by this relic of the barricade.

Gently placing the pages in Bojeanic's lap, he retrieved his gloves and lunch bucket and stretching as he stood, returned to his afternoon's work.

By the late afternoon Calmenté had made two trips to the pits outside the city and was well into loading his wagon yet again, when he heard deep rumblings in the east. Lifting his eyes, he marked mountainous clouds scudding across the sky, dark pregnant clouds eager to give up their water. The air was indeed close. Sweat poured burning into his eyes and he wiped them yet again with his neck cloth. Rain would be a relief, he thought returning to his work.

Then he noticed a flare of reflected sun winking deep inside the tangle before him. Thrusting a free hand into the snarl, he stretched his fingers toward the object, brushing aside shattered wood and old iron to find the treasure. Leaning into the mass, his shoulder against its bulk, he extended his hand till his fingertips brushed against the shining trinket. Straining, he coaxed the quavering bit until at last it surrendered to his efforts and his fingers closed around what felt like a delicate chain. Sighing, he relaxed and withdrew his arm, opening his closed fist to reveal a finely made gold chain with an equally fine, gold watch attached to it. Calmenté stared at the treasure, marveling at the delicate filigree of its casing and the three golden posts thrust into the air. With one blunt finger he depressed the center post, and the cover snapped open, revealing the skeleton-face, the gears, posts, springs and fly-wheels of the mechanism visible through carefully wrought, golden windows. There was no life in the machine at that moment, but when Calmenté turned the central post, tiny gears, rods and wheels began to spin and rock and tick launching the delicate second hand of the timepiece forward in measured grace. Calmenté gazed wonderingly at the elegant instrument angling it in the fading sun so that the burnished case and delicate crystal would flash. Then he depressed one of the smaller posts and the music of tiny bells floated up into the cloying air. For a second he held his breath and listened to the music drift upward, as warm drops of rain began to plop heavily into the Faubourg Saint Antoine.

ETIENNE'S WATCH

Etienne was a thief, and he had been born to his trade. His small wraithlike frame had been created, it seemed, for slithering and crabbing in shadows, for gliding along window ledges or down dimly lit alleys. He had certainly not been made for the day, though when in funds, he had covered himself with the couturier's art, mounting the affectation of civility, though his trade would hardly recommend him.

His left hand was his treasure. By its grace he had found more wealth than the common man could grub in a lifetime and through its skill, he had turned the atrocity of his youth into a reverie of the possible.

The idiosyncrasy of the man was such that he pampered his left hand, keeping it close in a lambskin glove, being content to use his right for all the routines of living, save perhaps in love. In his distorted mind there was no more precious a tool in his possession than a hand that could slip like vapor between the folds of cloth to the hidden and secure purse of a mark. So, like a physician who strolled the boulevard with his gold-topped cane, so the thief waltzed the broad avenues of Paris with only the one hand gloved.

In the year of our Lord, 1827, Etienne lived in the Rue Montétour in a fine three-room flat situated above the Café aux Pigeons. He had chosen the apartment for several reasons but primarily for its location near the busy markets and circuses of the city. He had made it his business to melt into the crowd, to touch and take, then vanish like mist. So it was that he always chose his residence with an eye toward escape. Yet, there were several other powerful reasons he had chosen these particular rooms.

In the first place, Etienne, while no longer wanting for currency, could not, or would not, part with more livres than was necessary. The rent was moderate and with breakfast included, the bargain was actually superior. In the second place, he enjoyed the atmosphere near a café. Every morning, beginning in the very early hours, about the time Etienne was entering that magical half-sleep before waking, the seductive aromas of baking bread and brewing coffee would steal up the narrow stairs to his apartment, slip past the triple locks of his door and find the thief's imagination ripe and well-seasoned for temptation. It was in all aspects a pleasant residence.

Another powerful attraction of his rooms was, in truth, his landlady. The mature, but Junoesque, proprietress of the Café aux Pigeons was Madame de Sauvion. A widow without children, Madame ran the Café and let space in the building, apparently more for sport than profit. Madame had obviously lost

Monsieur de Sauvion prior to the expiration of her womanly desires, and so, when possible, she collected admirers as tenants, making what she considered a handsome return on her investment. Etienne, a lodger for almost a year had only recently graduated from knowing flirtation to taking his suppers in Madame's private chambers.

As a thief, Etienne was familiar with the delicate balance between gross larceny and elegant theft. In his experience, it was most often revealed in the lightness of touch. With Madame de Sauvion, Etienne was rewarded for his nimble touch by the enthusiastic application of carnal tribute, and on occasion, croissant and coffee in bed.

As the summer deepened and Etienne's relations with his landlady ripened, he took to keeping his bed for longer periods in the day, sometimes not leaving the premises from one dawning to the next. It was an agreeable arrangement, and he often lay with his plump and welcoming mistress on her fragrant sheets, remembering all the nights he had shivered on stones in the street, covered in filth, smelling of the sewer. Starving, he had learned the hard lessons of Parisian society, first as a sweeper, then as a beggar, then as a thief. And each time his mind recalled the bitterness of those days, he would pull Madame closer, losing himself in her luxuriant flesh and her pleasant scent of baking and rose petals.

But as time passed, Etienne began to develop a nagging suspicion that his trade, the art of his vocation was beginning to suffer from lack of practice. As the days advanced and the heat of each afternoon increased, so Etienne's concern intensified and his connubial attentions to Madame became distracted. Eventually, as he and Madame shared a quiet afternoon before supper the thief confided a suitable fiction to his mistress, begging a pressing engagement too long ignored. His words, flattering but lustrous with a kernel of truth, were well-turned and Madame de Sauvion, ebullient in her contrition, insisted on helping him dress, all but pushing him out onto the street to accomplish his will. She would, she promised, put back a meat pie for his supper and a glass of sherry as he liked. She had been a fool, she persisted, and only wished he could find it in her heart to forgive her. Etienne smiled and patted her cheek affectionately with his right hand, having already protected his left with its glove. Then he strolled away down the street into the throngs of afternoon passersby, his stick in his hand and his head held at a casual tilt.

Emerging from the Rue Montétour, Etienne proceeded north past several shops and a flower vendor with his pushcart, on with the press of people seeking their own several errands, each alone in his thoughts oblivious to his presence and the itching fingers of his left hand. He inhaled deeply of the earthy smells of the boulevard; the pungent tang of dung and horse sweat, of overripe fruit too long in the sun, of the vagaries of unidentified perfumes and the harsh, woody scents of cigars floating from the many clutches of men chatting the market up or the government down. He was, he knew, a creature at liberty after confinement, like a falcon released from its perch and hood he thrilled to see, even sense the prey in innocent gambol all about him. His left hand tingled in anticipation.

He did not actually see the watch at first, but heard it. Etienne had been leaning against a hitching post, admiring a particularly fine woman who, at that moment, was laughing at a coarse jest, while smoking a very small paper cigar, when the many voices of tiny bells declared themselves, as if from the very air. Snatched from his reverie, the thief took a pair of steps away from his station and held his breath attempting to catch the sounds again and as if on cue, the bells chimed, twinkling in lockstep with the bells of the district clock. It was a repeater, Etienne smiled, scanning all the gentlemen as they pulled their timepieces to correct their settings. Carefully he noted the style of each man's watch and in short order he identified the owner of the marvelous trinket.

He was fat as many gentlemen of the 'Change seemed to be, dressed in a snuff-colored coat and breeches, frilled shirt and starched cravat. His pudgy hands were naked except for a thin band of gold that bit into the flesh of his little finger and his nails were clean. He fidgeted with the timepiece, adjusting its mainspring, while talking to his compatriots. Satisfied at length with his manipulations, he pressed one of the short secondary stems and held the device to his ear to again hear the chimes. This was an obvious performance, as Etienne noticed the fat man's beady eyes appraise his circle's appreciation for the expensive bobble, before he nodded and replaced it in his waistcoat pocket.

The group of gentlemen laughed raucously, as the pretentious fat man quipped and blew cigar smoke into the air. Etienne sidled over to the group affecting to admire some garments displayed in the window of a nearby shop, while he removed his left-hand glove and secreted it to his coat pocket. As he stood, his back to the group of men, his hands folded on the knob of his cane, he listened curiously to their conversation and watched their inverse reflection in the glass.

"Mon Dieu, Baudiére, but you are a ferret! When did she first discover the fiction?"

"Weeks! On my honor, she was interested only in the theater or sherbet while strolling the promenade. I assure you, my friends, this one cared for nothing beyond the comforts of society."

"You mean the comfort of your purse, don't you, Baudiére?"

"Could you mark it? She had not heard of the troubles, had not even noticed the National Guard closing the streets near her flat! I declare, except for the exercise she gave me, I doubt I would trouble to make her acquaintance."

"If Madame Baudiére had not been afraid of the troubles and left for Calais, you would not have made her acquaintance.

"'Tis true. I am too soon a lonely man."

"Your loneliness is a seasonal occupation, Baudiére. If it were not the students or street revolutionaries, it would be the summer heat or spring flood."

"Ah, my friends, I am afraid I must now look elsewhere for my comfort. The fiction of my too recent bereavement has been discovered and the tart has flown to the arms of another."

"Poor Baudiére, alone in a city torn by strife and revolution. How will you support such torment?"

"A man is born with fortitude, *mon ami*. It can not be manufactured."

"Why not join the coterie at the Fauberg Saint Antoine? You would not be lonely at la Barricade."

The group of men snickered at this image and the fat adulterer shook his head. As the men all puffed on their cigars winking at one another, reveling in their prosaic and shabby sin, Etienne adjusted his cravat, took a deep breath and then turned on his heel to instantly collide with the fat banker.

The abrupt and distinctly painful impact, followed by a flurry of curses, a few weak and ineffective apologies, arms and elbows and reaching hands, Etienne's dropped cane and battered hat, cigar ash on the wing and the general confusion of the melee…all played a part in the subtle street theater that, in the end, charmed the fat man's precious musical watch out of his waistcoat's pocket and into the thief's.

The modest collision that Etienne had engineered was a common fraud, one he had perfected in the early days of learning his trade. Yet, sometimes the oldest dodge is the best, he thought, caressing the heavy roundness in his fob. Besides, he needed to jump a few low hurdles after so many days on holiday. Etienne moved smoothly away from the group toward the furthest end of the promenade with the intention of making a wide leisurely circuit of the park, eventually finding his way back to Rue Montétour and the comforts of

Madame de Sauvion. In this manner, he would most likely avoid any gendarme called by the fat banker and perhaps get a glimpse of the rotund weasel scrabbling in street filth looking for his missing treasure.

As the thief approached the trees and box hedges of the park's far border, he noticed a number of soldiers drawn up in regimental lines under officers, and others, muskets held at the ready, standing at the open mouths of bordering alleys and streets. The glint of afternoon sun on the narrow blades of the many swords and bayonets sent chills into Etienne's bones and he turned to follow the promenade away from the marshal dealings of the civil government. Nodding a fainthearted acknowledgement to a youngish officer's salute, Etienne turned casually and began to retrace his steps. At that moment the hollow thunder of a not-too-distant explosion, followed quickly by the splatter of muskets and the screams of men, blustered through an adjoining street like an eruption. Etienne stopped on the path clutching his stick and then quickly putting his left hand back in its glove. At the same moment, the nearby troops formed into line and under desultory commands, quick marched from their parade toward the tumult.

"Pardon," a smooth voice murmured from behind, "do you have the time?" Absently, staring at the flashing blades, his ears full of the desperate clash so close at hand, Etienne reached to his fob and pulled the repeater into the waning light of day.

"Thief!" the man shrieked, seizing Etienne's wrist and, as he twisted around saw to his horror the scarlet, enraged face of the fat adulterer. Wrenching his hand free, Etienne bolted from the shouting banker, away from the park and the gathering crowd, past the astonished officer he had so recently saluted and into the desperate clash of arms just beyond the closed streets.

Panic exploded in his chest as he sprinted down the alley, his hat and stick lost in the confusion, his hair wild in his tearing race to get away. Frantically, he ran past boarded doors and bricked archways toward the glimmer of light at the far end of the tunnel-like passage. As he neared the alley's terminus, he saw a riot of furniture and refuse piled against the opening, creating a inclination he would have to climb. Quickly he glanced over his shoulder and saw in the dim obscurity figures running behind him. Without another thought, he leaped upon the cascading garbage and clawing his way up its flank. The battle he had heard from the promenade was in full riot when he emerged from the alley. The sizzle of flying balls and the haphazard discharge of rifles was a cacophony of sound, shocking his ears to deafness and stopping his upward progress on the flanks of la Barricade. Stretched on the edifice, pinioned like a butterfly, he lingered to gain his bearings and received for his trouble a musket ball that shattered his jaw, forcing a garbled scream from his lips.

Etienne clung to the barricade, stunned and disoriented, staring wildly at the confused sights, deafened by the crash and bang of pistols and muskets, choked with the acrid smoke of spent powder and warm blood running down his throat. To his left the high wall of the barricade seemed to teeter over him, irresolute but substantial, threatening to tumble down and bury him alive. To his right the shadowy figures of soldiers floated in and out of the indistinct light, unreal in the tilted and insane present.

The thief looked below him toward the alley from which he'd emerged and thought of the fat banker so furious at the loss of his musical watch, and then he looked to where the golden treasure had been thrown when he fell, a few feet away its chain tangled in garbage. Then out of the gloom he saw the bestial face of a guardsman and the slender, wicked blade of his bayonet. With deliberate, measured cruelty the soldier thrust the blade through his body, transpiercing his chest and siphoning the air from his lungs, stealing his screams.

For a heartbeat he thought of telling the soldier he was only a thief but the ludicrous idea vanished when the steel was jerked from his ribcage. Without a word he expired, his gloved hand twisted under his body.

The rain had been falling in earnest for several hours and the Fauberg was awash in liquid filth flowing from the partially dismantled barricade. Crushed and broken mortar liquefied in the downpour and mixed with tattered paper, bits of cloth, torn and shattered paving and the blood of guardsmen and students, running sluggishly around Calmenté's boots toward the overflowing gutters and the sewers beyond. The afternoon had vanished in the gloom of the storm, but Calmenté could sense the coming night and tossed one last bit of debris onto his wagon. He straightened up and stretched his back, looking at the other men as they, too, began to stand and glance about.

The warm rain had done little to alleviate the oppressive heat and as evening came on it seemed the whole tableau had been given over to greater horror. The Faubourg was more like a splayed corpse being tugged and picked at by sodden colorless birds, the stones of the square strewn with wine-red puddles, the fetid reek of death saturating the thick air. Calmenté pealed off his soaked gloves, stuffed them into his tunic and walked through the drizzle around his wagon to his despondent mule, hobbled between the poles. It was time to go.

With his head bowed beneath the limp straw of his hat, Calmenté shuffled from la Barricade, leading his mule toward the checkpoint and on further eventually to his home. The persistent rain ran from his hat brim in a thin stream and he kept his eyes on the paving as his booted feet slogged through muck. The few *livres* he would earn from this work no longer appealed, and though his wife would thrill at the gold of the watch, he was becoming disgusted by the thing ticking in his pocket. There had been no blood on its intricately worked skin when he had pulled it from the barricade, but it was most assuredly the fruit of death, and his nose was too full of the stink of it to look kindly upon its harvest. Whatever the gain he would count out into his wife's hand, the legacy of this day's work was an acquaintance with murder and it sickened him.

At the check point, Calmenté received another chit into his outstretched hand and then pushed on into the glowering night.

BY MENTAL HOMICIDE

"If only I could understand the reason for my crying. If only I could stop this fear of dreaming that I'm dying. If only I could understand the reason for my crying. If only I could stop this fear of dreaming that I'm dying."

—Laura Palmer

SWEETIE

PART ONE

Sweetie sat in Dr. Hilburn's office on the blue paisley love seat and stared with deadened eyes through the blinds, out the window. The world beyond the glass existed as a typical winter's day—typical in its grayness, typical in its loneliness. A naked red oak huddled next to the building, planted by some architect who had designed the office complex eight years before. Now its stripped limbs reached around the corner of the window, lightly bobbing with the wind, one of its fingers barely missing the casement, almost as if beckoning the occupants of the office suite, "Come talk to me." It existed alone, no leaves, not a bird or even a nest to enliven it. She's stripped, Sweetie thought, looking at the dull charcoal color of the bark through the slatted portal.

Sweetie sighed and lowered her eyes.

Earlier that morning, Sweetie had slipped away with difficulty from her receptionist job at the packing plant, having to rush to make her 10:30 appointment at the counseling center. Burl Friend, her boss and the owner of Nature's Friend Meat Packing had reluctantly allowed her to leave, but only with the stern admonition that she would work through lunch to make up the time. Sweetie nodded quietly, gathering her things and hurrying out the door. She couldn't afford to be late or miss this appointment. Over the preceding four months, ever since she had decided to get help, there had been several other attempts to see Dr. Hilburn, but something had always come up, forcing her to cancel. The last time she had missed, it had been to stay home with her 5-year-old because her regular baby-sitter had begged off. That day had not only cost her a sick day from work and Mr. Friend's scorn, but her mother had called and persuaded Sweetie into spending the day working on the Baptist Ladies' Blood Drive. By 7:00 p.m. when she finally turned the key in her apartment lock, she staggered in under the weight of a migraine headache, with her daughter Tulia in tow and running a slight fever. Shuffling to her small couch, she dropped her purse and a single package of powder donuts on the coffee table and collapsed into the worn cushions. Fighting nausea, she closed her eyes and lay her head on the low couch, back pulling her tiny daughter to her lap.

"Mamma," Tulia chirped, laying her head on Sweetie's trembling shoulder. "I don't like Granny's friends. They treat me mean and make me sit by myself in that other room."

Sweetie licked her cracked lips and whispered an apology of sorts and began to stroke her daughter's cropped hair. The fever burned her hand through the fine strands of blond hair and she tried to ignore the vision of her morning call to Mr. Friend asking for one more sick day.

"Mamma?" Tulia again squeaked. "Why did you have to work for Granny? Why didn't we stay home today?"

Good question, Sweetie thought, sitting forward a bit and kissing her daughter's forehead. Yes, it was fever all right. Sloughing the little girl to the side, Sweetie stood from the couch with effort, shimmied out of her coat and walked to her bathroom where the Tylenol was kept.

"A half-teaspoon for her and three extra-strength for me," she mumbled. As she ran the tap and filled a yellow plastic cup, she looked at herself in the mirror. Tulia came by her looks naturally, she frowned. Except for the dark circles under her eyes and the crows feet beginning to form at their corners, she still looked the way she had when she left school to have Tulia. Turning the water off and tossing back the tiny capsules, she took a long drink of tepid water and then refilled the cup. It seemed longer than five years she mused. When the cup was filled again, she set it aside and turned the water off reaching into the open medicine cabinet for the bright red liquid that would soothe her daughter. The water was necessary since Tulia suffered at taking any medication no matter what the taste. She had been that way since the beginning, since Rob had left. Till then he had been the only one that could charm her into taking medicine solo.

"I'm doing my best," she said to herself holding the dosage vial and the cup in her hands. "I'm doing my best."

For a moment she stared at her reflection, pale under the sterile bathroom lights. At 24-years-old, she felt used up and worn out, though the youthful aspect of her figure belied her feelings. She was on her own and yet she felt owned by everyone and everything in her life; her job, her boss, her family, her absent husband—even her child. Her gray eyes ran the contours of her body and she suddenly felt a pang of regret for the years of abstinence since Rob's departure. Beneath the baggy sweat suit blood rushed to her thighs and breasts, and her cheeks and neck blushed pink with desire. Then the pain in her head surged and reminded her of Tulia. Glancing a last time at her figure, she ducked her chin and exited to the other room.

The events of that day had cost her several weeks of condemnation from her boss and it was only after several abortive attempts that she finally screwed up the courage to request an hour for the appointment. Mr. Friend had squinted at her across the stainless steel butcher's counter and with an abrupt and violent motion of the reddened cleaver in his hand, he had dismissed her to her appointment. If things went well, she thought, maybe she'd look for a new job as well.

Dr. Hilburn had seemed like a nice enough man when he had brought her into his office. After seating Sweetie on the small couch, he had excused himself to get a cup of coffee, asking her if she wanted anything before he left. When she declined, he had quickly disappeared around the corner and she was left alone. As she watched him leave, she observed that he was not especially tall and with his casual pants, plaid shirt and Birkenstocks he did not fit the picture of the significant influence with which Janet had praised him. His youth and his closely cropped hair and beard reminded Sweetie of a college student, not a professional counselor.

Janet Willis, the meat buyer for a local restaurant had never really spoken much to Sweetie before two months ago when she had placed a personal order and decided to wait for it instead of coming back in the afternoon.

That day, Janet had started by pacing the small reception area, flipping through the month-old magazines and staring quietly out the window, and she had finished by taking a seat across from the reception desk to relax with a cup of coffee. Sweetie observed the tall, slender woman in her business frock, her auburn hair braided and twisted up neatly on top of her head. She seemed so confident and capable, and for some reason that day, she seemed safe. It was a relief when Janet finally struck up a conversation.

For the next hour, they chatted about most anything—clothes, the weather, Sweetie's work, Janet's work, their families, their children. Often Janet seemed interested in Sweetie's past, her family in particular. This wasn't strange to Sweetie since to her mind, her family—parents and brothers—had always been a source of pride for her. Finally, after what seemed only a moment, her order was brought up and Janet vanished out the door with a cheery wave of her hand.

From then on Sweetie looked forward to Janet's bi-weekly visits, and was strengthened at the thought that she was finally developing a friend. It wasn't long before Janet and Sweetie met outside of work, first alone for lunch a few times, then with their children for dinner, then a birthday party for one of Janet's children, then for a movie. Finally, a day arrived when Sweetie collapsed under the weight of her loneliness and confided in her new friend.

Janet listened, stirring her tea and nodding her head thoughtfully as Sweetie poured out her heart to her friend.

"Something must be wrong with me," she cried. "My family is so sweet and helpful, my parents love me and support me but I just can't stand them!" Blowing her nose loudly, she wept into her hands, never lifting her eyes from the table. "I've got a good job, I make decent money, I mean, you know, I'm not educated or anything! Mr. Friend is so good to me, but I just hate him." Again she blew her nose. "I'm getting older by the day, and I've got no prospects for a husband. Husband?" she gasped, wiping her eyes on her sleeve and squinting at Janet, "I've got as much chance of getting a husband as the hooker down the street. Worse! At least they'd know what to do with a man; I've forgotten where to start!" Janet frowned, taking a sip of her tea and then replacing her cup.

"Sweetie," she interrupted gently. "First off, let me tell you something. God's got the right man out there for you, don't you worry. As for sex? Trust me, you never forget how. Second, from what you've told me, your parents haven't done much to help you since Rob left. In fact, they seem to be oblivious to your needs, they seem to only care about themselves. And as for Burl Friend, well…"

"No, you've got it wrong," Sweetie interrupted, looking up from the table for the first time. "They're not the problem, I am. I've never appreciated what anyone's done for me, never. I've always taken from people, always. And every day, I have this hatred in me that keeps coming up, toward my parents, my brothers, Mr. Friend—all of them. I honestly think I'm going crazy, I think I'm losing my mind."

The words hung in the air and echoed in Janet's mind. Quietly and deliberately, she reached out and grasped Sweetie's hands. Speaking firmly she made her friend look up into her eyes.

"Sweetie? I want you to talk to a friend of mine. Jeff Hilburn. Remember I told you about him? He helped me through a bad time a few years ago." Janet stared at Sweetie, the warmth of her hands covering her friend's smaller, colder hands. "Do you remember, I told you about the time my Dad died? Remember?" Sweetie nodded without speaking. Janet continued.

"I'm going to write his name down and I want you to call him and set an appointment. I want you to tell him exactly what you're telling me. He's a good man and I think he can help." Releasing her hands, Janet reached into her hand bag and pulled out one of her business cards and flipping it over, she scratched the name and phone number of her counselor, Jeff Hilburn. When she had finished, she handed the card over to Sweetie, waiting until she had taken it. "You call him," she said firmly, holding Sweetie's gaze until her friend nodded silently.

That was three weeks ago, Sweetie thought, staring at the swaying red oak outside the window. Three weeks and here I am.

"So Sweetie," Dr. Hilburn said entering the room and closing the door behind him. "That's an interesting name. How'd you come by that?" He sat across from her and took a slow sip from his coffee mug on which was a picture of a little girl hugging a teddy bear. Sweetie stared at the cup and then at Dr. Hilburn, and then she broke open and began to cry.

PART TWO

She dropped her teddy bear and held her hands in front of her "privates" looking only at her feet and shaking her head. 'No' was not a word she was allowed to verbalize, but her body could, she had found out lately, tell her attacker a very definite "no!" But it really didn't matter. Her attacker was bigger than she was. They had always been bigger than she was.

So she submitted. In the end she gave herself to them but she kept her tears inside along with her anger.

"Hurry up, Bobby," the youth said, looking back from the door. His brother was oblivious to the encouragement, but in just a few seconds he shuddered, gasped and spent himself inside the girl.

"God, you're sure taken your sweet time. Come on, it's my turn."

"Keep your pants on, Billy."

In a few seconds, the younger boy climbed off his partner and stood pulling his jeans up then walking to the door.

"Next?" he said, smiling as he took his brother's place as lookout.

"'Bout time," said the other, stripping his pants and kneeling down over the girl. "Hey Sweetie."

"Hey Billy," she mumbled.

"Mamma, I don't like the way the boys are treatin' me," she said staring up at back of her mother's apron.

"What don't you like, Sweetie?"

"They're touchin' me...they're touchin' me in my—in my privates." For a few seconds her mother kept kneading the bread dough, occasionally stopping to sprinkle flour over the lump. Then, after wiping her hands on her apron, she turned around to face her daughter.

"I don't want to hear talk like that in my house. Your brothers are good boys. They would never hurt you or doing anything like that. Now you go on back to your room and stay there till supper. You think about what you're saying and then you come back and apologize. Now!"

Turning she left the kitchen, taking her bear with her—taking Tulia with her.

"I love you."

"What?"

"I love you, Rob. I do." She scooted across the seat closer to the tall teenager and snuggled close into him.

"Well, I'm not sure…I love you."

Smiling into his shirt, Sweetie reached down and began to unbuckle his belt.

"Hey," he said, swerving the truck, snapping his head down to see her head. "What're you doin'?"

There was no verbal reply, only the inevitable connection. She knew what love was, she had always known.

She felt the surge of warm blood running down her face onto her new dress, the one she had made over six weeks before just for that night. Rob looked at her as if she were something he had hit with the car, and she realized she had been there before. Turning from him she took her handkerchief from her purse and began to clean herself. Behind her she could hear the engine of Rob's Camero roar to life and then the heavy tires tearing at the gravel drive.

He loved her, she knew that. It was just nerves because of the prom and them being promised.

She had just pushed him too far.

"Daddy?" she looked over at him sitting in his chair, the evening paper before his face.

"Yes?"

"Daddy, I…"

"What is it, Sweetie?'"

Grateful that her father had not looked at her, she took a deep breath and let it all out.

"Daddy, I don't think I can marry Rob. I just don't want to do it. I'm scared, Daddy. I want to stay here, I want to stay with you."

In a matter of seconds the paper came down, and Sweetie's father stared at her across the den floor.

"Sweetie, this weddin's been planned for nearly a month. There ain't no turnin' back now. You're just nervous about your weddin' night, that's all. It's just nerves, don't you worry about it. If I know ole Rob, he'll be easy with you. You just don't worry yourself."

And the paper went back up.

"Well I'll be damned, a baby already?" Her father seemed ready to bust. "That's great, Rob, really great. Good for you!"

There was a round of general congratulations as the family made happy noises and floated in Rob's vacinity. Sweetie stood by the fireplace running her hand over her newly swelling abdomen and thinking of a Saturday three years before.

No one had congratulated anyone that day, she thought. There weren't any happy noises in that cold, sterile room. Only the sound of gurgling machine and the smell of antiseptic and ice cold hands where there should have been none. And there was pain and nausea and fear and desperation and shame.

Rob had taken her there and dropped her off.

"They say you'll be through in a few hours. I'll be back then." There was no conversation to be had. The decision had been made for her and that was right. She was too young to be a mother, too immature and ignorant to raise a child. She needed a few more years to grow up and Rob needed to graduate and get a job. Being a dad at his age would ruin his life. This was best for everyone.

Everyone.

Sweetie glanced over at a framed picture of her brothers and mother and father. In the front of the picture she could see herself at four years, toddling by dragging that old beige teddy bear.

"Tulia," she mused touching the picture.

The pain tore at her inside as if an animal was ripping her apart. Lying as she was, there was nothing to block the onslaught of the pressure, the searing agony as it approached.

"You're doin' fine, Sweetie, you're doin' fine. Jes scream your head off, if'n you want."

The old midwife wheezed as she worked, pulling and pinching at her as her mother, father, Rob and her brothers nodded approvingly on all sides of her.

"How'd I do, Jim?"

"Fine, son, jes fine."

"Man, Rob, that's a goddamn big boy in there," her brother said slapping him on the shoulder. Sweetie heard the horses coming, the thunder of their hooves and then she screamed.

"Ok, here he comes," the midwife panted. "This is the big one, Sweetie, push, push hard!" All at once the blister was lanced, the gush of her life poured out onto the sheets and she exhaled the joy of her new motherhood.

"Hey, Rob, looks like you got yourself a gelding there," her brother remarked sarcastically.

"Shit," her father whispered under his breath and turning, left the room.

"Well, Sweetie, it's a little girl," her mother soothed. Leaning over, the older woman brushed her hair out of her eyes and tried to dry off the perspiration from her forehead. "Boys don't always run in families. I was just lucky I guess. But you'll have other children, you're still very young. Never know, next time might be the charm."

Sweetie could not hear her mother, nor really acknowledge anyone else in the room. All she heard was the cry of her child, of the angel she had brought forth.

"Tulia," she whispered.

"Where are you going?"

"As far away from you as I can!"

"What about us? What about Tulia? We're your family!"

There were no words, just the door slamming and a few seconds later the roar of his engine and the squeal of his tires.

He'll be back, she thought. He always comes back.

"I don't see how you think we can help," her father snapped angrily. "You ran him off, plain and simple."

"I'm sorry, Sweetie, but your father's right," her mother said, sheepishly turning back to her cooking. "I don't know how to put this easily for you but it is a fact of life—if Rob was being satisfied at home, then he wouldn't be looking elsewhere."

Sweetie stared at the undisguised revulsion on her father's face and realized that he was right. I ran him off, she mused, I suppose that's right. Her father turned from staring at her and looked out the back kitchen window at her youngest brother who was just arriving from work.

"Well, I'll tell you one damn thing," he said without turning around. "You can't come back home, we got no room. Not for you and that *daughter* of yours. I'm sorry."

He didn't sound sorry, Sweetie thought. Her mother stood like a statue at the counter cutting board preparing that evening's supper. The knife snicked at the celery she was preparing. She did not turn around.

"Well, I guess I'll see you later," she said taking her purse off the chair back, finding her keys and then grabbing Tulia up from the floor. Pausing at the back door, she looked back at her parents and sighed. "I love ya'll."

There was no response as she pushed through the screen past her younger brother. "Hey, Sweetie," He quipped passing her on his way in. He ignored Tulia as usual.

"Hey, Billy," she sighed.

PART THREE

"Sweetie?" Jeff Hilburn leaned over to try and catch her eyes. "Are you all right?"

She slowly brought her eyes to his and nodded as if in a daze.

"I'm sorry," he frowned. "I want to make the hurt go away. I want to revenge you. You and Tulia. I want to take you back and right all those terrible wrongs but you know that's not possible." Sweetie nodded and wiped her eyes and nose. She shifted her position and put her hand over her eyes, as if she were having a headache. Jeff moved to get more tissues and then pulled his chair closer the small couch.

"You're a brave person." The way he said it was more a statement than an encouragement. "The life you have led to this day has required a courage that I'm ashamed to say I probably don't have. Especially these last couple of months," indicating the many sessions since that first gray winter's day. He paused, taking his glasses off and rubbing the bridge of his nose. For a moment the two sat in silence, just the quiet between them.

"I think you know now that your family and your upbringing were not normal." He paused again waiting for a sign from Sweetie that she was again with him. "Please understand that you can get beyond this, beyond your past. You are not "crazy" as you said months ago. In family systems similar to the one in which you grew up, the person like you who goes for help is very special—very brave." He stopped again connecting with her eyes and nodding as she understood. "That's right, you went for help because you're strong, strong enough to leave the system. Strong enough to get help."

"I'm proud of you."

Sweetie began to weep again, but this time it was a different crying. This time she cried because she was glad and she felt more like a person. She no longer felt so stripped. After another minute or so Jeff spoke softly.

"Are we at a place where you can stop?" She nodded and smiled, beginning to gather her things to go.

"Sweetie?" he ventured as she stood to leave. "I'd like to know what your legal name is, your *given* name. Is that OK?"

She nodded and looked down only for an instant, and then glanced back into Jeff's eyes. "Sarah Renee."

Jeff smiled and nodded as she turned to leave.

"That's better," he said.

By Self-Murder

"You can be a king or a street sweeper, but everybody dances with the Grim Reaper."

—*Robert Alton Harris*

THE EL

Sinclair looked at his finger and at the great crimson drops of blood sliding from it to the ground. The light, brilliant from an overhead fixture, glistened and infused the round drops with a fierce animation he had never seen. At his feet, at platform level, the blood spattered freely, coloring his shoes in abstract fashion and mingling with the gum wrappers, newspapers and litter.

For a moment he could only look at the blood, at his finger sliced neatly by the turnstile spindle, and at the growing puddle by his feet. Meanwhile, though he did not see them, the people on the platform pushed past him, hurried forward by the grating and screeching of metal on metal from the incoming Green Route Elevated Train.

It was at this point that the pain struck him. Murderously, it lanced across his finger and deep into his hand, closing his fist as he winced and cursed to himself. Beside him an elderly woman who was passing, looked up briefly from her habitual gray slump, first at his face and then at the thin red line running down the side of his clenched fist. Almost at once, she altered what had been her course and steered around him, her lips tight in determination and her eyes frozen to his hand. Then, like a group of pigeons alerted to danger, the crowd instinctively squared away from Sinclair, leaving him in a pool of isolation in the middle of Philly's Union Station.

That's what I get for hurrying, he thought. He stood for a second and the settled emptiness of an old song wended through his mind, "…*just a drop of water in the endless sea…*"

Glancing up beyond his hand, he saw the train, *his* train—the second-to-last train of the night—as it accommodated the few straggling passengers before the conductor could blow his departure whistle. As if snatched from a dream, he jolted awake and rushed across the yards that separated him from the train and thrust himself between its closing steel doors. For a moment it seemed he would be smothered by the black rubber vise which held him, but then in another he was through and standing alone in the transom.

Around him the other passengers took no notice of his successful battle with the Transit Authority, or his bleeding hand, which for the moment he, too, had forgotten about. It took several seconds, in fact, for him to again register the searing pain which he had recognized only moments before. It was strange how the pain was affecting him, he thought, finding a seat among the scattered empties at the back of the car. It appeared he was becoming somewhat dizzy, and though it was only a cut finger, for some reason he felt the urge to cry.

Clenching his lacerated finger tightly in his fist, Sinclair reached his free hand into his jacket pocket, then his pants pocket searching for something with which to stanch the blood flow. Finding nothing, he glanced down at his feet and seeing a section of the *Times* he snatched it up and began wrapping it tightly around his finger. Somewhere in his mind the fact that a newspaper was actually sterile whispered a pathetic form of consolation. Yet fashioning the smudged newsprint he grimaced and noted that the headlines he had seen had never struck him as particularly clean. And who knew to what the floor of the El would expose him. What was that about hurrying?

The makeshift bandage finished, he leaned carefully back against the swaying metal body of the train and elevated his hand resting his elbow on the back of the seat next to him. Taking a deep breath and exhaling, he closed his eyes and tried to calm the storm that seemed to be rising within. But in seconds he was overwhelmed, his battle against the pain lost. Coughing once, he adjusted his posture against the cold metal of the train and brought his free hand up to shield his eyes. Then his resistance broke and the tears began. *"Nothing lasts forever but the earth and sky...it slips away...and all your money won't another minute buy..."* The song slid from his coiled mind like wire from a spool. He couldn't stop it or the tears.

She was beautiful, he remembered, tall and athletic, with a face that would silence a room and lips that tasted like candy. Best of all she had loved him—more than anything or anyone in the world. What he wouldn't give to hold her one more time, to kiss her even briefly on the cheek—to hear her voice, even if only over the phone. But she was gone and bringing her back was impossible.

What had it been?

His job, he thought, his friends? His family? What one thing in the complex pattern of his life had turned her so decisively away so that she no longer even tolerated his presence? Turning it over in his mind again, Sinclair slowly found the shabby trail of his failures, the rusted gates of his memories reluctantly giving into the weight of his regret.

The fight under the Franklin Bridge—when he had slapped her in his rage? Images of her distorted face boiled back into his mind, sharp features, wickedly vengeful and bitter, her words lashing out as him in cruel, razor-like attacks. He could see himself, his back to her, pacing near the wall and shaking his head. He felt the rage again, the churning of his stomach and the sick, pathetic retaliation that was coming.

Not again, he winced, not again. But in his mind the cinema of his past persisted and again his hand shot backward, again his hand found the high, delicate cheek of his beloved and again he felt the recoil in his arm, the soft, but solid resistance she had been. And he felt her blood. Pain and blood running down his hand, down his arm all over again.

Drawing his sleeve across his wet face he glanced at his wounded finger and realized the makeshift bandage was failing and his blood was seeping from under its edges, oozing down his arm. Yet, it would be enough, he thought, feeling the motion of the train and knowing the nearness of his destination.

It had not been that fight, he remembered, again closing his eyes and smothering his torment. She had loved him even after that, maybe even in spite of that. No, he knew what it had been that had turned her away, changed her from his into another's. It had been something else, something much more violent.

That moment had come, as it probably did for many, he grimaced. In the heat of tender passion, on the edge of the abyss into which their foreplay had taken them. They had both been virgins, to that moment uninitiated into the realm of passion. And when they had finally embraced in the solitude of her parents' empty house he knew that the moment he had feared and longed for was at hand.

She struggled, he remembered, though strangely not with him. With him she had been unsheltered and open. But he remembered sensing the torment of the decision deep within her, the violence of her struggles as they drew nearer to the moment. What was it she had said later?

"We should've waited. I wanted to wait…it was important to wait…" But they hadn't waited. They had proceeded and in a few brief minutes concluded what had been a long, desperate battle with desire. A battle he now realized they had both lost.

She had never been the same after that. He remembered. Her kisses became strange—distant. Her words, once light and full of joy, grew morose until he no longer cared to hear them. Eventually she told him she simply no longer cared for him and they parted, though not in anger. The horror of their parting, the gruesome aspect of their separation was in the listless apathy, which choked them. Numbing their hearts and minds so that they drifted apart, bruised rather than broken. What had been between them as a mountain, a prize to be achieved, had been removed and all that remained had been the emptiness. It would have been more honest had they shattered and cut each other to pieces, he thought. *"...dust in the wind..."*

The train slowed as it descended and began its long right turn into Center City. Outside the amber lights flickered sporadically as the train scraped the power rail and passed through the underground darkness. Sinclair wiped his nose and mouth, rubbing his hand dry on his jeans. His mind was torn and shredded, traumatized worse than his hand. Coughing against the tears, he felt his mind appealing to this body to shelter it, almost pleading with his flesh to distract it from the *real* torment. But the pain he sensed in his hand failed in magnitude. The only wound that could eclipse this pain would carve out his heart.

Through the glass he saw the green and white tile of the platform sliding by and he felt the train slowing. In a moment the rocking car stopped and the steel doors slid obediently open. Sinclair followed his fellow transients and exited. All disappeared across the platform, through the shiny metal gates and up the stairs to the cold night of Center City. He remained, staring past the bland shadows of the people to the turnstile at the base of the stairs. In his mind familiar words crept haltingly along the muffled walls of his pain *"...dust in the wind, everything is dust in the wind..."*

What he would give to have those moments back? What could he have known than that would have prevented the suffering he now experienced? Where were the warning signs, the lifeguards—the friendly, neighborhood cops? It seemed to him as he stared across the platform to the stainless bars of the exit gate that what had appeared an entrance had really been a trap. But now, all that was history and he was standing on the El platform alone, bleeding. And he knew from where he stood, that all the tears in the world wouldn't change history or heal his sliced finger.

Distantly, he heard the hollow whistle of the conductor and in a few seconds the doors to the car in front of him slid quietly shut. After a beat the train that had carried Sinclair pulled away from Center City and slid off into the darkness, trailing behind it a muted shower of sparks. For a few minutes Sinclair stood in the clammy silence of the tunnel, listening to its underworld echoes and feeling the cold creep up his legs and into his body. *"…dust in the wind…"*

There was a buzz in his ears like the fat black flies that torment horses or bite your legs in the summer, but it was only the fluorescents above his head. They were high above him, caged in filthy wire mesh and lost in an intestine of cables and conduits, casting down their autopsy-room light to the tile below, cold and pale and terrifying.

"…all we do crumbles to the ground, though we refuse to see…"

The last train of the night rattled toward him, its headlight snaking around the walls of the far tunnel like an insane watchman's flashlight. Sinclair turned his head to look into the darkness seeing the beam, his vision stuttering like a film gone bad. *"dust…,"* the voice whispered in his ear, *"…dust in the wind."*

In seconds the car blazed into the station and the next Green Route El clattered toward him, its headlight brilliant and blinding, a huge eye staring into his misery. The whoosh of cushion air being pushed in front of the train suddenly wrapped him like a warmed blanket, powdery motes swirling about him, his feet shuffling forward. The sing-song murmur that had been his companion coiled about him as he stepped from the platform.

BY JUSTICE

"There are so many little dyings that it doesn't matter which of them is death."

—Kenneth Patchen

THE ICE BULLET

Doc Munós crossed himself and rose painfully from the kneeler. He was pretty much alone in the church, just one of the acolytes trimming the altar candles and a very old woman with a traditional, but worn black embroidered veil covering her iron gray, hair praying. In Spain, those are called *mantillas*, he thought, making his way stiffly out from the pew and into the center aisle. *Mantilla*, he thought again, easing himself down on one knee and once again crossing himself, much more attractive. His deep-set eyes rose from the stone floor up to the dimly illuminated altar and beyond to the life-sized crucifix which hung from the apse wall. For yet another moment he studied the familiar figure.

Over the seven decades of his life, Raul Munós' eyes had grown accustomed to the brutality, which so often has been perpetrated upon the human body. Sadly, he had been called upon time and again to bind up broken limbs and sew together torn flesh caused by one man's cruelty to another. He had also been called upon to sometimes tend the dying. This duty he had not minded, nor really the repair of the terrible consequences of violence, after all he had been trained to heal. But it seemed the Dear Senór had yet one other duty for him to accomplish, one he would have rather avoided. Crossing himself again, he struggled to his feet and stood with his face uplifted. Now he would have to end life, to take from some otherwise healthy person that gift of God no man should by rights take. And yet, he would use his skill and training and kill, and then at the end of the day, return to his home and wife and even sleep, but by the grace of God.

The hand-carved horror hung from the rough hewn cross before him exhibited the classic rigor of the many corpses he had seen. His head was locked into his neck at a downward angle, his chest expanded to bursting, arms distended unnaturally from loosened, if not dislocated, shoulders, all clinical symptomology of a savage, protracted death. Doc Munos appraised the gaping thoracic wound with its inflamed lips of crimson paint. It was made by the iron tip of a Roman lance and was well-positioned to produce the pericardial event described in scripture. He had surely been dead already, he considered for the thousandth time.

The other wounds inflicted on this ancient Jew were not as easily seen in this crucifix, but he knew them all too well. Scourging tore the victim's back to ribbons at the hands of an enthusiastic Roman with a short but dense braid of iron and glass tipped leather; broken and loosened teeth, bruised and lacerated muscles, eyes swollen shut and his beard torn out in bloody clumps. Finally, brutal thorns forced onto his head, beaten into place with rods until they penetrated his skull. State execution, once upon a time.

Doc Munós left the dim coolness of the Cathedral de Guadalupe and stepped into a brilliant Texas day. Even his dark glasses couldn't protect him from the searing pain that pierced his mind and he bowed his head. Now he would travel the sixty-odd miles to Huntsville and to The Walls, the Death House of the State Penitentiary where his duty for the evening lay. Some desperate, pitiful, evil man would be waiting for him there, waiting for death at the end of his needle.

Louis Able "Skeet" Rossitter, spun out his last few minutes in the Polunsky unit of Texas' death row by sitting on the stainless steel toilet suspended from the wall of his cell. In little more than the time it would take him to button up and flush, the guards would unlock his cell door and escort him to the van and then on to Huntsville and the Death House. In fact, he could hear the heavy, steel clash of doors as they entered Pod A. His breath rattled into his lungs and his rough hands quivered slightly as he stood and buttoned his white coveralls. He did not flush.

Skeet Rossitter had spent his 11 years on death row in predictable fashion. While his court-appointed attorneys pursued the staggered appeal process, Skeet lived in a steel box, six feet by nine feet, with one narrow, horizontal window to the outside, too high for him to reach and with one sliding drawer to receive his meals. He had not watched television since he arrived on death row, since no TVs were allowed. But he had listened to the radio religiously.

He also got to exercise three times a week, an hour at a time. He loved it out of the Pod, outside with whatever weather offered. At least the harsh clash of steel on steel was muffled out in the yard, though not completely banished.

Still, with the sun on his skin and the few natural sounds that heaved over the fences and walls, he felt, at least for an hour…human.

Human.

He had been called many things since it happened, but human was not one of them. His lawyers called him Mr. Rossitter, the guards called him *scum* and sometimes *nigger,* but this last only under their breath; Pod A was populated mostly by blacks and Skeet knew it. Fear, Skeet had decided, was not necessarily a bad thing, especially if it kept you from getting hurt or tormented. Anyway, most of the guards were just bored and did their job without conversation at all, except maybe when they had to control the other inmates. Captain Morgan was actually nice sometimes, and called him Skeet. But Captain Morgan wasn't in the Unit much anymore.

The other inmates in the Pod called him *zero,* because he never spoke. For that matter, he never made any sound at all. When they had closed the door on him in the Pod, he had stopped speaking with anybody, even his lawyers. When they visited he would only nod or shake his head in response to their questions, which, at first, was alright with them. He supposed they thought they could use his new-found silence to their advantage during the appeal process. Lately, they were just resigned to his silence like everyone else. He didn't much care what they did or thought; he didn't care what anybody thought; his not talking had nothing to do with legal strategy or some stupid game. He just realized when he had arrived at Polunsky, his life had ended, and his words, never very eloquent or very many, were no longer worth hearing. His mind…his spirit had already died and was just waiting for his body to catch up.

On the outside, they called him the *Woodlands Monster;* at least that's what one of his lawyers told him and to prove it showed a newspaper clipping when he came during the trial. He guessed they were right he was no longer human. Ever since it happened, ever since that horrible, bloody afternoon, he ceased walking the earth as a man. He was a monster.

Doc Munós arrived at *The Walls* early in the afternoon as was his custom. He liked to get to the Death House early to review his materials, to make sure he spoke with the tie-down team and other guards that would be involved with the execution, and view the death chamber itself, not that he hadn't seen it before. This was his twentieth execution in the three years he had been on the rotation. As one of only three physicians authorized to administer lethal injection in Texas, he had become familiar with the routine in a very short period of time. Shaking his head he barked a humorless laugh, turning his car off and sitting in the rapidly warming interior, he stared up at the red brick structure before him. Nothing about this process was routine, he thought. Taking some pathetic, insane person's life would never be routine to him. After another moment staring at The Walls, he picked up the thin manila folder from the empty passenger seat and opened it. Inside on a single sheet of paper was the TDCJ brief on his patient for the evening. The black face staring out from the small black-and-white booking photo looked no different to him than twenty others he had seen. Flat, dead eyes stared out past the booking sergeant—perhaps at the years that lay beyond, perhaps only at a crack in the plaster wall.

What in the world caused you to do such a horrible thing, he wondered again. Dropping his eyes beyond the personal information, he read again the circumstances of the crime.

> "Convicted in the slayings of his girlfriend Caroline, and her 14-year old son, Damian, inside their Houston home. Both victims were beaten to death with a baseball bat. Following his arrest in Katy two days after the murders, Rossitter said he took the bat and began to beat his girlfriend when she awoke and found him standing over her in the bedroom. Fearing that Damian might discover his murdered mother, Rossitter walked into the living room where he was sleeping and struck him repeatedly in the head with the bat. Rossitter did not harm Damian's ten-year-old sister, telling her instead to go across the street to a neighbor's house and stay there. No motivation for the murders was ever given."

Why? Sweat was beading his face and running under his coat, soaking his shirt. My God, why? Yet he knew his prayer would be unanswered, at least this side of the grave. Closing the folder, he placed it back on the passenger seat and took his keys. The time was getting away from him and he needed to prepare. Stepping out and closing the door, he adjusted his tie and walked on into the death house.

The forty miles to Huntsville passed quickly. Skeet, chained and placed between two guards, sat in the van listening to the road noise and the rushing wind, looking out the tiny, mesh windows of the van's doors at the retreating Texas countryside and the bluebonnets lining the highway. The first weeks of summer were the sweetest, he remembered. It had been a while since he'd been in it, seen its color.

"Hey, get him," one of the guards said. "The monster likes flowers!" The other guard grinned behind his dark aviator glasses, but Skeet ignored them both continuing to stare out the windows as the road unwound.

"The I.V. is started with normal saline solution. A dose bag of sodium thiopental is hung and introduced into the saline to sedate the condemned," Doc Munós explained, walking the new member of the tie-down team through the execution procedures. "Pancuronium bromide is added to relax the musculature including the diaphragm," he continued in his clipped, accented English, "and finally, potassium chloride is injected and the heart is stopped. From the introduction of the saline to the stopping of the heart, only five to seven minutes elapses." The new guard stared at the small plastic bags laid out on the stainless steel tray and the sterile tubing and needle packs.

Painless, Munós thought. The murderer will simply go to sleep. No trauma, no agony or shattering, convulsive paroxysms, just…sleep. And it only cost the state $86.08. Munós stripped off the latex gloves he'd been wearing during his prep. How ironic that I should wear gloves, he thought, like it matters that I might transmit bacteria.

"Hey, Doc," Sergeant Michaels called from inside the death chamber, "you gonna give em the ice bullet?" A slight grimace turned down the corners of Munos' mouth as the senior tie-down officer, Major Hilger, turned a stony face in his direction and shook his head slightly. Munos placed his stiffened hands on the small bags of liquid, neatly arranged atop a white towel on a stainless tray.

"Leave everything as I have arranged them here on this tray. If anything is disturbed I will halt the execution until I am satisfied." His voice was loud enough to be heard in the death chamber and he looked into the eyes of Major Hilger. The officer who had made the comment came into the room after a few seconds and waited, one hand on his duty belt. His face was hard underneath the grin but not evil, Munós considered. He had seen it all before—too many times. He wants more than the process can give him, just like everyone else, and he will be disappointed just like everyone else.

The practice of chilling the drugs prior to injection was an old, and in his mind, a cruel tradition. Other doctors rebelled against the painless termination process and refrigerated the drugs so the condemned's system was shocked by the flow seconds before they lost consciousness. He supposed the custom was meant to emulate the hum of electricity as the power surges before an electrocution, or the hissing of gas just before the cyanide flows in—sort of like the footsteps you fear will overtake you in the dark. They *wanted* the condemned to feel a jolt of terror before death, like some sick *gotcha*, a joy-buzzer for the soul.

He hated the practice.

Rossitter climbed down from the van with difficulty, requiring the assistance of one of his escorts to keep from falling to the pavement. The shackles and cuffs chained to the belt around his waist restricted his movement to the point that lifting his feet more than a few inches above the ground was next to impossible.

"Move your ass," the death house guard barked, shoving him into a well-lighted bay between facing walls of heavy steel bars. The buzz and click of electronic locks and the screech of metal-on-metal accompanied his passage through the bay and into *the Walls*.

He had heard many stories of the death house and he now realized that most of them were fear-induced fantasy. The walls were neutral-colored, as were the floors, the guards all wore black baseball caps and except for the clang and clank of steel doors and locks there were no sounds, no talking of any kind. Rossitter followed another, new officer to a small room where he was unshackled by two youngish, white guards, and then left alone. He stood in the center of the room for about a minute, getting the sense of the space, inhaling the antiseptic smell of the air and listening to the silence. Eventually, he turned and took the two steps over to a shelf cot and eased himself down. Once again he quieted himself to listen.

Doc Munós sat in a tiny room adjacent to Major Hilger's office and stared at the colorful paper fragment that clung to the drab gray wall. The three-inch triangular scrap clung to the wall as if it had been glued, probably one of those cheap, give-away calendars you get from an insurance agent or the local pharmacy, he thought. He gazed at the faded blues and the one tiny bit of red, and began to think it had been a reproduction of some kind of painting, perhaps an impressionist. The irregular brush strokes looked right. He remembered spending hours in the Dallas Museum of Art two summers back when they had hosted a collection of French Impressionist masterpieces. On loan from the Musee de Orsay of Paris, the works of Monet, Manet, Pissaro, Degas and la Trec had fascinated him to the point that his wife had finally left him sitting in one of the smaller alcoves, preferring to browse the gift shop instead.

It wasn't the subject matter that intrigued him so much, or really the ground-breaking stroke treatments. It was the colors that had captured his mind. Blue was never just blue, it was a cerulean wave crest on a deep sea of cobalt, with azure skies above it and indigo eyes within. Red leaped from the canvas in a parade-ground spray of crimson or a slash of scarlet upon opaline skin. To his mind, color was the nature of living, the context of vitality. Leaning closer to he scrap, Munós narrowed his eyes to get a better look and then frowned. It wasn't a painting after all, he decided sitting back in his chair and losing interest. It was probably some damn NASCAR ad.

Rossitter stood under the hot shower, letting the jets of water cleanse his mind. It had been days since he last washed, and the harsh impact of the water felt particularly good on his back and shoulders. Letting the water pound him, he stood with his arms limp at his sides, his eyes closed to the bars and two guards just beyond him. His *last* shower, he thought. Everything was now a *last* something or other, his *last* trip, his *last* meal, his *last* crap. The shower was good, he considered, better than the other stuff. Well, almost everything. The quiet was good. He liked the quiet of the death house after the incessant clamor at Polunsky—it was soothing, like being wrapped in a blanket or a cocoon of sorts. To be clean and quiet were good things and he was glad of it, even if only for today.

Munós was standing in the death chamber when the minister came in and stood back against the wall. He didn't recognize the man, but that didn't signify anything, he was probably not a prison chaplain, rather someone from the outside. Maybe the condemned had asked for him in particular. That would be a good thing, the old doctor considered.

Turning back to the table, he looked down at the tall thin black man who was being strapped down, the heavy leather buckles being secured efficiently by the members of the tie-down team. Major Hilger nodded approval as they finished and the team stepped aside. The condemned was staring directly above him at the lights in the ceiling and seemed almost calm. Almost, but not completely, Munós decided. He could see the rapid throbbing of the carotid artery in his exposed neck, the slight compression of his lips and the occasional bobbing of his Adam's apple. His mouth must be dry, he considered, and reached for the needle.

Did he have any *last* words? Once again, another *last* something. No, he didn't have any *last* words; he had spoken any *last* words over eleven years earlier. No *last* words, no plea for mercy or forgiveness, no spitting vengeance or hatred at his executioners or the spectators beyond the glass walls, no begging for understanding, no *last* anything for anyone else, except himself.

A few *last* sensations were all that was left for him. The comfortable tightness of the leather buckled restraints, the compressed, quiet air around him in the death chamber, a momentary coolness and tingling from the alcohol wipe as the doctor prepared his arm for the needle, the abrupt stab of steel entering his flesh and the slow dull ache as the needle was pushed into his vein and settled there, the efficient hands of the doctor and their confident pressure as he taped the I.V. in place. For a breathless second he waited for the icy shock he had been warned about back at Polunsky, for the serrated impact of the *ice bullet,* but all he felt was a slight fluid sensation as the saline and drugs entered his blood.

Skeet looked up at the doctor as he adjusted the I.V. drip. He didn't look happy about his job, he decided, but he didn't look too bothered either, just competent. His brown hands were sure and his touch measured like the old, black doctor his granny had used when he got sick or hurt as a kid. This Mexican had the same gentle surety that never failed to comfort, even when he was doing something scary. Just like that old, white-haired, black man years before. When he had had to get shots as a kid or get a cut sewed up, he had noticed the touch. There had never been hesitation or a jerky, overly forceful application, just deliberate, measured action, sure as the mail. Yes, he thought, looking back into the overhead light, this old Mex is a good doctor, he'll do just fine.

Munós completed his tasks and stepped back to wait while the drugs had their effect. He had felt Rossitter's eyes on him while he introduced the cocktail, but he hadn't noticed any hatred as he had in the past. In fact, when he had glanced over at him, he had noticed that his pulse was actually slowing toward a normalcy, losing some of the internal panic he had discerned moments before. It would be only minutes now, just a few last ticks of the clock.

Looking beyond the open black curtains at the witnesses seated outside the death chamber, Munós noticed something. Among the official witnesses, for there was no one in the family section, the overall demeanor reflected boredom more than any other emotion. However, there was one man whose expression leaped across the space that separated them and would have screamed rage had it possessed a voice. The man appeared in his late sixties, deeply black with salt and pepper hair cut very short, military fashion. He was perched on his front-row seat, arms crossed tightly hugging his chest, pulling his ill-fitting brown suite out of whatever shape it once held. He appeared to be trembling. His face and neck were suffused with blood and his expression was contorted into the single-most, virulent snarl of hatred Munos had ever seen.

Shifting his gaze, Munós consulted the large clock on the wall and then leaned over the motionless prisoner and listened carefully with his stethoscope. The tall, lean black man convicted all those years before of so terrible a crime was dead. He listened patiently for a full minute and then straightened his back, removing his stethoscope and nodding to Major Hilger. It was over. And out of the corner of his eye, he could see the black man on the front row start forward in his seat, releasing the powerful grip he had held on his arms. In that single moment of realization the older, black man blanched, and then slumped forward, beginning to sob into his hands. The witnesses around him looked away uncomfortably and then stood to shuffle off, leaving the man to his passion. His once-rigid military frame was no longer infused with power, but had wilted as if all the cords that had held him together were suddenly transformed from steel into fibers that pulled apart under the strain, rotted from within. The object of his hatred was clearly no longer in the world.

Munós put the stethoscope in his pocket and left the death chamber.

BY INDIFFERENCE

"He has outsoared the shadow of our night; envy and calumny and hate and pain, and that unrest which men miscall delight, can touch him not and torture not again; from the contagion of the world's slow stain, he is secure."

—*Percy Bysshe Shelley*

LA GUARDIA'S SIN

"Don't cry."

The words were a pleading, not a command. Simm stared at the boy and recognized a face he had seen all too often over the years. Somewhere in the haunt of this youth's thoughts was a question released and soaring. Somewhere there was now a why.

"It's okay, he's gone now."

The boy gathered himself together, bruised and aching, wiping large salty drops from his red cheeks. Squatting down, reaching a hand out to steady the boy's dressing, Simm spoke calmly avoiding the issues.

"I understand how things are, believe me. Nobody's going to hurt you now. Not now. And don't worry, I'm not going to tell anyone."

The large dark eyes of the boy stared into Simm's face without notice. Black panels of fear were closing his recognition, all that remained was automatic.

Breathe.

Simm glanced over his shoulder toward the chapel to see if there was anyone around, but the large, carved doors were closed, the poor box hanging on its nail. Father Frank was evidently already gone for the day. Looking up at the dwindling beauty of the weathered stone church and the graying sky beyond, Simm knew he had to get the boy home. Shadow birds bristled in the cornice of the chapel and braced against the wind. Silent witnesses. Turning back, he smiled gently and pointed at his watch.

"It's getting pretty late, why don't I take you home?"

There was no response from the boy, except a few furtive looks past the hedgerow where they were. Simm tried to make him understand, but the only indication he received that the boy understood was a jerky shaking of his head, the same look of fear on his face.

"OK, look," he tried again. "I'm going to help you up and then we'll go over to my car. Do you think you can stand?"

The boy shook his head in the same disjointed way, eyes looking now in wider circles.

"OK, let me put my arms around you…" The boy panicked, shaking his head vigorously, stiffening as the older man tried to pick him up. "Relax, relax…you're safe now. Don't worry, it's okay, it's okay…" His strong left arm scooped up the boy's awkward lankiness, his free hand snatching at scattered papers and a trampled school cap. For a moment, he just stayed in the same position, holding the trembling boy to his chest, trying to calm him.

There were no words.

Soon, there was no sound.

Eventually there was no protest at all.

He trembled and submitted, just like before.

"That's better," Simm whispered, standing from the dense foliage and proceeding across the neatly cut grass to his waiting car, the boys long legs and arms dangling loosely from his embrace. As he crossed the sidewalk, an elderly woman passed by; she was walking an overweight dachshund that growled the closer they came. The woman just stared with her mouth open. Simm ignored her, and proceeded to open the back door and place the shivering teen on the blue vinyl. Once he was sure the boy would stay, he placed the crumpled papers and the school cap on the rear deck and closed the door. Stepping forward he climbed in through his open door and slammed it behind him. Hard. Then, after looking over his right shoulder, he pulled into traffic and proceeded into the dusk.

The heater in the car felt good to his feet. The early autumn weather was turning a bit cooler than normal and squatting in the wet grass had chilled him. Simm was sure the boy would appreciate the warmth since he had been much more exposed and he glanced at him in the rearview mirror to check. For the briefest of moments fear flashed into his mind that the boy had somehow gotten out the door before he left the curb. He was not visible in the mirror. But when he jerked around and looked over the seat, Simm saw the long body laid out on the back cushions, curled, more or less into a fetal position, no longer shivering. Taking a deep breath, the man tried to calm his racing heart before he spoke. His mind flashed again a picture of the struggle in the hedgerow, and he winced.

Ugly.

Terrible.

Repulsive.

Unforgivable.

"So, you must live around here, right?" There was no answer. Stopping at the light he bit his upper lip and tried to think what to do next. Hospital?

"Hey, listen," he started, moving forward through the intersection. "Why don't I take you over to hospital and have them give you a once-over. You know, you got it pretty bad back there." Still no response.

Simm wrestled in his mind with the rightness of what he needed to do. The hospital was six blocks away, and it didn't appear his conversations with the boy were going to yield much of anything. He really didn't have much choice, the more he thought on it, despite his assurances to the boy that he wouldn't tell anyone. So he nosed his car over to the center lane and looped around the traffic circle till he was headed for St. Michael's.

In moments, he saw the rising soot-stained edifice which all but dominated the east end of the city. He had been here only a few times, visiting or dropping off a friend. He had never really sought medical attention for himself or anyone else. This would be something new.

Following signs, he quickly found the emergency entrance and pulled past parked ambulances to glowing fluorescent lights and broad glass doors. When he looked back, the boy on the seat appeared asleep. God, what a shame!

Shame.

The nurse at input was formal and professional and quite sincere. The doctor on call was also professional and very thorough. The boy, when they opened the door and tried to bring him out, was hysterical. God, how horrible!

Horrible.

"Well, he's definitely been…molested. He's in very bad shape," the doctor said with evident anger. "You say you found him?" The words stung, reminding him of the look on the fat lady's face. There was insinuation in his voice. Simm didn't like it but he could see how the situation might look.

"Yes, I found him," he responded meekly, "in a hedgerow beside St. Michael's." The doctor made some notes and was tapping his pen on the metal ridge of his clipboard when a constable walked into the room. Simm could see the pleasantries were over.

The duty nurse stepped lightly past the discarded blanket by the boy's bed and reached over to check his pulse.

Rapid.

Withdrawing a thermometer from her uniform pocket she shook it out and placed it under his relaxed arm. In a moment she withdrew it.

Very high.

Slipping the vinyl cuff off the bed post and over his arm she puffed air into the tube and then released it in a long hiss, counting.

Very bad.

Reaching down by her feet she reclaimed his lost blanket and re-seated it around the long-boned lad, tucking him in tightly. She then stepped back three steps and took a long hard look at his sleeping figure.

Pain.

Dreams.

Questions flying.

Shaking her head and clucking in sympathetic precision, she strode out the white door, on to her next paid assignment.

Father Frank knelt quietly before the pottery statues of Mary and Joseph and the infant Jesus, blowing out the folding flame from the match in his hand. The three candles he had just purchased blazed gaily on the altar before him, sheltered as they were in scarlet glass votive. Dropping the now cold stick in the tray, he turned his attention to the figures before him.

In automation, his right hand flew to his forehead then straight down, then one shoulder then…he faltered, his hand failing to make the final gesture. In that moment he realized that his knees hurt. The once-brilliant, red velvet beneath him was worn and the hardness of the wood pushed through its previous padding. His knees hurt and he was tired of his knees hurting. Leaning back on his feet, he stood and walked a pace backward to the first of the pews and sat down, massaging his knees and contemplating the trio before him.

Frank thought he understood Jesus, at least the theology of the man. He understood redemption and sanctification, and he even thought he understood transubstantiation. Well, almost. Looking that moment upon the crudely modeled features of the babe, his tiny hands held aloft in awkward sign of blessing, he couldn't for the life of him construct one valid thought toward prayer. What do you say to a clay figure when you realize they're just clay?

And Mary. She was there too, with her blue shawl trailing down over elegant arms. She had always looked so tender to him, so loving. That evening she looked brittle, cracks showing through the paint. What had he ever found to talk to her about? She held a baby inside her body once—what had he done close to that?

Finally, the carpenter. That strange, innocent bystander of scripture, caught as he was in a web of Divine intrigue, hardly spoken of in scripture at all. Frank had never understood praying to this one. Never. Joseph, as important as he surely was, never really impacted anyone as far as Frank knew. No one except perhaps once, a little boy. The art of this statue was even more vague than the others. This guy wasn't even the boy's father, and yet, there he was. Always.

Looking down at his empty hands, Frank thought of the approaching 6:00 a.m. Mass, and the scripture texts he would read. "Are not two sparrows sold for a cent? And yet not one of them will fall to the ground apart from your Father."

Birds.

Frank stared at the statues comfortably placed in their brown stone alcove, and he thought about sparrows.

Outside birds fall.

Inside they aren't allowed.

So birds can't fall inside.

Sighing heavily, Frank pulled himself off the pew and walked past the kneeler and the flickering candles and the faded statues. He passed in front of the altar, and for the first time in 15 years, didn't kneel or cross himself, he just kept walking. The back door slammed and echoed through the vaulted ceilings of the empty church.

The boy soared and tumbled, banking first to the left, then sharply to the right. He was awash in the sky, crystal blue heights beckoned him and azure depths defied him. He was released. Below him, the earth flared out like brown sludge, molting its winter coat. It was all ugliness, flat and labored and tedious. But where he was then, all light played. He was beyond the depths, past that damp shallow existence that the earthbound knew. He was free to extend himself to those places mortals can't know, through the illusions of luck and happenstance, over the bridge of faith, besting hope in its own race.

He was swift.

He was cool, liquid speed and he gifted any who touched his wings, all those who blessed his flight.

Fluttering momentarily, he hovered above the place, the God-place. Its skinny, inky finger reached out to touch him in his gamboling, but he avoided it. Circling, slicing the air with fixed wings, the boy glared down at the structure of the thing, glued to the mud, trembling with despair. Flashing past its windows in descending spiral then upwards once again, he realized the God-place was empty of everyone, everyone but that one who could do nothing but watch.

La guardeian numas oberva!!

Fly, escape, upwards, reach out to emptiness, to the wind, to the storm. Away from the one whose eyes stare from the door, the witness...the *witness.* Closing his eyes and thrashing with all his strength Timothy thrust his tiny brown body through the sky, past the power of his wings to carry him and burst in agonizing splendor.

Away.

Beyond the sky to a place where falling doesn't exist. Where gravity is extinguished and the blue is all there is. Into hands that protect, alighting on fingers which don't retract, far above the pretenders, the shadow birds who, do nothing but watch.

By Infirmity

"I wanted a perfect ending. Now I've learned, the hard way, that some poems don't rhyme, and some stories don't have a clear beginning, middle, and end. Life is about not knowing, having to change, taking the moment and making the best of it, without knowing what's going to happen next. Delicious Ambiguity."

—Gilda Radner

DELICIOUS AMBIGUITY

I can still feel his hand surrounding mine, large and warm and comforting. Yet the entire world around me, except for his hand, is a haze of muted whirring and mumbled conversation. Perhaps it's always been that way.

The pain is no longer an issue, *thank God*. As I lay here, even the memory of it escapes me. But I know the memories are still in my mind, still alive, still…angry with me. In the front of my brain I have an area—a clearing of sorts, stacked with receptacles…boxes. One box holds all the memories of my pain. It is not a file box with neat hanging folders carefully labeled, such as is found in an office. Nor is it a sagging, stained cardboard box, covered in cobwebs of neglect, like I used to find in my attic. No, it has been used too much to look so abandoned, opened and closed, filled and emptied over this past year many, many times. It is a box like the ones I've seen in all the rooms in all the clinics and hospitals I've visited. It is a large box, and it has an ominous biohazard label on it, and it is made of a semi-opaque substance, so that I can see a hint of its contents. I have often seen it from a distance, seen the shadowy writhings within, like alien creatures struggling against each other, clawing to get out, scrabbling against the smooth sides of the box to get at me. I can't remember at this moment how it felt when the box lid creaked open and they swarmed out into my flesh, I only know that in the past I dreaded waking and hearing that coffin-lid sound and then the scuttling of the pain. But as I said, the pain is no longer an issue.

I am not afraid. This is not to say that I have never been afraid; I have. I suppose it is best to say…I am not afraid anymore. When I was young and sick, I would run very high fevers and in my delirium I would see visions. The most common of my visions was of a monster machine, its mouth yawning open, a conveyor transporting into it everything placed on the belt. I would hover above, observing the malevolence of the mechanism, the cold, relentless tearing and rending as objects were drawn into its waiting jaws. Terror would seize me as I floated above, a horror that at any moment I might fall upon the conveyor and be drawn inexorably into its pitiless depths. I remember screaming out loud, thrashing in my sweat-soaked bed, in my father's arms, staring wild-eyed at my parents' distorted faces, struggling to flee the machine.

Now I lie placidly on the conveyor, aware, I think, of my destination, but no longer afraid. Fear, like the pain, is boxed up and stored in the clearing. It, too, is a large box but not plastic or even wood, because fear is too corrosive. Fear is housed in a carefully sealed and locked steel box. Actually, a box within a box, the smaller one holding the fear, the larger, stronger box with the seals and locks, contains the smaller. It's safer that way, I think. Fear can get out of the smallest cracks and seep into your life, like the common cold, so eventually, everyone catches it. But fear is contained now, stored with other items that I no longer need, or that no longer need me.

Strange how I remember fear, can describe its effects, can see my life's struggle with it, but now, even when I remember, I have no anxiety. I wonder if it's the drugs or simply the fact that I've conquered this one terrible enemy, at last. I mean, I have the keys to all the locks on all the boxes. They were given to me a while ago.

He has taken his hand from mine, its warmth radiating away and my hand left alone on the sheet, cooling. I wait for a few seconds and know he will be back. I can feel the course texture of the sheet beneath the tips of my fingers and the presence of tape on the back of my hand. I also know that my hand rests against the side of my leg for I feel its long shape rising beneath the sheet comfortably close. There is movement nearby, a waft of air crosses my face and drifts down my arms and then his hand envelopes mine once again. His hand is strong and large, mine is as a child's within his grasp.

I cannot think too well right now, my mind is so fuddled, by my condition and more than likely, the drugs. I know that I am glad to be resting now. It seems so long since I have truly rested, since my body felt at ease. Maybe the reason I can rest now is because my mind is so insensate, so numbed. I have always had difficulty making my mind accept the mortality of my flesh, its need for rest. Even in succumbing to a nap, I felt I was letting someone down, disappointing my husband or the kids or myself. I suppose I can understand this in the young, we were all indestructible then.

I remember the music most, pounding out heartbeats with velvet-covered mallets. My body was hardy and hard, sensitive to the touch, but bulletproof. Long legs and fingers, baby-soft blond hair to my shoulders, clear eyes and skin with the force of life throbbing and pulsing through me like nuclear adrenaline. When I was awake, I was a meteor ablaze in the heavens, when I slept, it was because my body gave out and I slept where I fell exhausted—embracing eternity, adrift blissfully in the ether. Maturing was a good thing, though. After all, meteors burn to ash.

The following years mostly kept me running *and* guilty. I don't remember having much time, though there were obviously years and years of the stuff. They are now a distorted smudge, like so much of my life and all I can remember is the aching need for a rest that never came. Now it is here or just about here anyway. I'm drifting again; I can feel myself going under, being pulled away with the tide. But he is holding my hand, he is anchoring me to this moment, his hand is anchoring me here.

I want to speak to them but my tongue is disconnected. I want to gaze upon them, but my eyes are turned off. I need my children. I want to hold them again, nurse them, tickle them, phone them, change them, tumble them, wake them, *make* them again...I sense them—their scent, like fragrant fields, like rain-washed clothing hanging on a line. I remember, I know each of them from inside the studio. The canvas of their flesh bears my brushstrokes, the swipe of my palette knife.

My thoughts haven't made much sense for some time. I've felt the illness take my mind apart one piece at a time. It seems I could actually feel slices of my intellect dissolving, like someone pouring acid on it or allowing some devouring insects into my head and letting them feed off my brain. At times, I could actually hear the workings of their jaws, reducing each of my dreams to mush. Now, all I know is that he holds my hand, and I am still tethered to this life...for the moment. I suppose I know I will be leaving soon. Will he go with me? I know he will not let go of me but will I let go of him?

I would love a cup of coffee right now, a really *good* cup of hot coffee. Even if I couldn't drink it I could at least smell it. There is nothing quite like the perfume of coffee whispering through the house, making its way into all your quiet corners. In many ways, coffee's been a greater consolation to me than all the drugs...except, perhaps, the morphine. At least it was something I could hold, something I could feel. If they just let me have one cup, I could savor the warmth of it, hold it gently against my skin. They could put a few drops on my tongue and I could taste its singular essence. I would have it served in a translucent glass cup so its rich color would comfort my eyes and the glass would fog with its moist, living heat. Oh, that would be nice just about now—a cup of coffee in the afternoon with my friend.

I can no longer feel any part of my body, except my hand. Is it my hand or is it only the warmth that surrounds what used to be my hand? The stuff of Neverland is sliding into my place, pink clouds, green pools, a ticking clock and the laughter of children, so much laughter. Somebody needs to tell them not to fix my shoes…

The nurse reached up and flipped off the alarm, returning the room back to its relative quiet. She also turned off the respirator and closed the I.V. valves. For a moment she stood without moving, looking down at the figure in the bed. Then, stretching her hand, she pulled the sheet from beneath the now-lifeless hands and lifted the fabric, placing it over the quiescent face. With one last glance around the empty room, the nurse swept out, turning the light off and shutting the door behind her.

By Accident

"It's not catastrophes, murders, deaths, diseases, that age and kill us; it's the way people look and laugh, and run up the steps of omnibuses."

—Virginia Woolf

DANCE UNDER THE PINK HIBISCUS

ONE

The man who opened my car door was impeccably dressed. The dove gray of his uniform along with his doeskin gloves contrasted starkly with the scarlet waistcoat peeking from beneath his lapels and the brilliant white shirt hinted at his collar. Cold, lifeless drizzle fell from a doleful sky, covering the doorman as he leaned out till he glistened like a lawn awash in morning's dew.

He swung my door open and tipped his captain's hat with quiet dignity, then stepped aside, allowing me onto the sidewalk. His face was brown and deeply lined, and the smile he wore was kindly, showing genuine pleasure and that strange patience which so often comes with age. Yet it told me nothing of his life. I could not return his smile, but tipped him generously and took from his gloved hand the polished black parking disk with *Hawthorn's* trademark flower etched pink in its center. Turning, I proceeded through the heavy steel doors into the building.

The entry foyer was as nondescript as the exterior had been, little more than a five-by-ten threshold facing a rough brick wall into which a heavy oak door had been set with one gas-light fluttering softly to the right. I allowed the street doors to close behind me before I proceeded. Shaking the mist from my trench coat while I looked around, I perceived the effect of the small room as quite Creole and as I wiped my feet on the coconut-fiber matting which extended to the door, I was overcome by a forgotten memory of New Orleans and the night I had first visited the French Quarter. Listening carefully in that closet-like room, I could almost hear the horses hooves on the blue-stone streets, the ghosted echoes of liquid jazz and the clink of glasses together; I could even smell the wet, pungent odor of the city.

But I wasn't in New Orleans any more.

Proceeding through the interior doors I was, at once, greeted by a serious young woman with shortly cropped brunette hair, wearing a smart-looking man's tuxedo. She had been standing just inside the doors behind a large, antique captain's desk talking quietly on the telephone. But upon my entering, she quickly replaced the receiver on its cradle and stepped toward me, at the same time snapping her fingers for another hostess who came almost immediately.

"Good evening, sir," she said simply, reaching for my coat. "I'm sorry I don't recognize you, is this your first time to visit *Hawthorn's*?" Nodding my head, I told her I had a reservation under the name of James, which she turned and verified in her book. At the same time, I relinquished my coat which was immediately taken by the other hostess into a substantial coatroom which, at the moment, appeared practically empty. Apparently, I was to be among only a few patrons for the evening.

"It doesn't look as if there are many willing to come out tonight," I remarked casually, pocketing yet another disk, this one lavender.

"Apparently," she replied smiling. "Monday night, you know. Football and all that." Her British accent which at first I had not noticed, floated pleasantly into the room. "Oh well," she sighed, "we shall endeavor, Mr. James to make *your* stay that much more pleasurable." Again she smiled and motioned for me to follow her down the paneled corridor to the larger rooms beyond.

As I proceeded along the richly appointed hallway, I noticed the enormous wealth of art lining the walls. Paintings, spotlit and golden-framed, and sculptures sequestered in plant-lined alcoves were positioned on either side to afford me the greatest possible view. As I moved forward, I realized the artisans, whose work I viewed, were individuals about whom I had only read.

I wondered if they were originals.

Passing by, I marveled at the startling colors and styles of impressionists, moderns, primitives, even the impaled realism of Flemish masters. The beauty of their works washed my mind so thoroughly that I slowed my walk and eventually stopped, staring into the most beautiful eyes I had ever seen. "*Reclining Delilah*," as she was titled, stared out at me with veiled seduction so marvelously blue and clear; executed so realistically that I momentarily flushed, thrusting a nervous hand deep in my trouser pocket.

The canvas was elongated so that the resting figure was, for all practical purposes life-sized, as was the couch upon which she lay, as well as the tapestries and ornamental palms and objects surrounding her. The effect was, to say the least, hypnotic. In particular, the diaphanous material of her costume was so fantastically tangible and delicately translucent that for the briefest moment I discerned the swelling of her breasts in a sigh, as if my presence wearied her. It was unnerving.

At the bottom of the painting, a single pomegranate reposed in a bowl near a careless, bejeweled hand, while another partially eaten fruit was held aloft with scarlet stained fingers to glistening lips. The artist was unfamiliar to me, but the work so effused life and desire, luxury and opulence, peace and rest into me, that I was at once embarrassed, when the hostess, who had gone on, discovered me lost.

"So you've come to the barber, have you?" she remarked, stepping in close beside me.

"I don't recognize the artist," I said awkwardly, pointing to the signature scrawled near the girl's jeweled and painted toes.

"I believe he's local," she said simply, clasping her hands behind her and gazing directly into the work. We stood together, there in the long paneled salon, gazing at that marvelous painting for two or three full minutes, until finally she turned to me and asked if I would like to continue. I nodded without a word and turned again down the hall. I followed obediently the steady gate of my hostess, but I stole one last glance at the beauty reclining on Persian pillows. It was amazing what pigment could capture, I thought. As if she read my mind, the young woman ahead spoke over her shoulder as we came to the end of the corridor and began to descend into the main hall, "The model for 'Delilah' is here tonight, Mr. James. If you'd like, I can introduce you to her."

My heart started within me, and I momentarily hesitated at the top of the broad, sloping stairs. Below me, the room fell away into an immense, multi-tiered hall, similar to the lobby of the Fairmont across town or the Plaza in New York, but populated with only a few individuals and couples scattered at semi-secluded tables. The hostess continued on down the staircase and, after a second, I followed catching up to her quickly.

We stopped at the foot of the stairs and she whispered something to a maitre d' there who nodded and quickly produced a crisp vellum card presenting it to me for my signature. That small task completed, the maitre d' signaled for a waitress and the hostess whom I had followed down, turned to go. Realizing she would be returning up the stairs, I reached for her and touched her arm, leaning over closely so as to be heard in a whisper.

"I *would* like to meet her," I said, trying not to sound too anxious. The hostess nodded and smiled her same smile.

"I'll introduce you after her performance. She should be on shortly," she said and turned back up the staircase to the main lobby. I followed a velvet-clad waitress to a small table near a grand piano and settled myself into one of its round-armed leather chairs. Once I was comfortable, my server reached past me, removed a small reserved sign from the sparkling white tablecloth and handed me a leather-bound menu.

"It's good to have you join us, Mr. James," she said, shaking out the white linen napkin and placing it in my lap. "My name is Laura and I'll be serving you tonight. The wine steward will be over in a few minutes to take your order but in the meantime, is there anything I can get for you?"

"Just water."

Smiling, she excused herself and in seconds returned with a crystal pitcher and filled my waiting glass. In the moments after she had served me the lights of the hall began to dim till it was at once illuminated only by the small candles on each table, like dozens of muted fireflies hovering beneath twilight trees. It was then the pianist lifted a light, romantic composition that I did not recognize and my eyes were taken to the stage.

TWO

Shrouded by thick shadows and almost unseen, a diminutive seated form started and rose as an amber spotlight came up and in that instant this small woman feigned to capture the light's golden shimmer with reaching, grasping movements of her hands. She shifted from the low bench in fluid ease, swelling with the music, advancing down-stage to its glittering edge, then bowing in seeming obeisance to the floor. Her gown shimmered under the lights like an exotic stretch of sand, neutral and windswept, strewn with pearls and bits of shell and clasped to her waist by a thin cord of gold. Beneath the membrane of this gown, fleeting images of her vigorous body compassed by exotic panties and bra caught my eye, provoking my desires. Turning she continued away from the audience and fell again upon the divan.

Her motions were well-defined and rehearsed. They were, to me, elegant and refined presentations of classic choreography, rather than sideshow vulgarity. My past had acquainted me with the latter, and this woman who glided upon the sunlit stage did so in lyric poetry compared to others of her caste. I leaned forward, one hand clasped upon the table the other at my lips and attempted to put aside the awkwardness I felt and receive the combustion of her dance amidst the soothing timbre of a music I had never heard.

The song that poured from the piano was elegant and carefully tender, and yet, as I listened and felt the surge of the composition, I perceived that it was also comfortably masculine. I did not recognize its melody, but the strains of it rose and fell like the sea. In that similitude it flowed about me like the warm water of a gulf, as if I, seated on the sand, allowed its deliberate glow to wash around and over me, to pulse through my mind.

On the stage, she was extraordinary. Moving as she did about the raised platform from one edge to another, alighting upon the divan for an instant, then skipping to the shadowy edge of her aurora, she played like a muse. She was as a barefooted girl in a summer's meadow with wildflowers in her hands. At a moment of the song when the tempo stepped up slightly, with a simple motion of her hand she released the golden cord which had bound her garment upon her and as easily as one removes a glove, twirled out of its confines.

Strange. I can see her now in my mind's eye, moving in mime, in rhythmic disport as unconcerned as a child, and yet so mature, so finely sculpted a woman. Her remaining garments accentuated her olive skin and voluptuous curves; her face a mask of passion, full lips parted, brows arched. Yet now, I can think only of her eyes. They were blue; a light almost frosted cerulean—like sapphires under the sun. It was the girl in the painting.

I was stunned.

Abundant, sweeping curls of deepest brown fell around her shoulders and face as she danced. Her hands moved over her body, molding her luxurious bosom, hiding the lace of her panties in faux modesty as she advanced to the stage edge, toward the darkness where I sat. In a moment when the music reached out and held its breath she stopped her motion and stared deeply into the audience, into my very soul. After one painful and desperate beat, she slowly drew her legs and arms together and demurely cast her eyes to the floor. My mouth was dry and I could feel my heart through my suit, my body throbbing with arousal. The next second, she turned, lifting her hands above her and swept back toward the center of the stage, where she had started.

She began using her chair as a bolster now, skipping around with a petite hand on its back, extending one leg then the other over its upholstery. Finally averting her form, she confided her figure to its fabric, arching herself in its cushions and intensely pulsing with the rhythm of the piano. Her illuminated form was a spectral visitor, released to my examining eyes. I could not stay from exploring her as she glistened upon the pew. It seemed to me at that moment that the moisture on her skin, the softness and shadowy reticence of her femininity whispered to me of passions I had never tasted, her eyes like shining stars promised a deliverance I could never know.

She was wending toward the conclusion of her ballet, blushed with exertion and yet animated with the life of her music. Her chest heaved as she whirled to the voice of the piano. Then, with scrupulous premeditation she found the peak of the music and abridged her movements so that she gracefully found her couch and kneeling forward into the cushions, gathered them to her body and reclined her head as the shadows descended once again around her.

A hush followed the conclusion of the dance as the music faded. For a few seconds there was a hollow silence, then substantial applause began and I instantly became aware of others in the hall surrounding me. To that point, I had been enraptured only by the dancer and the effects she was having on my body, my feelings. I had been deceived. Now I glanced to the side and noticed the faces of other men likewise charmed and began to realize that there was yet another aspect to this moment.

These men, their faces and attitudes, seemed to me to be of the basest character with vulgar smiles stretching their lips and depravity engraved on their eyes. And I sat in their midst like a toad, ignorant of other toads, engrossed in my own gluttony. Worse, I was one with them, an ordinary voyeur, lusting after an object without thought as to worth or nobility or even humanity. And I had fouled myself. My own body, brought to climax involuntarily by the living passion of the dance, now betrayed me. Hot blood rushed to my cheeks when I considered rising from the table, considered exposing my shame to callous eyes. But I could not stay for the next act, the dance in which Delilah would remove the rest of her garments. I could not endure it.

Choked with bitterness, I stood and left the chamber, retreating up the sweeping staircase and down the paneled hall. Arriving as before at the canvas, which I had so recently seen animated, I halted abruptly for a final look at the dancer. Her dark hair glimmered with myriad flecks of reflected light as did her shimmering eyes that gazed out at me with confident affinity. God, I was lost. But I knew this creature was not of this earth, not of my world, a coryphée of the imagination and not of the flesh. My throat caught, and I pushed onward toward the entrance.

The hostess was startled to see me and came out from behind her desk with a questioning expression on her face, but I did not indulge her. Commanding her eyes with mine, daring her to look away, I handed her the lavender disk for my coat, then paced away toward the doors and waited, my back to the cloak room. In seconds, she was back and I pushed a few bills into her hand while I shrugged into my coat and then fled the building. In moments I was in my car driving out into the wintry night.

Shame would be my escort that night, shame and an empty bed. The dancer had been only an illusion.

THREE

"Good afternoon, *Hawthorn's.*" The voice on the other end of the phone was a resonate baritone and not what I had expected at all.

"Hi," I responded nervously, "I was wondering what time…uh, when a particular dancer…mm, *performer* works. Is there a calendar or schedule or something, which…I seem to be making quite a mess of this." I laughed nervously, felt a complete fool and was about to hang up when the voice insisted I hold on for a moment and transferred me.

"Hello, this is Maryanne, how can I help you?"

Faced with explaining the reason for my call again, I physically cringed and hesitated long enough for the cigarette-roughened voice on the other end to inquire if anyone was still there.

"Uh, yes," I blurted, "I was wondering if you kept a schedule of when your dancers perform?" That sounded better but still pretty childish. I felt like an adolescent with a crush.

"Yes sir, we do, Mr.….?"

"James," I replied, quickly filling the pause.

"Our calendar is set down two weeks in advance Mr. James. Do you have a particular artist in mind?"

Artist! That's the word I had been looking for. "Yes," I said moving to the next and perhaps, most embarrassing aspect of the call. "Yes, I do, but I have one problem. I don't know her name." Silence. "I was wondering if you would be able to help me on that, too." This last revelation was followed by an awkward silence. I confess at that moment I was completely at a loss as to how to identify her.

"Obviously it would help, Mr. James, if you were able to…"

"I know who she is," I exclaimed, interrupting as my mind landed on the one piece of information I knew about her. "She modeled for a painting. It was called…um, um…'*Reclining Delilah.*' Yes, that's it."

"Oh yes, Delilah," she responded with obvious knowing. At the sound of that name being returned to me, the alarm klaxon in my brain began to sound loud and clear. A stripper named Delilah…"Is that her name?" I asked incredulously, suddenly wondering at the wisdom of this adventure.

"Delilah is her stage name, Mr. James," she said carefully. I could hear the characteristic metallic click of a Zippo lighter and her drawing of a cigarette. Exhaling, she breathed, "I'm sure you can appreciate how inappropriate it would be for me to give her real name to just anybody."

As a matter of fact I understood that perfectly. I cleared my throat.

"Yes, I understand. When do you have Delilah scheduled to perform over this next week?"

"I'm afraid she's not scheduled at all."

"Vacation?" I ventured.

"Well, not really. She's actually been quite ill. Fact is she's just out of the hospital and is recuperating at home."

For a second, I hesitated, and then, "I hope it wasn't serious. Is there anything I can do?" The question was silly in retrospect, but one I was used to asking whenever someone I knew was having difficulty. For whatever reason, be it the profound loneliness I was enduring, or the direct exposure to her intimacy in dance, I suppose I felt a perverted closeness. I knew it must have seemed abstract to Maryanne, who likewise hesitated but then responded in the negative.

"Well, please let her know that she'll be missed."

"I will, Mr. James," she intoned, taking another hit from her cigarette. "Is there another artist that you would be interested in seeing?"

"No, not really," I responded, mentally abandoning the conversation, "and its Morrow, James Morrow." I hesitated, awaiting a reaction but there was none. "I really only saw her that one time. Pretty lame really, calling like this. I really couldn't say I'd be interested in another performer after seeing her. Thank you anyway."

"Your very welcome, *Mr. Morrow,*" she returned, and I ended the connection.

FOUR

She stood near the beach house, in the cluttered sand near the road. The house's white-painted eves and dark, gabled roof stood silently, against a back-drop of the green and blue ocean, framed by white foam and seagull sentries. Evening was approaching on the sea-borne breeze and with it came ominous tokens of a storm from the deep. She stared out past the clean little structure toward the gathering thunder clouds, toward the purple horizon, where there seemed to be no division between water and sky. Perhaps there really wasn't, she thought, not caring either way.

For several minutes she stood content, feeling the warm sea breeze on her skin and the hot dry sand between her toes. Her mind went any direction that it wanted. There were, for some strange reason, none of the common concerns that normally crowded her thoughts, no worries about work or her friends or her lovers. The wind tossed her bangs in her eyes and lifted her white sundress well above her naked thighs. At that moment, as the ocean's sweet breath slid lightly over her skin, she recognized that she was indeed bare beneath her dress, that the white cotton garment which hung from her shoulders was all that covered her from stranger eyes. But on this beach, she thought turning to look in all directions, there was not a soul for miles. Extending her arms from her sides, reaching upwards to the darkening sky she drank deeply of the fresh, exotic air and then released it, feeling within all of herself, power and peace.

But at that moment, when no thoughts other than those of sand and wave and wind compassed her, there ventured a sound, tiny and pitiful and loose in the air. To her mind it was foreign but at the same time familiar, and it beckoned her forward like some erstwhile piper tasking her march to the water like the entranced children of old. The distance between where she had been and where she was going, for some reason was covered in an instant, the warm dryness of the wood on the porch comforting to her unprotected feet, like the summers she remembered as a child.

As she opened the door and stepped through, she ventured into what was almost twilight. The windows facing the ocean, while open to the breeze, were draped with tattered, graying curtains. The floor, barren of furniture and carpets, was coated with sand. It was as if the house had been abandoned, left to the wind and ocean—left to die on the quiet beach. Her ears pricked to the snapping of the tattered curtains and for a moment were unable to find the sound that had originally compelled her inside. But soon, standing quite still in the center of the large square room, her ears found the muted chirp that had wooed her from the sand.

"Hello," she called hopefully as she tiptoed from the main room down the dark narrow hallway toward the noise. It had sounded so like a bird or pipe from the outside, yet now with her being so close, she could tell it was a child, a baby whimpering as if just awakened from a bad dream. "Don't cry," she called again peering around a corner into an empty bedroom. The same tattered gray curtains and empty, sand covered floor met her gaze. Turning, she set her face toward the only other room situated toward the back of the small house. Taking a few quiet steps forward, she thought for a second that the child sounds had disappeared, but quickly, as if in fresh peril, the child cried out louder, more desperately. She quickened her pace and rushed through the last doorway, finding the origin of the sounds. In the center of the sandy floor, standing behind a stockade of grayish-white wooden slats, an infant cried, reaching pathetically away from her toward the open window, toward the torn and shabby curtains which slapped the weathered sill.

For a moment she stood transfixed, welded to the floor by the awful sight of a tiny form reaching out to someone in a house where no one lived.

"Don't cry," she whispered moving toward the child. But instead of comforting or quieting it, her words were startling, causing the child's limbs to quiver and shake as it turned toward her voice. As she approached and reached out, she noticed in the corner of the bed a stuffed animal, its plush face and features marred by age and sand and strangely, covered in a fine coating of dark, rust colored powder. At that moment the child screamed a sharp, penetrating shriek, halting her progress. She noticed, to her horror, that the fine dark powder that covered the toy was moving, swarming from the edge of the bed across its breadth and touching the foot of the terrified child. Ants.

The child screamed again, louder and winced in pain. Instinctively, she snatched the child up, and brushed furiously at the biting insects on its leg. "It's okay, it's okay," she wheezed, clutching the baby to her body and massaging its wounded leg. "I've got you, it's okay."

Rocking back and forth rhythmically, clutching the crying child she backed out of the room, eyeing the pulsing brown blanket which now covered the infant's bed. Cold chills raced over her skin and she averted her eyes. "Oh my God!"

Exiting the bedroom, she walked back to the main open room which faced the ocean, continuing to comfort the baby, until finally the child's cries had died down to ragged gasps for air amid small, snuffling whimpers of fear. "It's okay, nothing's going to hurt you now," she said, calmly surveying the main room once again. "How could anyone leave a child alone," she muttered brushing an angry tear away from her cheek. "What kind of monster abandons a baby…" she stopped her words, looking quickly downward.

The child, pale blue eyes open to her face was nuzzling upward toward her unbound breasts, its mouth working as if it would nurse. It was as if the child could not see. "No," she shook her head. "No, no, you can't nurse me darling." But the baby continued its search. Then it dawned on her, this baby really can't see, she thought. And she remembered the window and the ants.

"Oh, sweetheart, I don't have any milk for you," she said sadly stroking the softness of its new spun hair. "Oh no, "she began to cry, "don't…" But the baby had worked its way through the loose strings of her bodice and was already suckling at the edge of her left breast, insistent and determined. "Oh, sweetheart, oh no, oh…oh my God," she sighed as the baby finally took her now-erect nipple into its ready mouth. For a moment all she could do was stand and watch as the terrorized baby calmed itself, drawing passionately against the weight of her heavy breast. Then, as if the breaking storm she could now see out the back windows had brought it, her milk came, flowing sweetly into the baby's mouth, and the tension which had existed seconds before melted. Her mind, so tangled with concern for the child and herself in the strange house, stilled and peace entered.

The sensations which flowed through her, from her breast to the child; the baby's warmth against her warmth, its weight and movement covered by her strength; somehow replaced the contentment she had near the road and banished the panic she had begun to feel in that dreary house. What she would do from there, she did not know. She would just sit down on the floor and hold this child. Maybe she would cry. Yes, that would be good, she decided, sinking to the sandy floor. I'll sit here and cry and hold this poor blind child to wait out the storm. Despite the warmth close to her, she began to shiver and then…then she awoke.

Her first conscious thoughts were that her sheets were as wet, as if she had loosed her bladder—and that her arms were empty. Shivering, she sat forward and pulled at her clinging gown grateful that she had kicked her comforter from the bed. It would be one less item to change.

For a moment, she stared hard into the darkness and fought to hold the last images of the dream in her mind; the roiling green of the approaching storm, the toasted warmth of the sand beneath her feet, the feeling that had quivered in her breasts. But the cold stickiness of her gown chased the images from her mind forever.

"*Damn*," she whispered.

Her fever must have broken, she concluded crawling painfully from her bed and pulling off her wet clothes. Draping the soaked flannel across a chair, she stepped gingerly to the bathroom where she found a towel and dried herself, although it's texture was rough on her skin and hurt her as she rubbed. Finished, she went back to her bedroom and pulled on thermal leggings and a soft T-shirt that felt clean and smooth to her tender skin. Then it was across the floor to her armoire, where soft dry sheets awaited. The room in which she stood was cold with the early winter's morning and she moved stiffly beginning the process of removing her saturated bedclothes.

What had Maryanne said, she mused, eventually dropping the sodden bundle in a corner of the room. I need someone to care for me?

"What's new," she grimaced returning to her bed, and wrestling with the fresh sheets. Reaching out she tucked the far corner under and then reached for her comforter. I'm cold, she thought as she pulled its bulk onto the bed and slid back, into the welcome confines of the fresh linens. I'm cold and I don't want to try anymore. I can't try anymore. No more, Maryanne. No more, Daddy.

No more.

FIVE

"Hello, Maryanne?" I asked, certain of the husky, smoke-tired voice that had just received me.

"Yes, this is Maryanne. Who is this?"

"This is James Morrow, we spoke yesterday."

"Oh yes, Mr. Morrow. Have you changed your mind about visiting *Hawthorn's* again?"

"Oh no, that's not why I'm calling," I said quickly. "I wanted to ask you if you'd make sure some flowers I'm sending over will get to that sick young woman we spoke about yesterday." I still couldn't bring myself to call her Delilah.

For a moment there was a pause, and then she brightened somewhat.

"Certainly, Mr. Morrow. I often have the responsibility to deliver flowers to the performers from gentlemen admirers. I'd be happy to see she gets yours."

"Well, I think that when you're sick you need to get flowers, that's all. No big deal." Reaching for my pen and a scrap of paper I asked, "How do I send them and what does she particularly enjoy?"

In the next few seconds Maryanne relayed to me the address of *Hawthorn's* and the type of flowers she felt that Delilah might like.

"Not everyone asks what the ladies would like in the way of flowers, Mr. Morrow. That's very considerate."

"Yes, well, I wouldn't know about that. I just find it nicer if someone sends me something I like, rather than something they like." I could hear the metallic click of her lighter again and the expected muffled drawing on a cigarette. After a few puffs she added a postscript to our conversation.

"If you write a card, Mr. Morrow, address it to Courtney." Again another long pull on the cigarette. "She's been a pretty sick girl."

"Thank you," I said and hung up the receiver.

Six

"Can I help you?" the woman called, walking in from the back room. She looked about thirty-five, a little overweight with ordinary eyeglasses and a cheerful almost playful smile.

"Yes, I need to order some flowers."

"My goodness, middle of the week. Birthday or anniversary?"

"Neither. Just some color and perfume for Tuesday."

"She must be someone pretty special. Girlfriend?"

"Well, I wouldn't say...yes, actually...Yes, you could say that"

"My, my...what you young men won't go to these days to please us ladies. You know, when I was your age, a young man wouldn't be able to afford even one carnation, much less an arrangement." She smiled and looked as if she were remembering something from long ago. "I once had a beau that worked a second job polishing mirrors at a glass company, just so he could afford to take me to the picture show. But I never did get any flowers"

"Wow, you must be really old."

"Jimmy, you shouldn't say that. Oh my, I'm terribly sorry. He's very excited."

"I understand, don't worry about it," she said smiling. Putting her hands on the counter and leaning over so she could see little Jimmy, she took on a serious expression and posed the question. "So gentlemen, what will it be?"

"Hmmm, I'm not quite sure. What do you think we should..."

"Little tiny flowers, Dad, like on the wallpaper, you know, in the bathroom. Only they have to smell real good, and they have to be pink." This last he said grimly, eyeing the florist with what appeared to be grave doubts.

"I think some type of rose, but I'm not sure..."

Putting up one hand as if for me to hold that thought, the florist turned on her heel and passed quickly into the back room. Very shortly she returned with two stems of delicate, pink-throated flowers whose very entry in the room coated us with a deliciously luxurious fragrance.

"Oh, man, that smells great. What are those called?"

"Flowers that smell *real good*, as requested."

In a moment, the order was placed and the bill paid. All that remained was the card. Taking the small envelope and white card from the florist's hand I laid it on the counter and pulled out my pen to write.

"OK. What should we say?"

"To Mom, love me," he said with a confident grin.

"Hey, what about me? I'm paying for them, don't I get to say something?"

For a puzzled moment the two stared at the flowers, and then at each other. Finally the solution was found.

"How about this? 'To our best girlfriend, love James and James, *Two*."

"I like it," the florist said with a broad smile.

"Me, too."

Taking the completed card from the counter, the florist slid it into its holder and tagged the vase for delivery.

"This should make it over in the next couple of hours, Mr. Morrow. Mr. Morrow? Sir, are you all right? Sir?"

"Mom! Mom, something's wrong." The attendant blurted, backing away from the counter. After a few seconds an elderly, white-haired woman hurried to the counter where her daughter waited anxiously.

"He just stopped talking, Mom. He bought these tube roses and was filling out the card and then...then he just...Is he okay?"

"Oh, honey, it's okay. Mr. Morrow, sir?" the older woman said gently ignoring her daughter and placing her large hand on my sleeve. Turning toward her, I nodded with great effort. "Do you want me to call somebody for you? Would you like to sit down?" I shook my head and deliberately closed my pen and reseated it in my shirt pocket.

"No thanks," I said carefully and turning, left the shop to return to work.

"Wow, that was weird."

"Honey, that's Mr. *James* Morrow. You know, the terrible accident a few years ago?"

"But he was acting just fine, and then...zonk, he was gone."

Nodding, the older woman stepped up to the window and watched the street. "Celia, honey some things are hard to forget." Then she whispered more to herself than her daughter, "some things you never forget."

SEVEN

She answered the intercom from the confines of her bed. "Ye…yes?" The door-man's voice was considerate and direct. There was a delivery, would she like it brought up now? She forced her mind to concentrate on what he was saying, shaking the opiate cobwebs from her mind. "Fine…sure."

Releasing the intercom button, she lay on her side, legs splayed across the covers for balance just as she had when the buzzer sounded, her arm draped across her pillow. Though unmoving, she felt the dopey, irrepressible sense that she was sliding from the covers, slipping into another world. The numbing effects of her prescription entombed her flesh and shrouded her mind. It was a womb where she clung to her sheets and dreamed, but did not live.

The door chimed.

"God…" she muttered her fingers twined in her sheets. She was floating now above the fabric of her bed, past the white blandness of her walls and the hypnotic pulse of her ceiling fan into a featureless province. Her ears were deaf to music that surrounded her, yet she could feel the waft of wings and the presence of strangers. "Mercy," she whispered, sensing her flesh separating from her spirit. Thirst tore at her throat but she was unconcerned. Her insides ached and pleaded for attention, there was blood in her mouth but she could not taste it.

The door chimed again.

Jolted from the clouds, she crashed. Anger exploded from within, anger and the pain. "*WHAT*!?" she cried, dragging her face through the pillow and flailing her arm across the bed fumbling with the sheets and pillows, she thrust her arm wide onto the nightstand knocking her water glass to the floor and hearing it shatter. "Please, God, oh, please…"

The door chimed once again.

"Ju…just a minute," she managed, forcing herself up on her elbows feeling her tangled and damp hair before her face. "Just a minute…" she breathed in resignation, pulling herself to the edge of the bed and putting her bare feet on the floor. There was a sharp prick on the sole of her right foot…glass! Lifting her foot, she moved over and then stood, faltering a bit. Her head reeled in the cool shadows of her room and it took a moment to gain her bearings. Then, though she stumbled more than once, she navigated her way out of the bedroom across the expansive living area toward the apartment door.

"Who is it?" she asked hoarsely through the door, her head resting on its cool, steel surface.

"Flower delivery," a muffled voice replied. "I was asked up."

Flowers? Her mind could not find a place for flowers.

"Leave them."

There was a muffled response and then a soft rustle against the door.

Absently she moved away, faltering with each step until she found a softness—the leather couch against the far wall. There she reached trembling hands out, kneeled into the pliant cushions making her body into the smallest space she could, pleading for sleep, for the drug to take her again.

Mercy, she thought. Please, God…*mercy.*

EIGHT

"She said she'd love something to eat, Mr. Morrow." I could sense Maryanne frowning on the other end of the phone, "*and* a little company." For some reason this conversation seemed a bit strained. "She says she's been out of it for the last few days and hasn't yet made it to the store. She says you're very kind to offer."

"No problem really," I said. "I'll take it over around noon. Would you let her know when I'll be coming?"

"Certainly."

"By the way," I said, feeling the necessity of additional assurance, "I'm not really a pervert or anything. I actually am just trying to help."

Maryanne made no response on the other end of the phone although I could hear her smoking. After a few empty seconds I closed the conversation. "I'll talk to you soon, thanks."

NINE

Her apartment was dimly lit and smelled sweet like a hotel room with new carpet and fresh paint. She opened the door and stood to the side wearing a faded cotton robe—no makeup, unwashed hair and pale lips. She was not what I had seen on stage, nor was she unreachable, as I had imagined she would be.

"Hi," she said weakly." Come on in." I walked across the proffered threshold and down a ten-foot, cool, twilit hallway to an only slightly brighter living area.

"I talked to Maryanne at the club again today, and she said you hadn't been out at all since you came home from the hospital," I said, turning as she shut the door behind me. "I thought you could use some food, and she seemed to think it was a good idea. It's only a few basics I picked up at the store," I said, placing the small grocery sack on the bar. "I also brought you some soup and a sandwich. I figured you could use something already prepared, it's no big deal." It would have been ridiculous to tell her that a small Caesar salad and cup of soup had cost me 25 bucks at the penthouse club of my building.

"Yeah," she coughed. "I haven't gotten out much." Shuffling toward me, she received the sack lunch and went past into the little kitchen just off the den. Opening the refrigerator she placed the entire bag in on a bare wire shelf and clicked the door shut. "Why don't you sit down," she said and pointed, moving from the kitchen to the living room.

"Thanks," I said, and slid awkwardly into a soft, leather chair positioned opposite a matching leather couch. I watched her move from the kitchen to the stuffed couch against the far wall beneath a row of three, shaded, frost-covered windows. As she walked she held her side casually as if the pain she felt was invisible to my eyes. She knelt onto the couch settling back into the gray leather then pulling her legs and bare feet up under her. Her old robe gaped open to reveal a worn camisole covering her ample and unrestrained bosom. For some reason, the very absence of sexuality in her movements, the blandness of her features, was appealing.

"I hope you don't think I'm strange," I said feeling more a fool than ever. "The flowers, the lunch—I just thought...," I fidgeted with my trench coat belt, "I just thought it might make you feel better. I mean, I've been sick before, and alone. I think it helps to have someone interested, don't you?"

She nodded in an understanding way, looking toward me with those brilliant blue eyes ringed by purple bruising, like eye-shadow gone astray. Her face in the dim cool light was tired and weak-looking. Her eyes, into which I found myself staring, actually seemed to moan and plead with me. At this point the conversation became even more awkward because, for all practical purposes, it ceased. She sat looking toward me, and I sat, wondering what I should do next. Then, I noticed a large bouquet of fresh cut flowers set in a glass vase next to the couch. I could see the unopened card still on the plastic stand.

"Hey," I said pointing at the flowers, "they did a good job didn't they?"

"On what?" she asked continuing to look my way.

"On my flowers," I indicated, again pointing to her left.

"Oh, yes," she sighed and leaned ever so slightly toward them. "They smell wonderful."

"Yeah, the tube roses really smell good. I don't really care for flowers that look beautiful, but have no scent, you know? I mean, what's the point? They might as well be artificial without the smell."

She was no longer looking toward me but had closed her eyes as if pondering my words, dissecting them. Suddenly she reached out and brushed her hands over the blossoms, fanning the petals.

"If you caress them it releases their perfume." Her words came to my ears from far away. She seemed distant and mysterious, almost as if she were completely by herself in the room. As she caressed the bouquet and inhaled the sweet fragrance, I felt like an intruder, like I was interrupting a moment of intimacy.

The process of just getting in to see her had been ridiculous—cameras, guards, the locked and monitored lobby, dogs—I felt completely out of my element. And now I sat in her dimly lit apartment alone, she in a robe and not much else, watching while she indulged herself with the flowers I had sent her. Not only did I feel like a cheap voyeur, but I felt childish as well.

"So," I blurted out, rubbing my damp palms on my slacks, "what were you in the hospital for?" My innocent question seemed to fly past her, leaving the awkward silence even heavier and more tangible. Finally she opened her eyes and looked away from the blooms toward me and grimaced a smile, "I had an operation years ago," she shifted her weight and brushed her hair away from her face. "It seems they *botched* the operation a few years back and they needed to have a go at it again."

"Nothing serious, I hope?" This last question was really directed toward the mournful way she sighed, rather than her answer.

"Well," she again shifted her weight and sighed a little, looking past me to the hallway and the door. "That depends on your perspective. I won't have any children now—not that I would have before."

The casual tone of her voice revealed nothing of the trauma those words conveyed. It was as if she had told me her tonsils had come out. "I'm sorry," I said again, feeling impotent in the presence of her barren womb. "Is there anything else I can do for you?"

For a moment—a long silent moment in which her mouth was parted, but no words were uttered—I read the moistness of her skin and the flush of fever in her cheeks. It was as if she couldn't see me at all, as if all she saw before her was emptiness. And I just sat there feeling like a six-year-old, whose been shoved once too often, and stands, his feet planted and fists clenched. For a moment, I hoped we would find in each others' pain a common ground, I hoped she would see what ever it was she was looking for in me. But in her face, in the crystal-blue light of her eyes, I saw only cool indifference. It was more than I needed, and much more than I could take.

"Well," I muttered, breaking my gaze and standing from the chair, "I'd better be getting back. No, no—don't get up," I urged as she made efforts to walk me out, "I'll find my way." Turning quickly, I covered the ten paces to the door and opened it to the elevator lobby outside. Turning to tell her good-bye, I found her standing at the opposite end of the hall partially hidden, her hands on the edge of the wall.

"Take care of yourself," I said quickly, hoping to get out faster than I had gotten in.

"I will," she said quietly without moving. "Thanks for the groceries."

"Nothing to it," I said turning to go. But as I stepped out into the hall I heard her again. In fact, I almost missed it.

"I guess I'll see you?" Her voice was a whisper and I could hardly tell her meaning. For a split second, I contemplated the obvious answer, she was, after all, a spectacular attraction. But something in my gut terminated the desire. She was more than a mannequin, more than the flesh of my lust or anyone else's for that matter. She could feel and breathe and hurt and have fever, and she had become a person to me, a person that liked the perfume of tuberoses.

"I don't know—I'm not so sure that would be a good idea."

She was looking past me from the other end of the hall, and I stood by her door my hand on the latch. "OK," was all she said, and I nodded, closing the door deliberately. For a moment I rested my head against the door's cool surface, wishing as I never had before, that I did not care about people that hurt. Behind me the soft chime of the elevator sounded and its doors slid open. For a moment, I wondered how her pain could be stopped—how anyone's pain could be stopped, how *my* pain could be stopped. Then I turned on my heel, and caught the elevator as the doors were sliding shut. Glancing out the hall window, as I stepped into the car, I saw that the weather had changed outside. Tiny pellets of sleet were starting to tap at the glass and the day no longer sparkled.

TEN

"So what's his story?"

"Oh, I think he's a nice enough guy; a bit lonely." Courtney replied. "I guess he wouldn't have come to *Hawthorn's*, if he had any kind of life. You know what I mean, a woman or something?"

"Are you kidding? You and I've both seen many *happily married* men drooling at the bar."

"Yeah, I guess you're right."

There was silence between them for many minutes. Maryanne went back to the crossword she had started earlier that morning, and Courtney just sat with her face toward the window, absorbing the warmth of the brilliant sunlight flowing through the open blinds.

Maryanne bit her lower lip and tapped the paper with her pencil. In a second she grimaced and scribbled out a word, then thought, erased what she had written and wrote something else. Dropping the pencil she reached past a half-eaten grapefruit and extracted a cigarette from an open soft pack near her purse.

"You shouldn't smoke," Courtney said without turning.

"No shit," she replied, accompanied by the click of her ever-present Zippo and an acutely appreciative inhalation. "You're beginning to sound like my ex."

"Maybe he wouldn't have run off, if you'd quit smoking."

"Yeah, maybe he'd have become a priest if I hadn't slept with him, too." The sarcasm was bitter but not directed. "Hey, what's with you this morning? I thought you were feeling better?"

Courtney took a deep breath and turned toward her friend with a thin-lipped determined look. "I am feeling better—I'm getting better. The doctor says that pretty soon, I'll be ready to go back to work. He's says that if all goes well in a week or so I'll be, how'd he put it? Oh yeah, I'll be *dancing in the park*," she grinned mischievously.

"Hey, you didn't tell me this guy was a regular," she laughed, taking her dish from the table to the sink. Running the water she dropped her half grapefruit into the disposer and turned it on. The grinding noise was deafening, but lasted only a few seconds. When she flicked off the switch, the room reeled with a sudden lack of noise.

"Courtney?"

She had abruptly slipped out of her chair at the small breakfast table and vanished into her bedroom. "What's going on in there?" Maryanne called, but could hear only the sounds of her friend rustling through boxes or drawers or some such. In short order, however, she emerged with a broad smile holding out the object of her search.

"I think I've found a new song."

"Really?" Maryanne smirked seating herself again at the breakfast table. "Maybe this time it's something I've heard?"

"I don't think so, it's real old." Holding up the worn, cardboard LP cover, she turned her back and began to affix the vinyl platter to the turntable of her stereo. Carefully she fitted the record over the nib on the rubber footing, then picked up the arm of the player and brought the needle down gently, finding just the track she wanted.

There was a slight scratch and then the familiar hiss of a well-used recording and then the music. The initial acoustic melody was unfamiliar, but shortly the distinctive harmony of Seals and Crofts poured into the apartment.

> *Lost…lost as a child's first thought*
> *I must have arms to hold me,*
> *Lost without loving care,*
> *I must have my fair share…*

Maryanne watched as Courtney with her arms clasped to her body, sway with the music. She ignored the hiss and scratch of the worn vinyl and enjoyed the moment of her friend's creation.

> *Fair…fair is a changing word,*
> *But fair is an honored promise,*
> *Justice if your still there,*
> *I will have my fair share…*

The dancer released her arms above her head and twirled delicately as the song soared into the chorus.

> *Justice is a lady,*
> *Flaming out with justice in a long white gown,*
> *With a breath of love we can share,*
> *Share…sleep with me if you dare,*
> *Celebrate my fair share…*

The guitars and violins of the composition created a spun garment of gold for her movements. Releasing herself into the music, Courtney touched lightly around the living area avoiding the furniture, oblivious to Maryanne, the open blinds or the gown she wore.

> *Fair…fair is a changing word,*
> *Fair is an honored promise,*
> *Justice if your still there,*
> *I will have my fair share*

Maryanne watched in admiration, as her young friend freed herself in an ensemble of simple grace and delicate beauty. Each step, each hand gesture was as if it had always been a part of her, as if life was a choreography she knew instinctively. It seemed when the moment came, she could present the completed dance on command. As the music gently came to the chorus again, the passion of the dance erupted in renewed vehemence, Courtney's face open and searching, her eyes wide in innocent longing.

> *Justice is a lady*
> *Flaming with justice in a long white gown,*
> *With a breath of love we can share,*
> *Share…sleep with me if you dare,*
> *Celebrate my fair share…*

The melody quickly faded, guitars and violins echoing in the apartment for the few seconds between the tracks. Then the next song started, this one more upbeat and driving. Courtney, who had been oblivious up to that point, came back to herself and rose from her fallen posture of the finale. Walking to the stereo she lifted the needle from the record and replaced it in its cradle. She was breathing heavily and moisture bled into the fabric of her gown.

"You know he wants to see you again," Maryanne said, crossing her legs and watching Courtney's expression carefully. She waited.

"Maryanne," Courtney began, slowly, having recovered her breath, "what's he like? I mean, is he handsome, fat or skinny, is he tall—do you really think he's married?"

"I don't know," she replied, taking another puff on her cigarette. "I've only talked with him on the phone; you're the one who's seen him. You tell me."

Silence.

"Hey, he got turned on watching you wiggle that little ass of yours, just like all the other pathetic assholes that come to Hawthorne's. Is he a rapist? I doubt it. Is he Prince Charming? C'mon…"

Courtney did not look back at Maryanne, but with one hand holding up her damp hair she moved away from the stereo, back into the living area around the corner. After a silent moment, Maryanne continued.

"Look, Court, I don't think he's a freak or anything. If he'd been twitchy, he'd have blown when you let him in with the food, right?" After a second she continued. "I think he's okay, Court. I just don't want you getting hooked up with somebody else's problems, you know? Silence from the other room. Raising her voice she finished. *"I don't think dating customers is a good idea!"*

Stubbing out her cigarette, Maryanne rose from the bar stool and walked around into the living area. Courtney had left the room and gone back to her bedroom down the short hall. Her voice, muffled by distance floated back to Maryanne.

"I want to see him," she said quietly but firmly. "But not here—at Friday's on Greenville, for lunch, okay?"

"I don't think it's a good idea, Court."

"Will you drive me?" Her voice sounded more distant, as if she had gone on into her bathroom.

"Oh sure," she said, looking with dissatisfaction at the incomplete cross-word in her hand. "What are friends for?"

ELEVEN

The black Miata convertible, top down, pulled up to the curb silently and waited. The day was perfect, one of those comfortably cool, sun-filled days Dallas often got early in November. I recognized Courtney instantly, seated in the passenger, seat wearing small, round sunglasses and a white sweater. The driver, a woman with fierce red hair and similar sunglasses was unknown to me. I had chosen a particular table by the window in hopes that I would see her arrive, and now, I watched in anticipation as she finished her conversation with her friend, opened the car door and got out.

I had never seen a blind person's cane before that moment. It appeared an interesting device though, the way it was folded in several small sections and then, I supposed with the aid of elastic, was pulled into a long, straight cane when let go. She handled it easily I decided, as if she had been doing it all her life. Till that moment, I had no idea that she was blind.

A strange sensation moved from my stomach to my mouth, like when I was a child and knew that I would not be able to eat dinner without throwing up. It wasn't that I was sick exactly, but like I knew I was going to be sick. Reaching a hand out for a drink of tea, I steadied myself and then went to greet her at the door.

"I'm meeting someone, a James Mor—"

"Here I am," I interrupted somewhat out of breath.

"Hi."

"Hello again. Let's go this way, I've got a table…," indicating the direction with my hand and then, "uh, I'm sorry. I didn't know…"

"Don't worry about it," she said neutrally. "Let me take your arm." Reaching out a crooked elbow I noticed the hostess' face. What kind of look was that?

"Like this?"

"You're a pro. Lead on, McDuff." We proceeded to the small table I had arranged before.

Once seated, I signaled to the waiter and then sat back and watched Courtney. With practiced ease she broke her cane into its consistent fragments and then smartly wrapped it with an elastic loop. In seconds it vanished from the table onto the adjacent sill. Likewise, she quickly removed her sunglasses and looked directly into my eyes.

"Pretty slick, don't you think?"

"I don't know what to say."

"How about, 'Gee, I didn't know they made neat stuff like that.' Or how about, 'Wow, I didn't know you were blind.'"

"I feel like a fool. I'm sorry."

"For what," she asked, tilting her beautiful face to the side. I tried not to stare into her eyes, but at that moment I was helpless. How could she not see me?

"I suppose I feel a fool for thinking you were perfect. And then for feeling pity when I discovered you weren't."

The waiter bustled up and set a large glass of water before Courtney. "What can I get for you folks today?" he chirped.

I hesitated a second looking from Courtney to the waiter and then back again. "Uh…why don't we…"

"I need a little time to look at the menu," she interjected, looking up toward their young server.

"No problem. Just signal when you're ready," and he vanished.

"I don't know what to do."

"Don't worry about it," Courtney smiled reaching out to her water glass, "I do."

I was beginning to understand why I felt so stupid and worthless. Over the proceeding weeks I had all but fallen for this exquisite young woman seated before me. And in so doing had created in her all that I wanted: intelligence, beauty, sensitivity—perception. Only how could she perceive me and all that I was, when in her eyes I was just another voice out of blackness?

I *was* a fool.

"You don't look blind." I immediately regretted the observation.

"Well, technically I'm not," she said. "Not completely blind, that is. You see, while this eye is useless," at this she pointed to her left eye, "this one is not," then she pointed to her right. "Well, not yet. I can actually see a little light with this eye, although it's fairly indistinct. But the doctors say it won't last." Until that moment I could not have discerned the difference.

"How did it happen?"

"That's an interesting story," she said whispering as the waiter returned. "*I'll tell you later.*"

"So what have you folks decided on?"

"I think I'll have," she paused holding the open menu before her vacant eyes. "Hmmm, let me see. Oh well, I'll have half of whatever *he's* having," and she handed the menu back toward the waiter.

"Great. And what will you be having today?"

I was taken aback by this charade, but recovered quickly enough to order a club sandwich and a chocolate milkshake.

"Two straws, please," Courtney winked and the waiter grinned. In a few seconds we were alone again.

"How did you know I liked chocolate?" She was smiling at me and staring with those crystalline blue eyes. I looked away.

"I didn't...I'm not sure...you were going to tell me what happened. How you lost your sight."

"That's pretty boring stuff, James. You sure you want to ruin your lunch that way?" Catching myself nodding, I said yes under my breath.

"Well, I'm not going to tell you. How's that?" Then she smiled.

TWELVE

Courtney planted her feet in defiance at the pool's edge, hands on hips, one clenching her towel the other her swim goggles. Her brown hair, cropped just below the ear caught the sunlight and blazed reddish gold. Her great, crystal-blue eyes winced tightly closed.

"My heat's next, I need to stay over here," she insisted. Her father, shaggy blond hair blowing in the hot, Texas wind, mouthed over the noise of the crowd that she could just as easily sit with him in the shade and save her strength. "No," she wagged and turned to a group of girls a short distance from her and began to talk.

"She's twelve," he ventured out of the side of his mouth, "and a half." His Australian accent wound its way round to my ear and caused me to listen. "Used to be her best buddy til about a year ago—now I'm nothin' but trouble."

He smiled while he said this last.

"Ah, ya know these pre-puberty years. Heaven help us, eh?"

The gun went off releasing the girls poised on the starting blocks and a shower of water was thrown into the steaming air. Fifty meters, a turn, another fifty to the wall and the race was finished. Now Courtney climbed to her position in lane eight.

She was smaller than her age group. Waiting for the command to take their marks she shook out her arms, checked her goggles and tucked her hair into her silver cap for the tenth time. The loud speaker crackled, "Take your marks…" She reached forward, grasping the edge of the block. In a second the gun popped and the 200-meter Individual Medley was underway.

"Her best strokes are the back and free. Seems when she hits the breast she just sorta bobs up an down like some kinda toy." He was watching intently arms crossed, with each hand grasping the opposite arm. He did not cheer as the other parents did, only watched with thin-lipped intensity.

At the end of the 50-meter butterfly, the turn was made and she began to backstroke. Leaving the wall, Courtney immediately began to migrate out of the center of the lane toward the inside rope. In seconds, her left arm began to brush the floats and her head, in panic, began to turn, desperately trying to regain her direction. The whole 50 meters was a struggle to pull straight and she lost time.

"What's that about?" he mumbled dropping his hands to his side and stuffing them into his shorts' pockets. "She's never done that before."

The breaststroke back was predictably slow. Courtney did bob up and down as if she were some giants bath toy. Agonizingly slow, she reached the final turn 15 to 20 meters behind her nearest competitor.

"She's never swam this poorly," he insisted, raising one hand to shade his eyes for her last length. "We just got back from London a few days ago, and she's had a cold." He no longer seemed to know anyone was near.

Her free style was practiced but lethargic, she seemed fatigued. Passing the center of the grandstand where he stood, she began to double her efforts; her strokes became crisp and swift. As the wall approached she had closed the distance between her and the next swimmer, almost catching her as they touched. Then she was up and out of the water pulling her goggles and cap off grabbing her towel from a friend.

"I don't know what happened on that backstroke," he said shaking his head. "Ya know, she lost her sight when she was three—some kind of cancer. That's why she's pulling her head over so strangely—trying ta see the rope." He inched up on his tiptoes for a second to catch a glimpse of her in the throng by the pool end. "Yeah, she and I used ta be pals, but now..." He stopped as she stepped onto the bleachers and moved toward him.

Cancer took her eye. Cancer attacked a three-year-old little girl and with its blunt rage carved out her sight. At the moment when she was flush in the comfort of her family, just beginning to know her role, really just knowing mom and dad, she began her struggle with death. Plump and olive-skinned, with a fine dusting of brown hair, a star-field of freckles and eyes that lit up the morning like sapphires—she got sick.

Did he hold her in his arms when the doctor announced the arrival of the disease? What color was the carpet under his feet when he paced waiting for her operation to end? Did he care when she vomited on his hands after chemo? Did he hold her hand when they took the bandages off her eye? Did he calm her nightmares when she woke up in the dark?

Her loss must torture him. Her fatigue must terrify him. It's just jetlag, just the climate—the damned heat and the goddamned sun. She looks good. She looks strong and good.

Her hair was darkly moist and tangled, framing a round and sunburned, engaging face sprinkled generously with freckles. The juvenile roundness of her shape evidenced her pre-pubescent age, although her mannerisms were all woman. Climbing the bleachers, she began to wince in shame as she caught her father's gaze and in that moment her scar became apparent. Before, when her cancer had been unknown, the striking clarity of her light blue gaze had been able to hypnotize and transfix. Now as her expression revealed the asymmetry of the surgeon's design, it was a distraction to know that one of these startling windows to her spirit was forever sealed off, a window whose shudders were closed and locked for all time.

"Good swim, Court," he assured, reaching a tentative hand out to her face. Looking away from him she shook her head and wiped her nose.

"I've only swam twice in the past three weeks, you know. I'm jet-lagged!"

"I know," he responded, nodding in faithful agreement. "You'll get em next race."

"Oh, daddy," she exhaled turning to leave. "I'm really tired, can't you understand?"

Stepping after her he mumbled, "I understand…" and they were gone.

THIRTEEN

"I understand too. Where's your Dad now?"

"He died about three years ago," she said between mouthfuls. "He lost *his* battle."

After another pause, Courtney put down the crust of her sandwich and wiped her mouth with a napkin. Her smile, present since they sat down together, was now gone. Looking hard in my direction, Courtney took on a more subdued tone of voice and began to ask some questions of her own.

"What is it you want, James Morrow? Why are we here like old friends eating from the same plate?"

"I don't know. I just wanted to be with you, that's all."

"Do you visit *Hawthorn's* often?"

"No."

"Do you like the way I dance?"

"I suppose. Yes, I like the way you dance."

"Maryanne says you just like the way I wiggle my little ass. Is that why you and I are sitting here, James, because you like the way I dance?"

"No," I said strongly, shifting in my chair, "at least I don't think so." She looked at me, or at least in my direction. There was an awkward moment and I fidgeted.

"That was Maryanne that brought me," she said brightly, changing the subject. "Too bad she didn't get to see what you look like."

"Why's that?"

"Because I wanted her to tell me later," she said laughing a quiet, girlish laugh. I looked down at my napkin and then took a drink of tea, rattling the ice.

"Why don't you tell me?" she blurted.

"Me?"

"Sure," she responded, "Why not?"

I wasn't sure 'why not?' except that I was completely unsure of how to describe myself. How does one say 'ordinary' in an interesting way?

"I don't think I can do that."

"Oh, come on," she smiled. "Indulge a young, blind lady." I swallowed and moved again in my chair.

"Well, I'm a stockbroker…"

"Not what you do, what you look like." Her voice was emphatic and her face became profoundly serious.

"Um, I guess I'm pretty normal looking. About six-foot-three with brown hair and hazel eyes. I…"

"Do you work out?"

"About three times a week." I hesitated, expecting another question but nothing came.

"I, uh…Well, I usually wear suits, you know, to work and all."

"Not your clothes—you!" Again, she seemed very serious.

"I have a big nose?" I was completely unsure of where to go from there.

"Really," she said, sounding intrigued. "Let me see?"

I couldn't move, reason had left me. Slowly, with great deliberation she was reaching across the table with her left hand at approximately my face level.

"Help me," she said, extending even farther. Taking a deep breath, I closed my eyes and leaned in toward her reaching fingers.

It was as if butterflies danced across my skin. Her fingers read my features, gliding over my eyes, my nose, my mouth. Skillfully, she found my chin, my ears and hairline, and in what seemed only a few seconds, she pulled back and was finished.

"Your nose isn't big," she said seriously. "It's quite aquiline, very nice, actually."

"How's everything else?"

"You look good, James Morrow. Quite nice looking."

"Thanks," I replied placing my napkin on the table. "Can I ask you something?"

"Uh oh," she muttered with mock fear on her face. "Sounds pretty serious."

"Oh, not really. I was just wondering why you dance." The question was unexpectedly direct. "Why do you dance at *Hawthorn's?*"

"Because nobody can see me in my apartment?"

Her face held a wry expression, but it quickly faded.

"James Morrow," she said slowly, "I dance at *Hawthorn's* for many reasons. And each of them is mine, nobody else's."

"But everybody at the club—the staff, the customers—they all *see* you dancing. Don't you feel self-conscious?"

"You don't understand."

"You take your clothes off in front of strangers—how can I?"

"I took my clothes off in front of you."

I was suddenly embarrassed, my face flushing and I looked away from her out the window.

"I don't know how to make you understand." she continued. For a while, she seemed to be thinking, staring toward me as if I was in her full vision. Then there was an instant when I almost perceived her focus. "Um..." she continued, "do you believe in God?"

"God?" I recoiled. In my mind flashed a picture of two caskets—one large, one small. The building smelled sickly sweet, buried in carnations and lilies. I could taste the smell in my mouth, felt it on my clothes. The minister, pathetic in a gray wool suit that was too tight, was sadly taking my hand, leading me to the front. I could hear the others crying, feel the tremor of the organ in the soles of my shoes. My hands were cold but not as cold as...

"God?" I asked again, somewhat softer.

"Yeah, God."

"No, I don't believe in God. Do you?"

"Yes," she sparkled. "I dance for Him."

"*Dance* for him?" My skepticism was obvious.

"Yes. To me dancing is like going to church," she continued. "Well, some churches, I guess. I feel free when I dance, James. I forget the crap I'm going through; the loneliness, the pain, all that I would rather not feel. And in those precious few moments, I feel a clean connection with God. I think God likes it when I dance, at least when I dance for Him."

"How can you say you dance for God? I've seen you dance. *Hawthorn's* isn't a church."

"At *Hawthorn's* I dance for money—to pay the rent, buy clothes and food, to pay for the doctor. At home, I dance for God."

"That's some combination, Courtney. God and *Hawthorn's*."

"Is it so different than what you do? What most people do? Dress up and play office games all week for money, then on Sunday dress up and play church games for what, you tell me!" I stared at her and could think of nothing to say.

"You know what Nietzsche said, don't you?"

"Nietzsche?"

"Yeah, Friedrich Nietzsche," she continued. "He said once, 'If these Christians want me to believe in their God, they'll have to sing me better songs; they'll have to look more like people who have been saved; they'll have to wear on their countenance the joy of the beatitudes. I could only believe in a God who dances.' I'm with him. Me too!"

I stared dumbfounded by this revelation, and shook my head. She was quoting an atheist as a proof text for God.

"Well," I started, "You may believe in God, dance for him as you say, but I don't."

"Why not?"

"What do you mean, why not?"

"I mean why not? If you don't believe, you have to have a reason. Why not?"

"Why should I?"

"James?" she hesitated. "James, you sound as if *you* have a story to tell."

"My story isn't interesting, believe me. Besides, I'm listening to yours." She looked my way, and suddenly I felt the sickness rising again. I reached for my glass and tried to take a drink.

"What's wrong?" she asked, leaning forward touching my hand.

I shook my head and pulled my hand away, making an attempt to speak, but only coughing. It was coming now like it had years before. I felt the forgotten fear of not being able to stop it. I stared into her unseeing eyes, and worked my mouth as anger and horror crowded out the rest of the room.

The silence of the sanctuary overwhelmed me, as did the hardness of those around—on the podium and at the altar. And yet, most everyone cried, tears running down their faces like tiny dark rivulets across the slate and shale at the highway's edge. The air was thick with flowers—carnations specifically—and my mouth was bitter with their perfume. Still I watched with some interest, as the pastor attempted to paint for me a picture of life after death, of eternal joy for which this should be a celebration. And I wondered how it was he knew of these things. By what magic had he glimpsed the eternal home of those now gone.

His sermon was well thought out and kind; a three-point homily on why someone should give his heart to God. And as I reflected on this, I wondered why it was that he never raised himself to meet my agony, to explain the seeming incongruity between God's love and this abominable loss.

He failed.

He failed to meet my pain, when he called their deaths a great blessing. He failed to unmask the truth of this moment, when he called this funeral a coronation. And he failed to explain to all the rest who came, that if you think your heart is already given to God's hands, how unspeakably horrible it is to see it torn apart before your very eyes.

And so I realized the comfort I had felt in the sanctuary of my God had been a carefully wrought illusion. Just as the place I had had with my wife and son was destroyed in a moment, so now my ability to walk in comfortable religious ignorance was gone.

It was over.

Returning mentally to the table I coughed and reached for my tea. It was empty.

"Sorry," I said rattling my ice and sipping at the melting cubes. "You were saying?"

She didn't speak, but looked toward me with an expression I could not describe. Then I noticed them—her tears. They began to flow from her right eye, slowly at first and then in a steady stream.

"I'm sorry, I sort of ruined things. I'm sorry." She was shaking her head wiping her cheek.

"That's what I was talking about," she said finally. "You've been there, you understand."

"You're wrong. I don't understand anything…"

"*Yes, you do,*" she interrupted. "You understand the most important part of this. You understand the *pain.*"

I looked at her and shook my head, indicating that I was confused but she responded, "No, you do, really. And that understanding is the key."

Reaching her hand out she said, "Take my hand." I hesitated, but then slowly took her outstretched hand. "Do you feel that? Is that real?"

"Yes."

"Is your pain real, your anger?"

"Yes."

"Was your love for them real? The time you spent with them? Your memories—are they real?"

"Yes." Her grip was hurting my hand.

"You look me in the eyes but I don't see you. Does that mean you're not there?" I didn't answer.

"I dance on a stage before strangers, even you—but I can't see anything. Does that mean they aren't there? You aren't there?"

"You're trying to…"

"Because He took them from you, because they're gone, you think He's gone. With the simplicity of ignoring Him, you do away with the crime, so you won't have to deal with it. You protect yourself by hating Him, putting on an armor pain can't break through." She stopped. "You're wrong, James. You're wrong and you already know it."

I was stunned. The torment of the years was racing over and through my body and searing my mind. But she held onto my hand.

"Comfort isn't found in protecting yourself, it's found in plunging ahead." Leaning forward, she narrowed her eyelids and whispered. "He's not afraid of you, you know. He's not afraid of your questions, He's not afraid of your anger and He's not afraid of your love." Turning her head toward the window and then slowly back toward me, she smiled, "But you are."

Her statement greeted me like a slap. Instantly, tears seeped into my vision and I choked. If I could have left I would have, but she held me there with more than her hand. And though I barely knew her, though I counted the yesterdays of my life as dead, somehow the truth of her words thrust their way into my heart, into the very center of my soul and broke open a long forgotten door—and life peeked out.

"You're right," I gasped. The words almost hurt as they passed through my lips. "You'rr right."

Again we sat in silence, facing one another over the remnants of our meal. The exchange had been strong and not at all what I had expected from this meeting. She still held my hand, but was no longer gripping it savagely. And now there was a pleasant aspect in the lull of our conversation, a peace of sorts. The tension was no longer present. Although neither of us longed for conversation, both realized it must come. As for my soul—I would have to try again, though up to that point there had been no road.

"I can't believe I'm going to say this," I started, regaining my composure. "But I enjoyed lunch,"

"Me, too," she said quietly.

"So, do you think we can stand an encore?" My attempt at a casual rejoinder sounded stilted and awkward, but she grinned anyway.

"Are you sure you want to?"

"I'm sure."

"Okay," she said, releasing my hand and sitting back. "How about the traditional date thing? You know, dinner and a movie?"

"A movie?" I asked, "But how will you be able to…?"

"You can *tell* me what's happening," she whispered. Now it was my turn to smile.

"Deal."

"You stockbrokers, always closing."

"When do you want to get together?"

"How about tomorrow? Or are weeknights taboo for the Wall Street gang?"

"Weeknights are fine. I'll call for you around six." She nodded, and I signaled for the check.

"By the way," I said, turning back toward her. "Are you sure you'll be feeling up to this. I mean, according to Maryanne you were pretty sick."

"Maryanne's a worrier. I feel good. I'm fine and I want to go out." Facing in the direction of the street she continued, "I want to go out with you…" Her voice trailed off and she hesitated than reached into her purse for her sunglasses.

"What time is it?"

"Quarter to two. I'd be happy to drop you."

"Oh, no, my ride should be here any second," She stood to leave. "Maryanne, you know. She's hell on wheels, never misses an appointment." At that moment the black Miata flashed past the entrance and down the alley, slowing to make the U-turn at the end of the alley.

"Well, you're right. Here she is, right on time."

"Told you," she grinned.

Reaching for my arm she ducked her chin strangely, as if she were keeping a secret. It was then that I noticed the feeling. Whether it was the slight touch of her hand on my arm, the modest demeanor she presented or simply her fragrance, the result was the same. Unexpectedly and without premeditation, I was thrilled and saddened with an aspect of relationship that I had all but forgotten. Instantly and quite clearly, I was reminded of that prized and longed-for feeling of newness each alliance must know. That unmistakable character of anticipation, the tremulous sense of some astounding discovering just around the corner, worked its way into my heart and caused me to smile. As we exited the restaurant I relaxed, squinted into the sun and waved at Maryanne.

"I'll see you tomorrow," I said leaning in so she could hear me over the engine noise.

"Six o'clock, don't be late," and she descended into the small convertible allowing me to close the door after her.

"Good-bye, *Mr. Morrow*," Maryanne ventured, around the cigarette in her lips and in a flurry of red hair, she gunned the engine and they were off.

FOURTEEN

"Did you enjoy dinner last night?"

"Oh, jeez I was stuffed, you kiddin'?" Wheeler snorted walking around from behind his desk, rubbing his flat stomach, feigning obesity.

"Too stuffed to work, eh?"

"Yeah, but not to stuffed to go to a titty-bar," injected a passing conspirator.

"What? Awe, man! We were late getting out, what were you thinking?"

"Didn't you close the place up?"

"You betcha," he said, hands on his hips beaming a proud smile. "Did pretty well, if I do say so myself."

"I noticed you making three or four trips to the cash machine, Wheeler. You musta been havin a *real* good time," With that, his colleague went on his way.

"Yeah, I blew about $400 bucks last night. Jeez!"

"What time did you get out, Bob?"

"Two," he said flatly, and then stopping cold, he eyed me wickedly. "I really shouldn't tell you this but…" He lowered his voice, indicating that the door should be shut. When it was secure he continued, "I kinda continued the party on, after closing time. I uh, well, I wound up takin' out one of the dancers." His grin was proud, like a boy who just tore the wings off a butterfly. "She sat down and asked if I'd take her to eat and so we just left."

"At what time?"

"Two, I already told ya. Anyway, the taxi takes us back to the garage here and when I got out of the backseat to pay…*I wound up in that back seat, she was in the front seat for whatever reason*…anyway, I got out and she got out, and the cabby leaned over to get the money and he puts his hand on the passenger seat, you know to support himself, and then he starts yellin', 'Hey, she pissed in my seat!' Oh my god, I almost fell out. I mean, she was so friggin' drunk that she pissed in the taxi. Can you believe that?"

"What did you do?"

"I paid him and then we went back to my car."

"To get something to eat."

"God no! She gave me a hand job in my car, and I took her back to the club."

Wheeler laughed to himself, as if he had accomplished a great thing. Shaking his head he turned and went back around his desk to sit down. "This mornin' on the way in, I asked the guy in the garage that details cars, 'Don't wash it, don't wax it—just scrub the passenger seat out, okay?' Lots of soap and water, you know'"

"What was her name?"

"Oh, James, who knows. Some sleazy stage name."

"What club was it?"

"Some flower club, uh…I really can't—oh yeah, it was Cherry Blossoms over on Maple. Yeah, she was kinda skinny, but she had these huge fake breasts and that kinda bleached hair? You know, typical stripper."

Yeah, typical, I thought leaving Bob Wheeler's office. Reaching into my pocket I felt an odd smoothness and drew out a small black disk from *Hawthorn's* with its pink flower etched into the surface. Rolling its shape between my fingers, my mind went to Courtney. She was not typical, I thought. And while she may have danced under the pink hibiscus, she hadn't sold herself to it.

At that instant I felt an overwhelming passion, like someone who is only a few blocks from home after a long, lonely trip. In my heart it seemed only a matter of moments until I would be with her again. And she, so wonderful and strong, patient in the face of a life such as she had known; a person who could find God and peace in a crucible of cancer and its hopelessness; even to the point of seeing His very shadow in the words of Friedrich Nietzsche. So that when he declared the death of God, she drew from some reserve an ability to decode his anger into a cry for help. From one lost and wounded child to another, I guessed.

I was actually, for the first time in a very long time, not only content but hopeful and even a little happy. So maybe the disease was good, I thought. Maybe it had had a hand in her redemption—and mine. And if that were the case, then I would say a prayer of thanksgiving for cancer and for the young girl whose body *and* spirit were stripped in its care.

The flower in the center of the black disk glowed in softness, its color so vivid and real that I could almost smell its fragrance. My unfamiliarity with that type of flower had been replaced with fresh appreciation for its beauty, its brilliant color and its broad, sheltering petals. It was, to say the least, unique.

"Mr. Morrow, telephone call for James Morrow." The tinny sound of the intercom caught my mind back to work, and I turned toward my office, putting the keepsake back in my pocket. Stepping into the glass confines of my office, I glanced at my day-planner and the bold dinner notation circled on its right margin, 'Courtney at five—dinner & movie.' Picking up the phone, I answered in my usual way, "Good Morning, Morrow speaking."

"Is this *James* Morrow?" The officious sound of the voice on the phone tightened my stomach. Somewhere in the back of my mind a familiarity was emerging.

"Yes it is. Who's this?"

"Mr. Morrow my name is Jones, Dennis Jones with the Dallas County Coroner's office…"

FIFTEEN

Courtney lay silently at peace. Her lips were parted slightly so the inner blush of her life could be seen, had it been there. Her eyes had been closed by an attentive M.E. and yet her left lid was not completely shut. The bruise on her left temple, though large, was subdued and no longer angry.

I stood next to her, one hand on the cold metal table, the other on her right hand.

I had no words.

For the last two weeks, I had been captivated with the idea of Courtney in many different ways, but never like this. I would not ask why this had happened. I had learned a few years ago that asking why only made the ache deepen and the rest of life more a shadow. It was *how* that concerned me the most.

The young orderly standing in the corner of the room was fidgeting with the tie-string on the waist of his scrubs. He was black, about 20-years-old, and seemingly unbothered by the spectral aspects of his occupation. He was comfortable with the cool habitation of this place, but he probably didn't know what had happened. There was no one else in the room. Marianne stood outside a large window, her arms tightly locked around her, an angry expression frozen on her face. A fatigued, but gentle looking, detective stood next to her drinking coffee from a Styrofoam cup and watching me. He would know, I decided.

Motioning for him to enter, I turned again to Courtney. The freckles on her nose and cheeks had not faded as I had imagined they would. And though she was pale—almost alabaster in coloring—she was not at all repulsive. Her nakedness was somewhat indistinct beneath the cloudy plastic of the shroud, but in all still attractive, perhaps even more astonishing so at rest, than it ever had been on display. And there was a quietness about her that did not correspond with death, a repose that touched her form, more reminiscent of sleeping, than dying.

The detective entered quietly and stood aloof, not near but within reach. Our muted conversation felt blurred and unreal.

"How did it happen?

It appeared an accident. Seemed she fell and struck her head…

Then it wasn't the cancer?

Did she have cancer?

Yes.

No, it was not the cancer.
Was she alone?
Yes.
Do you think she suffered?
We don't know, but it's unlikely…
Who found her?
Her friend…
Why did you call me?
Again, her friend. She said you two had gone out and we found this card in a flower arrangement on her dresser."

Reaching out I received my business card from the officer's fingers and read the words scribbled on its back,

> *I'm sorry to hear you're sick,*
> *please get well soon.*
> *James Morrow.*

Nodding, I handed the card back to the detective, then turned to face Courtney. The detective withdrew quietly, signaling the orderly to follow.

"So," I said quietly, "here we are again." I gazed down at her, and then out the glass to Courtney and the men in the hallway. Then slowly and deliberately, I leaned over and laid my head gently upon her breast, closing my eyes to weep.

BY AGE

"A dying man needs to die, as a sleepy man needs to sleep, and there comes a time when it is wrong, as well as useless, to resist."

—Steward Alsop

ANNO DOMINI

The breeze riffled the pages in his lap, one slip of newspaper fluttering away from his fingers, dancing gaily into the fall morning, tippling along the grass then across the flagstones and onto the pond, where it hovered for a second, then laid itself down in the water, melting to a gray-black smear of yesterday. He was sleeping now, 83 years of memories at his feet, scattered about him like toy blocks from his childhood. The black leather of each volume muted with age; red, green and gold tags, like ribbons of valor decorating their spines. The open book in his lap was similar, though newer, its gold edging pristine, winking at the new sun.

It was a rarity when he failed to write in his journal. Business, family obligations and travel not withstanding, he was diligent to record the events of his life, some inane, others profound and a few, nothing but froth. Only for one period had he purposefully put down his journal and refused to write. It began on the date his grandson had been killed 12 years earlier. Lifting his pen mid-sentence and setting aside his journal, he had not picked up that one volume for almost eight months. There was never an explanation given for his silence, other than the one panel he prepared for his next entry, a full-page ink drawing depicting a chubby three-year-old boy, wielding a small plastic shovel by an incomplete sand castle. The words—My Spencer, 2012 to 2031—were printed in his familiar block letters beneath. On the very next page, his journal resumed much the same progress it had known in the past, but without the general enthusiasm.

To be sure, his take on profound social or political events once again found their way into the pages, as did sporadic chronicling of his daily tasks. And he still inscribed pages with ferocity and cutting insight concerning the spiritual issues he felt the succeeding generations of his family would need to understand. And while he recorded special moments spent with his children and their children, embellishing them with the best ornamentation his mind could conceive and his arthritic fingers could execute, it seemed to him *(and to those who occasionally pulled a volume from the shelf and scanned its pages)* that he could no longer bring to bear the fullness of his passion. In a way, Spencer's hand prints stained every page since that day in May, 2031, when he was lost, staining even those pages unwritten during eight months of silence, locked away as they were, somewhere inside the chambers of his heart.

The initial volumes of his journal had all been of the same structure, uniform in appearance and function. Each began with a half-plate ink drawing of special significance as to the year, depicting some unfolding global or family event, or even his particular feelings. One 200-page book usually lasted between five and eight months, making for a total of 161 volumes and over 32,000 pages since his 40th birthday. A lot of words, a lot of memories.

In October of 2003, the half-plate opening page was of a clock, its glass shattered, hands warped, the smoldering works glimpsed through a jagged hole in the face. His purpose, he had explained when asked, was to put a face on the sudden increase of terrorism in those times, and what he felt was happening as the universal clock wound down. In another book, he drew a detailed spray of flowers, replete with a tiny bumble bee sampling one blossom's nectar; in still another, he depicted the instrument panel of a car, its gauges indicating high speed and no fuel. Each book, he would say, should speak a different and subtle message to the generations to follow him, who would read his thoughts. An image, he contended, spoke all at once and didn't have to be unwound like words.

When he had first begun to journal, he diligently recorded his daily routines, thinking his children, who were small at the time, would find his daily schedule fascinating or at least anachronistic. Later, as they matured, he became less prosaic about the meals he ate or the deadlines he achieved, realizing slowly that the pages he filled should contain accounts of those people and places he loved, not schedules. After all, what were schedules but itineraries of the mundane, checklists before takeoff, manifests of cargo less important than the aircraft itself, or the storms through which it passed.

When he had been a boy, the passage of time had been sluggish. Waiting for Christmas seemed a lifetime of days and nights—a virtual eternity of weeks. Time passed like paint drying or hair growing—imperceptibly, almost tortuously. Tedious school days crawled to his birthday and Christmas, both of which were at the end of the year.

He actually remembered sitting in first grade as the teacher explained how to read the clock *(by that age he had been capable of that task for months)* and trying to calculate how many minutes would pass before the class ended. He then extended this series of calculations to how many minutes would elapse before the end of the day, the week, till his birthday.

He didn't extend this calculus to the balance of his life until he was in the tenth grade, at which point he considered the decades most likely ahead of him, and gasped to postulate a life of 36,792,000 unwritten, unprogrammed minutes. And even then, he cringed to imagine the span of time between his present and the date he would turn 18.

Eighteen, that wonderful, frightening age. Eighteen-years-old and the dawning of a new, limitless horizon of possibilities—it had stormed into his mind like a rapist. Life's rarest and most delicate sweets awaited him, sex being chief of among them and his burgeoning adulthood had defiled him, taking the glorious beauty of his manliness and degrading it into pulp trash. He couldn't have imagined that moment 420,480 minutes before the instant it happened, nor could he have foreseen that his initiation into the mysteries of sexual love would have been so mishandled, so achingly fouled up. The thousands of pages of memories recorded over months and years still had not seen that moment addressed.

He had always been honest in his diaries, even when the content with which he filled pages was less than appetizing. He had described his frustration with his children through their various insanities, the passion for his wife and its cooling with age, the shock and disbelief at personal betrayal, the magic of birth, the emptiness of death, his fears, raw and unadulterated, and his hopes, however unrealistic. And yet, when recording his sin, his failures, he withheld the fullness of his mind.

He had read the diary of Samuel Pepys in his late 30s and had been appalled by the casual blandness of Pepys' description of his sexual liaisons with chamber maids, friends' wives and daughters and tradeswomen. He was repulsed by the graphic, vulgar details of his physical manipulations and the pathetic attempts to disguise his vulgarity, by using fragmented speech in French, Latin and Spanish as a code of sorts. *"mi mano was sobra her pectus, and so did hazer with grand delight."* What an ass!

And yet, he remembered comparing his own mental infidelities with Pepys' physical ones, finding little difference and absolutely no moral superiority. He had become disgusted and ashamed, and determined to plunge his most secret self into a void of bland allusions and references. His children could speculate as they read his words, wonder what "Dad" had meant by his struggles, but would not have to face the ugliness of his thoughts, the odor of his vulgarity. What purpose would it serve, he reasoned, to spill the details of his wickedness across all those empty pages? "My pain is my pain," he declared, "my weaknesses are my mine."

But a year or so before his 70th birthday, he had made an entry in which he had revealed with brutal honesty, the personal war with sin he had waged for most of his life and from which he had been finally delivered by a loving and very patient God. It was a struggle that was long past him now, as were most struggles. Now he slept in the autumn sun, at peace with himself and with his God.

He had observed teens since he and his wife began having children and had always viewed them as fresh—like newborn peaches, hard, covered with a slight down on their translucent, richly tinted skins. Yet, as he had often written, so many teens, and peaches for that matter, were raised in industrial nurseries, rushed to market and ruined by mishandling that their quality was unalterably damaged. Most, he bemoaned, had been plucked prematurely from the parent tree, had been opened, their flavors greedily consumed by transients, their beauty marred by rough, casual usage so that their essence was changed. When their love was offered in the future, sometimes in desperation, it was tart, nothing like the mellow sweetness of sun-ripened fullness. They didn't look bruised as much as they looked mechanically picked, packed and shipped…commoditized. To him it was sad.

By his late teens, time had accelerated. Strangely, it was no longer crawling but tramping along at a fine pace—a good, solid healthy walk, able to be measured and predicted, the minutes stretching out into semesters and vacations and breaks and weekends; seasons punctuated by periodic eccentricities and deadlines, imagined and real. Most of his days were an emotional, physical blur, adrenal activity stressing his machine, till the flesh and bone of his body lay limp in bed, still clothed. And he had slept soundly in those days, deeply relaxed in the bliss of perfect exhaustion.

Not till he had entered early adulthood did his sleep begin to disintegrate. Then the passing of time accelerated, like a rushing wind in his hair. Marriage, children…debt? Life flew past him like an apparition fettered with anxiety, from those moments in the delivery room to those at the little league diamond. His journal, carried with him like an appendage, barely kept the pace and many, many days received short shrift.

In mid-life the panics grew further apart, but time itself leapt from beneath him, pulled away like the cloth in a magician's trick. His children left home and married, he and his wife entered into a more easy companionship and God began the process of settling his mind and heart. In a few years, the husks of which scattered before his step like leaves, he was settling into maturity. He still journaled, but the days of frantic one-line entries had long passed, the easy, casual use of time replaced the passion of an uninformed youth.

The days, however, actually moved along quicker, the intervals between sunset and sunrise actually seeming to compress. As a life-long observer, he contemplated the sudden quickening of time and determined, much the same way he had in tenth grade, that it was a natural occurrence, that hours and days passing so quickly did so, not because time had been accelerated but because his perception of their passing had been altered. In his journal, he calculated that a year in the life of a five-year-old was in fact 20 percent of his life, practically an eternity and yet, a year in the life of a 50-year-old was only 2 percent of his life, a fraction that vanished as quickly as morning dew. At 70, he no longer took time to consider how quickly it passed, for it was too precious a resource. In his 80s he awoke each day, tasting each moment as if it were his last sip of water.

And now the sun had moved further up in the sky, warming the cool breeze that loosed his papers from his lap and his sleeping fingers. A slender, orange cat stretched on the flagstones near his chair, rolling on the warming pavement then collected herself for a bath. A mockingbird began to bicker in a nearby tree as the cat strolled over to the man and leapt effortlessly into his lap. She kneaded contentedly on his lap and then settled comfortably on the fading warmth of his hands and the open journal. It was a place she had occupied for many an hour in the past two years, and today, though beginning like most others, would end this practice.

The old man was gone. His body and his mind, wrung out by the mangle of his life lay still and unmoving in the chair. His soul now free, pondered with grave curiosity the long-desired exploration of the Peaceable Kingdom.

BY SACRIFICE

"Greater love hath no man than to lay down his life for his friend."

—*Jesus of Nazareth*

THE EXCHANGE

The shattered B-17 trembled like a wounded bird. The elegant, streamlined, silver wings were now scarred and pitted, long, gray tendrils of fuel streamed from perforated tanks. Once-powerful engines screamed through each air pocket spouting flames and coughing black liquid. Yet even though the battle had been fierce, no one had been lost. The experienced commander had brought the plane clear of enemy shore batteries, and now, engines sputtering, the aircraft was falling even nearer to the gray waters of the English Channel.

The mission had been a qualified success, thought the captain as he gave the command to abandon ship. When the bomber group had first crossed the Channel, crews of each ship were enthusiastically anticipating the sting of battle. There were several young recruits among them but they seemed confident enough. So confident in fact, that even he began to relax as they ventured toward the mist-shrouded French coastline. All his instruments showed normal and the rest of his wing signaled "All green!" This day would be a medal winning day, he thought, for himself, as well as his crew.

It wasn't long before Smiley called out their coordinates and announced they were in German air space. His voice lacked any hint of fear, however, which seemed strange to the captain, who remembered that Smiley was never not scared. Usually it was a matter of fact to see his bombardier frowning by his charts and instruments, swearing at his luck and praying to his God. He was a Jew and wore a funny little round hat all the time, even in battle. The name Smiley, however, was not his real one.

The label of 'Smiley' had been bestowed on him by the overhead turret gunner, Jack Saunders, who always teased him about his frown. Jack was a likable sort, almost like a big brother to the rest of the guys. He was tall and husky with blue eyes and black hair, always present with a joke and cleaning his prized German Lugar. The gun had been purchased from an intoxicated G.I.

on a night he said he would rather forget. Jack was alright, and that morning as they flew on toward battle, he was no different. Whistling some crazy tune he had joked that they would have to take Smiley to the flight surgeon as soon as they returned, simply because he was happy. Same old Jack.

The two waist gunners, Peter Finney and Red McCheon, laughed at Jack's remark, even though Smiley outranked them all. Both Pete and Red were full of fun, inseparable as kids and since joining the service together, ready at all times for a good joke or a good fight. Red had once been decorated for a fight he had started in a bar. It seemed that the man Red took to be a Norwegian sailor had actually been an escaped P.O.W., and when the police broke up the brawl and arrested the German, Red was brought before the British commander and decorated for valor. Pete, who had been a small part of the bar fight, received only stitches and a smile from a sympathetic nurse.

The rest of the crew, tail gunner and ball turret, navigator and copilot, were newcomers to the Captain's flight crew—replacements all. But that day they were cheerful as per the theme of the flight. "Hey you guys, it's gonna be a blast," they said. "Yeah, on Hitler, sorry bastard!"

But they were all so young and inexperienced. And this was the part that halfway scared the Captain to death. He had learned from several terror-filled nights that the paps of inexperience often bred false security. The tail gunner was Harold Phillips, a lad with a blond crew cut and a noticeable tennis tan. And while Harry never admitted it, the Captain knew his age to be barely 17. My God, thought the Commander, he probably hadn't even had his first girl yet.

The navigator and copilot were both semi-friends; they had met in the Officer's Club two weeks prior, after a particularly hairy mission. They had struck up the kind of communication common to smoky English pubs of the time—"Rotten weather, Hey?" "Yeah, clear as a bell; guess we'll have to fly!" But even though the talk had been brief and the beer stale, the Captain and the others became friends of sorts. All three depended on that tie, but knew from somewhere that with a crack in their well-sealed cockpits and a second run of bad luck, all ties, all friendships could dissolve. The three were veterans of the war, surviving missions, outliving most of their crews. And by virtue of their records, all realized the truth in the statement, "There are no atheists in fox-holes or any pretenses under the scrutiny of God."

The ball turret gunner was a nice boy, peach fuzz barely grown on his softly turned cheek. Had he been home, he'd have been playing baseball or fishing or lazing barefoot in the sun with an old floppy dog, something other than killing his fellow man. But he was a soldier fighting the same war as the rest of them—to preserve freedom, to warrant a new life for destroyed peoples, to play savior.

Yes, he was a soldier, but with the cracking and flashing of the shore batteries, all in the craft realized that war was an inappropriate time to play anything, especially God.

They had crossed the French frontier by this time, and already one ship in their bomber group had been destroyed. The captain recalled how it arched orange across a sunrise sky and finally, reluctantly, touched the passionate landscape. The ship died instantly, yet, it fostered the eruption of an oil-black flower which seemed to grow in slow motion, its interior alive with the frantic licks of orange-peel flame. It was alive, thought the captain, as he kept the corner of his eye on its retreating shape. And it was tragically beautiful.

Another thirty minutes and they were over their primary target, some railroad center operated by Vichy. But in those brief moments, the ship had taken a merciless beating. Tiny perforations gleamed sunlight through most of the plane's fuselage and fuel poured from plate-sized holes in the wings. Flack was a hideous weapon, thought the captain. It popped softly, deceptively all around like firework torpedoes. And as several popped around the ship, he felt as if he had been spared, his sentence reprieved.

They were playing with popguns, he said to himself. Until he looked down at the neatly cut hole in his leg. It wouldn't even bleed for another minute or so, and he stared at the clean wound, his lips white with effort as he fought to control the tears.

"Bombs away, Cap, let's get the hell outa here!" said Smiley. The Captain gritted his teeth and began to bank the ship slowly around to make their escape. And that's when it happened.

There, as the plane swung slowly around its belly upturned in the pepper sky, was the wrenching blow to the center of the craft and a scream from the youth in the ball turret. It had taken a hit. The waist gunners disconnected their tethers and were there in an instant, opening the convex hatch and reaching inside to pull the boy out. Strong hands closed around the limp boy's arms and warm blood ran between their fingers as they gently tried to ease him out of the shattered ball, but something caught. They tried again, with more force this time, struggling to pull him out. McChoen shoved Finney away and stepped into the glass sphere, placing his feet on the mangled seat back, trying his own brute strength at getting the kid out, but it was hopeless. The cold wind whistled up from the broken glass, fluttering the pant legs of Red's flight suit and swept back his hair. He was crying and swearing and jerking at the wounded boy, until Finney was forced to pull him away from the turret to the other side of the aircraft. There, anguished, Red whistled through his mike to the Captain, "The kid's been hit alright, but he's still alive. The only problem we're having is getting him out of the turret, he's stuck fast."

The captain listened helplessly, as he fought to control his twisted plane. If they were very lucky, perhaps blessed, there would be another night of cowering in the Officer's Club, drinking the fear away and laughing at their close call with death. But the Captain knew—knew right down in his soul that that would never be.

His ship was losing altitude fast and though he struggled to keep it aloft, it sank, always deeper toward the gray of the Channel. Shortly after they crested the Channel Zone, he called to his crew and told them of his decision to abandon ship.

There was silence for a short time, followed by mumbled prayers from Smiley, as he disconnected his headset and made for the hatch. Saunders was down from his turret and grabbing Red who was numb, silent and hostile. Moving him carefully the two and Finney got ready to jump. Only a very few minutes were passed but the Captain felt as if it were taking hours to clear the ship. His navigator and copilot didn't look at him, as they released their harnesses and left the cockpit. There alone, sitting relaxed and watching the sea through the crack in his cockpit windshield he wondered why it was always the babies who were taken, why the helpless and the innocent. The whitecaps were barely perceptible as he viewed them through his broken window, along the diagonal crack that ran the length of the glass. Chuckling slightly, he moved a gloved finger along the crack as he looked at the ocean below. One ocean is trying to climb into the other, he thought, but it can't do it, the crack is stopping it. Again the captain grinned, dropping his hand to the harness release and depressing the button. Standing up and looking one last time at the churning ocean outside, he turned and left the cockpit.

As he entered the main fuselage, a cry went up from the ball turret, from the wounded boy inside. He had regained consciousness when the Captain was ordering the ship abandoned and attempted to free himself. But finding himself stuck, he waited for his friends to help, but they never came.

And now, as the crew left the ship, one at a time through that gaping green door, he cried out in understandable terror. He had never thought of dying alone, not in a bomber. But now understanding fully the death he would experience, the lad screamed and reached out toward his friends only inches away.

Yet they left all the same, that sick feeling in their stomachs and the horrible memory of the young boy's scream etched in their brains. First Smiley went, then Red and Finney, followed by Saunders and the tail gunner. Finally, the navigator and copilot leapt from that door. But just as the copilot was leaving, his foot reaching into space, he turned to see a sight that he would never forget.

There, on the floor of the plane was the Captain. He had taken the wounded boy's hand and was speaking softly to him. "That's alright son, we'll ride her down together."

And then the copilot was gone, falling in space, tumbling end over end till his silken brown bag popped. Hanging motionless in the air, he watched the plane fall slowly to the sea and once down, disappear under the grey froth. Staring out at the waves, his heart was tugged. He would remember.

A week or so after, in the warm, peaceful confines of a California office, an officer from the Adjutant General's office sat quietly at his desk reading reports and, occasionally, banging out one of his own. His job was a simple one. Bolster the morale of a war-weary people by his radio reports. He was qualified for the job to be sure. He had been an actor before the war and even now had a few jobs from time to time. As in all war posts, and this one was no exception, there was stress. Yet, the anxiety of this job was not found in the doing, but in the feeling, the enduring, the caring.

So each day, he tried harder to reach the people, to understand their emptiness at the loss of a loved one, to penetrate that scornful, apathetic detachment that a foreign war fosters. But the adjutant was not only a soldier; he was a man as well. At times, his heart would sink and be saddened at considering the prospects of the war. And though he was a God-fearing man, he sometimes wondered if freedom was such a holy struggle. So to guard himself against the day when disgust would overwhelm him, he secreted away the citations awarded men overseas, reading of their daring, their courage, to inspire himself again.

When five o'clock came that day, it blew in off the coast, balmy and nice. Walking to his window, he opened the glass, leaned out and smelled the sweet air. What a beautiful day, he murmured. Returning to his desk and at the same time loosening his tie, he lifted the blotter and withdrew the citations he had hidden there earlier. He arranged them neatly on his desk and read carefully the actions of his country's brave men. So many medals, he thought, and so much to fight for. He made sure he read every detail, trying to visualize the courage it took to die alone or save a platoon or sink a battle ship. Making himself an actor, he tried to live the war from their perspective. And then he came to one paper which slowly, naturally, gripped his heart.

It was the highest tribute his country could give a man for bravery. The man, a pilot of a B-17, had flown a mission over France. The report described a sacrifice of life, an exchange of one thing for another far more important, so that the adjutant read on hypnotized.

The paper described how the plane had been shot down coming home. The ball turret gunner had been wounded and jammed into his seat unable to move or get out. When the pilot ordered "bail out," every one left the plane—everyone that is except the ball turret gunner and the pilot. As the copilot was exiting, he saw the Captain sit down on the floor of the plane, take the wounded boy's hand and say, "That's alright son, we'll ride her down together." The report ended with a commendation, the Congressional Medal of Honor, posthumously awarded. That was all there was to read, and the adjutant put the paper down on his desk, placed his head I his hands and wept.

For years the adjutant remembered the story. When he felt himself becoming disheartened with his country, he would remember that pilot and realized that there were still people who cared and had compassion, who were willing to make so great an exchange. And being comforted he went on.

In 1979, some 30 years after his service as a California military adjutant, the former actor strode confidently onto the stage to speak his piece on 1980s politics to a crowd of more than 20,000. There was a feeling of great astonishment in the audience as they finally recognized who the speaker was. And in like manner, the speaker could be seen to blush at the roar of welcome he received. No one in the arena had known who the featured speaker was to be, and as this witness affirms, the adjutant was as little-prepared to receive us. There were screams, sobs and sniffles from men, as well as women. Deafening cheers and applause from people who choked down the laughter that bubbled up from somewhere unknown. It was as if Santa Claus had stepped onto stage and smiled at us.

All these feelings rippled from one end of the crowd to the other. Finally, the ovation past, the speaker began his talk. As he spoke, it occurred to me how sincere this man was, how genuine. I did not take notes but sat in limp excitement, feeling the history of the moment. During his speech, there was one moment that fell silent as he gathered his thoughts. As he stood there, about to resume his talk, the melody of a thousand, reaching voices floated up out of the darkness and gently touched the speaker's ears. "God bless America, land that I…"

He fumbled with his notes and blinked a few times. We could tell that he had been touched. But when he again began to talk, he told a story I will never forget. It was the story of a World War II pilot who gave his life to comfort the last few minutes of a dying boy's life. In trembling tones he finished the story, "There is much to love in this country of ours." And the people overtook him.

"He's crying," I said, stopping to realize that I was too. Looking around at my friends, men, women, I noticed their tears, as well. Blinking hard, I tried to catch a glimpse of the adjutant as he left the stage, his wife in tow. But I failed. He was gone, but for some time the audience refused to admit it. That experience still echoes in my mind, all those people and one tender man. Now, when I became discouraged, I remember the adjutant and his story and that there are still men of compassion in this world.

I doubt he ever saw himself in the position he eventually achieved, with so many people looking to him for strength. But I'll wager somewhere in his heart, he thanked God for that man who died so many years ago. I know I thank God for him, and the officer from the AG's office who became president. For I realize that, although there is suffering in the world, there is so much more overcoming of it.

BY DESIGN

"Death not merely ends life; it also bestows upon it a silent completeness, snatched from the hazardous flux to which all things human are subject."

—Hannah Arendt

SURF SLEEP

We walk among untold multitudes lost in quiet, desperate moments, although their struggles are unseen and terror's expression lost to the expansive sea. Yet, the surf brings to us the remnants of their lives, the glittering fragments which once danced whole and complete.

Along with us, quiet sentinels stand ready to receive from the sea. Their colors like marble and granite, they set themselves like pickets just out of the water's reach, their eyes immovable, fixed on the waves. They are, for a season, like us, our children skittering between us and the water, playing along as we pick through this bone-yard.

Our God did not put ornate gates or fences or signs or any hindrance between us and this cemetery. No, and no markers either. We would drown in them!

Under our feet they are crushed. We scan their remains with our eyes; we reach our hands to extract one, like gods.

Are we, in fact, their gods, we, who reach into their world from another? Our minds cannot recognize our godliness or our divinity. Do we not bare this form of godliness one to another?

We touch one, then another, brush some aside who are broken, pitted; we do not want to see the shattered ones, the drab ones. What benefit will they be to our conversations, our appetites, our dwelling places?

And some are too small. Our hands are covered in their wet clinging. It becomes melancholic, them covering us…so many, so desperate, so small. It suffocates!

And others are so ordinary. They are powdery white and fan shaped, splayed out in our hands neat, clean, un-pitted, un-scarred and ordinary; one among trillions. Where is the brilliance, the color and design, the single taste unique to itself? One fluted orb is lifted out, the sand brushed away. It is as delicate as a porcelain cup, the hue of which is pale and sweetly translucent to the sky's fire.

Shall we be like that dark Danish prince who when gambling by Elsinor port happened upon a vanquished and lost friend, "alas, poor Yorick. I knew him, Horatio." Shall we hold it to our faces and long for those quick and feisty jibes of yester-year, the agile dance of its youth? Shall we muse of a past we can know nothing of?

And what is it to us really, but broken pottery from some other world? They are vessels constructed and fired for an alien purpose, whose users we know not. The colors and shapes amuse us and nothing more.

Then we walk, we among these crushed and fragmented multitudes as though through a graveyard. The crimson of a western sun stains the velvet coast before us, their markers, rivulets in the sand.

They are there and here, about us at every turn. They who were born in obscurity, in a moment we knew not, the insignificance of which boggles the mind, they saturate the landscape with their beauty. Some are golden and graceful, more fluid and clean; another is turned with a unique style; and yet one more gloats with black ink stains and blood on its gown. They are beautiful, but created so for whose eyes? Rare is the maiden who has been offered one flower as striking, one gem as single.

Before us the sand is stretched out as a warm blanket over the sleeping. Snugged into their cozy cover, the countless fallen sleep the sleep of anonymity. But those we shall walk past, those whose skin will never again tingle with the air, does their existence then have no meaning? If a maiden's eye appreciates not the curve and color of the thing, never beholds, enjoys, savors or wonders at the object; was then there a purpose in their lives, is there now a purpose in their deaths?

Yards away, the waves pound the new arrivals relentlessly. Without thought, with no conscience and with casual ruthlessness, the sea commands the newcomers and tasks them to sleep. The sand awaits, its embrace is all that remains, all that is hoped for. All except perhaps the sun and a wandering, passing, vaguely curious person.

Are we in fact their gods? Or do they recognize that one day soon we will join them as broken pottery asleep among multitudes?

BY SURPRISE

Death—the last sleep? No, it is the final awakening.

—*Walter Scott*

THE TAXIMAN'S GOD

"Make no mistake: if He rose at all
it was as His body;
If the cells' dissolution did not reverse, the molecules reknit, the amino acids
rekindle,
the Church will fall."

"Let us not mock God with metaphor,
Analogy, sidestepping transcendence;
making of the event a parable, a sign painted in the faded credulity of earlier
ages:
let us walk through the door.

Let us not seek to make it less monstrous,
for our own convenience, our own sense of beauty,
lest, awakened in one unthinkable hour, we are embarrassed by the miracle,
and crushed by remonstrance."

—John Updike, *Seven Stanzas at Easter*

ONE

Oh, God!

His mind replayed the events of the past hours furiously and his hands rubbed together in visible turmoil. He sensed the dry roughness of the clotted blood that covered them and looked down to see the blackened, red flakes drop to the floor. Though numb, the stark contrast of the white floor and the dark blood started his stomach once again. The accident had been a horrible mess. God, he wondered, would he ever forget what he had seen?

Everybody else had, apparently, left—police, doctors, coroner—everybody. Only he remained, like some schoolboy, unsure of the appropriate behavior. What of the family? Where were the friends? It had been nearly five hours and no one had shown up, he thought, looking across at the still figure on the table. A muted and vague jazz riff floated indifferently down the hallway past triage and security, seeping under the drawn curtains and closed doors till it entered into the cubical where he sat, finding his ears.

"Excuse me, it's Frank isn't it?" the charge nurse asked, softly touching him on the shoulder.

"Yes?"

"Frank, I think we might be more comfortable in the waiting room. The police still have some questions and we might be able to rustle up some coffee. What do you say?"

Why was it always we, he thought, like she knew what we were thinking or what we needed.

"Have you tried to contact any of her family?" he asked, without looking up.

"I'm sure everything's being done that can be done. Let's go to the waiting room."

"I think I'll stay here," he said, moving his arm away from her gentle urging. Her emotion was fiction, he thought, she was like a prom date on the arm of the ugly rich boy. He was cold to her.

"Really Mr. Teska, there's nothing else you can do here and well,…" her voice trailed off as she looked toward the table, "we have to take care of Sarah now."

"So that's her name?" he mumbled indistinctly. She hadn't looked to him like a Sarah, not in the car and certainly not here. But then he hadn't really had a good look at her yet. Turning mechanically and looking up into the nurse's face he shook his head slowly, "…no, thank you. I'll stay."

"But Mr. Teska…"

"She doesn't have anyone here," Frank said incredulously. "Thank you nurse, but I'm *staying*. You can go now."

The nurse straightened next to him, stiffening at his coldness. She looked imperiously down on the top of his head and hesitated. She was pretty, he thought, she's pretty but her eyes are hard and she really doesn't care. Go away! His mind suddenly screamed and he looked down, anger welling up within him. Tears began to form in his reddened eyes and he blinked hard, once again wringing his hands.

After a few seconds, he heard her rubber-soled shoes squeak out of the treatment cubicle and back towards the nurses' station down the hall.

It was quiet now, very quiet. The only sounds he could hear were muted and far away—voices, music, laughter—outside the curtained cubicle where he sat. He could see the world outside if he looked through the small opening in the curtains. Except for last year's tiny Christmas lights lurking along the edge of the nurses counter, it was white and sterile; plastic and stainless and clean.

What a damn awful lie! His mouth curled into a rage he had never before felt. The world outside *wasn't* clean, it was messy and it was brutal, disorderly—*un*clean! And it was malevolent, too. He had not always thought that way. No, he had never thought that way. And to do so now, having never processed the thought before, was strange and unsettling. Sure, there had been Hitler, Stalin, Mao, the holocaust, and the inquisition. There were even earthquakes, tornadoes, serial killers, rapists, gangs; he had read about all of these, seen them on the TV…but he had always thought they were random, unconnected events; things and people that went wrong, like a tire out of the factory with a flaw, a bubble just under the surface. Perfectly good until, at the right speed and temperature, under the right amount of pressure—bang!

But now, where he sat, with what he had been through, seen and tasted; now, he knew the truth of the world and of his life. It was not an accident, not unusual for evil to spring forth. It was much more unusual to live the life he had lived till that day; peaceful, content, always comfortable.

Horror wasn't accidental, it wasn't an aberration of the norm, it *was* the norm. He had only to look back over the last few hours to see that. Somehow it was clearer now than it ever had been.

Reluctantly, he got up and moved across the room. He needed to change his point of view, to see everything from a different perspective, to feel differently than he did. But the ragged edge of his sanity provided no footing. He stumbled near the precipice and flailed with his arms for something, anything but the night. Before his eyes the gloaming skirts of twilight played out its passage once again and he panicked. He did not want to go there again, he was afraid to go. But in a strange way he felt the trip was necessary, decreed by the heart of flesh that pounded within him. He was alive, never more so than at that moment, and *in* that moment he had to review the evening regardless of consequence. He would go back and live his life over while she died—again.

His eyes moved from the sterile hall outside and covered the room. Before him, fragments of the trauma lay scattered, torn and saturated, like leaves following a storm. As he surveyed the quiet frenzy in the room, his eyes came to rest on a pair of ripped patent-leather shoes forsaken in a corner alongside a pair of bloody surgical gloves.

For a moment he stared at the pitiful white objects, at the broken straps and the water which clung to them, at a smudge of oil on their shiny surface. And then he closed his eyes, rushing the long route back to the morning, to normalcy, before the phantasm on the road, before the accident. And he began to weep into the recess of his elbow, his mind shuddering, fleeing the hospital and running for home.

TWO

Pleasenten was just thirty more minutes along the little blacktop and then a shower, a beer, a squeeze from his wife and sleep. Man, was he ready.

Six hours at the gas station punching buttons and putting Snapple and Ho-Hos in plastic bags, followed by five hours in the cab—was he tired of that! Feeling the weight of his shifts closing in, Francis X. Teska, convenience store supervisor and part time cabby ground the palm of his left hand into his eyes and turned his two-way radio off and the tinny dash-bound AM radio on.

Greeted with a burst of static, he quickly spun the volume knob. God, what an awful sound, he thought, tapping the dial, exciting a crackle with every touch. "Come on!" he hissed, twisting the worn plastic to try and find a clear station.

"Why don't I get this fixed?" he whispered to himself. "I know, probably the same reason I don't stop talking to myself—because I like it." And so he smirked, continuing to tune the radio. This habit of talking to himself had developed over the last four years with the advent of his second job. With the eternal lack of sleep and the aggravation of traffic, Frank thought it a defense mechanism for his sanity, "Like the porcupine has its quills," he would say. Besides, many a night found him out alone, with no fares in sight and only thoughts of his wife and the kids flowing through his mind. So what if these thoughts were eventually given voice, so what if he conversed with the air, what did it matter if he sometimes only spoke to swear?

Looking up from the dash, Frank saw the flickering white center-stripe passing under the middle of his hood and jerked the car back into his lane, cursing his stupidity and the battered radio. After he was certain there were no cars coming down the other dark lane, he reached back to the stubborn instrument and fiddled more aggressively, till he at last found a song that he liked and could hear.

"At last," he sighed, taking his hand away gently and gazing ahead through the white beams of his headlights. Tunes at last; the natural narcotic he had gotten hooked on over the last year in the cab. It had become, literally, the only crossable bridge between Philly and the spindle-thin trees of his home.

The long, hour drive from Philadelphia was, compared to many drives, one of the more beautiful. After fleeing the city and crossing the massive blue steel of the Benjamin Franklin Bridge into Jersey, it was another thirty minutes to the Mt. Laurel exit and from there, twenty minutes of trees, cold creeks and clean, white houses. Finally, at the end of his day, he arrived home.

Pleasenten was a postcard hamlet, population 4,706. *(His seven-year-old had remarked once after seeing the sign, that the six added to the population was her, her mother and father, big brother Frank, Jr., little brother Stephen and Papa Teska. The mayor obviously hadn't counted Jack the dog because, as she said, he wasn't quite human.)* The hamlet had the standard, white-spired church, an old and venerated city square with several revolutionary cannon proudly displayed. And finally, secreted away on a quiet cul-de-sac was a neat, three-bedroom, two-and-a-half-bath frame house with a second-hand swingset nicely repainted robin's egg blue—like the eyes of his smallest boy. But that was in the daylight.

Regretfully Frank's trek occurred at three a.m. And in those sleepy hours, in the very early morning, this otherwise picturesque drive was solitary, unlit and terribly lonely. So music, music in the dark became his lover.

THREE

"Franky," a grossly fat, older man snorted, waving him over to the curb as Frank backed his cab out of the driveway. "What you doin' tonight, Franky, some last minute shopping?" the man chuckled, as he waddled over across the snow-covered median. Paul Mansour, his across-the-street neighbor, had been the only person in the first few months of their residence in Pleasenten, who had made any effort to befriend Frank or his family at all. The others eventually were met, always by accident, at the store or walking the dog. But Paul had been direct. The only person, in fact to make a point of welcoming the newcomers to the quiet softness of Pleasenten. He was Italian, from the "old school," as Paul would often remind him, and to an old, Italian, a neighbor, especially one with Italian blood in his veins, was practically family and he was responsible to "open his arms."

"Pauly," Frank smiled, reaching across and out the window, grasping the slab-sized hand his older friend extended. It was funny, Frank thought, squeezing his neighbor's round, hard hand and smiling up into that olive-colored, moon-shaped face; he had moved out of the city, in part, to leave the vulgarity of his ethnic heritage in South Philly where it belonged. But it had somehow found him out, weedling its way into the suburbs. Paul even used the quaint, streetwise name modifications that Frank had always thought marked young Italian males as punks or Mafia wannabes.

Just another *Johnny* or *Sonny* or *Freddy* or *Tommy*, with no future, no respect—just family and the Catholic church. Yet, when Paul Mansour smiled and called him *Franky* with that heavy accent, for some reason he was able to remember, in a special way, the years he had spent in the old neighborhood. It was like the delicious taste of a Pat's cheese-steak, the smell of incense in the church or the feel of a broomstick in his hands. In fact, when his neighbor called out, "Hey, *Franky!*" the whole golden panorama of his childhood came back, the endless games of stickball, his mother and sisters sitting on the stoop gossiping and their father walking the six blocks from the bus stop arriving home right as the church bells rang for evening mass.

"Another late night, eh Franky?" Paul continued. "When you gonna take some time with that beautiful wife of yours? Why don't you take her to the city and have a real dinner? Huh?" Paul was an Italian gourmet, if there was such a thing, and he seemed to know all the best places where a man could take his wife and have a little Chianti, a large plate of pasta and a special dose of romance.

"I don't know, Pauly," Frank responded meekly. "Gotta a lot of bills, you know? Life gets a lot more expensive with kids."

"Kids *are* life, Franky," he wheezed, resting his bulk against the front quarter panel of the cab and pointing back at the house. "Those angels you got come straight from the Holy Mother and you know it." The sweat was beginning to pop out on his forehead. It never ceased to amaze Frank how much Paul could perspire even when it was cold. "I tell you what," he continued. "You leave those sweet angels with me and your Papa for the evening and you take that princess out to see the city, have a little wine, a little dinner. Old men and children belong together, Franky. It's the way God created the world."

"Good idea, Pauly," Frank smiled, dropping the column shift into gear and looking back over his shoulder. "I'll talk to Papa and set it up." Paul Mansour and Frank's father had fallen in together as co-conspirators a week or so after they had moved in. It seemed the tangible memories that Paul evoked in his father were even more powerful than those Frank experienced. So other than sitting on lawn chairs together and arguing in Italian or playing with the children, these two old-timers set about scheming to find ways to enhance Frank and Marie's marriage. It was endurable, though sometimes it complicated things.

"You drive careful tonight," Paul said pushing off the fender and mopping his brow with an ever-present handkerchief. "Don't worry about talking to your Papa, I'll take care of everything."

Smiling and nodding, Frank pulled away from the curb and rumbled down the street watching in the rearview as the huge man made his way to his front door. After a second there was a muffled squeal, the door flew open and his children ran out tackling Paul's giant legs.

Life indeed was sweet.

FOUR

The tires of his cab hummed against the asphalt in a rhythm that dulled Frank's mind. Twenty-five more minutes, he thought; half-way home.

To Frank this was always the hardest part of the day, the last little bit of driving. Invariably, Frank's eyes began to burn early in the drive, in a subtle but persistent rebellion. He had tried everything to cope; vigorously rubbing them, driving with the window down, drops, no-doze, gum; but nothing worked. He had even tried smoking a cigar, but that had only made him sick to his stomach. So he lived with it, like everything else, like the static on the radio.

His legs ached too, the product of long hours stiff-legged behind a counter, breathing stale cigarette smoke and making change. From his driver's seat he could stretch his left leg and relieve a little discomfort, but the right was frozen behind the accelerator and each passing mile exaggerated the disparity of irritation between his limbs. Wincing, he adjusted his body for the hundredth time, realizing after all that this one unfortunate circumstance *did* keep him awake.

The radio crackled sharply and then settled back into its soothing friendship. Oh man, Streisand, now there was a beautiful woman, he thought. And God, could she sing. Feeling the velvet strains of "Evergreen" wash over his mind, he leaned his head back against the rest and tried to summon an image of his wife.

To him, Marie had always been a mystery. In his mind she represented that untouchable, unknowable quality of life he had only witnessed, but never really experienced, never consumed. Over the years, he had envied his friends who earnestly and recklessly jumped into life's depths, devouring its opportunities, and ignoring the dangers. It was not that he was afraid, he thought, only prudent. He had always, eventually, gotten wet, but he had first observed and calculated the costs, the potential liabilities from the relative safety of the shallows.

So Marie's presence in his home, his bed, was a constant reminder that what he held was probably for someone else, a stolen flower from a neighbor's garden. Even their first meeting and the bewildering outcome of that hot summer night was something that even now he really could barely grasp.

The 1950s in Philadelphia were quite like the rest of the nation, only more so. Frank, like the other natives of the city's Italian neighborhoods, attended public school faithfully each year. And like his friends, he also felt imprisoned from the world of seasons, though only able to witness their turning from the windows of his classes.

Fall semester was torture. Frank's mind wandered through the glimmering autumn days when the trees in the parks all but sparkled with the hue and glow of fading life smoldering in their leaves. It seemed to Frank a defiance against the coming snow, yet he loved fall, if for no other reason than it prophesied the sheltered closeness of winter and the inevitable intimacy generated among his classmates.

The winter months were the best for Frank in school. Viewed from outside, the dirty, oil-stained snow seemed to crowd up along the curbs and shove in close to the building like a redoubt, behind whose walls the inhabitants were shielded. Inside, the boys and girls lingered in the hallways and by the doors, before and after school, looking out at the bleak, shrouded pavement and swirling wind, and then turning around in the building's comfortable embrace, like lovers who resist leaving one another even though they will again kiss the next morning.

The long, sticky spring semester was to Frank the most painful. Minutes dragged into hours, as he stared past the smudged glass into a burgeoning world, longing for the liberation of summer. The prospects were limitless and dotted with the sublime elements only youth enjoy. There would be ferocious, street-rivers cascading joyfully from their hydrant fountainhead, his family's annual trek to Jersey's packed and lubricated shore, and stick ball vigils, that seemed to last from breakfast to the dinner bus with his Dad's long walk home.

Yet in all the seasons of his life, most nights and every weekend, it was not the school, but the Catholic church that presided over Frank's maturing. And for all her meddling and eternal duties, it never felt to Frank that the Church was harsh or, as some of his friends like to gripe, "frigid." The Church, in often ponderous ways, literally structured the substantial aspects of Frank's growing, much like a strict but favorite great aunt, and it was never more evident than one very hot and sweltering summer evening.

FIVE

School had let out the fourth week of May, much to the delight of students and teachers alike. Parents, however, rarely shared this joy, and immediately pronounced judgment in the form of monumental cleaning tasks, that were ever well-intentioned, but rarely, if ever, completed. It was the bane of summer to have convenient, live-in help and yet, have that help teased, diverted and stolen from under parental control into the wildness of play.

The temperature the week of Frank's final eighth-grade class had climbed unseasonably into the low 90s. By Friday afternoon, when the very last bell of the very last class sourly announced the official beginning of summer, the inmates and keepers of PS #64 revived from their lethargy and emerged onto the streets of South Philly hungry and impatient. The neighborhood collectively cringed.

Frank and his friends had dreamed of this moment for months, and once released rushed with abandon onto the streets, propelled by a froth of eager, fellow parolees. From that moment until Labor Day, there would be nothing in their lives but hoagies, orange cream soda, rock-and-roll, street ball, and of course, the annual Catholic social.

This first day of vacation had become, quite literally, the best day of the year *(next to Christmas, that is)*, not just because it was the start of something big, but because it coincided with an event Frank and his friends had only recently began to enjoy.

The Catholic social at St. Bartholomew's Church had been a neighborhood recurrence for the past 10 years, but had only now caught the boys' interests. This change of heart was partly due to Father Al's newly relaxed musical tastes, which included some of the more recent, up-tempo numbers, and partly because these events began to draw on a fundamental need that the boys were only just beginning to recognize—the need to be near girls.

St. Bartholomew's basement was huge. It was so big in fact, that it had become, for all practical purposes, the meeting place of choice for almost the entire neighborhood from 15th Street to the waterfront. Since the fire of 55 and the succeeding renovations, chief among these the opening of the cavernous basement as new meeting space, the room had been reserved and used by any and all organizations in the neighborhood. There had been the unions, the scouts, the Italian-American League, the Knights of Columbus, the Masons, *(Frank had always suspected that these groups, while publicly separated, were somehow intimately connected. Yet if he ever mentioned this speculation to his parents his father would always stop what he was doing and look sternly at his mother. His mother would then cross herself and whisper behind her hand for him to mind his own business.)* Regardless, most groups eventually found themselves under the sheltering stonework of Mother Church, especially when they felt the need to spread out in a private place.

Frank had been coming to St. Bartholomew's ever since he could remember, having been christened in the sanctuary, confirmed at the altar, forgiven and counseled in the confessional and instructed in just about every room including the basement. In Frank's 14-year-old mind, these lower rooms were comparative in appearance to the first century Roman catacombs he had read about. This last aspect had at first unsettled Frank, conjuring images in his mind of musty and sinister apparitions emerging from the shadowy recesses. But as he'd matured, he had become increasingly comfortable with the rambling structure. Indeed, he actually began to look forward to the possibilities of privacy that these dim alcoves might provide.

In any event, every year, the Catholic dance began with a lengthy speech and prayer by Father Al, and every year the boys and girls from the neighborhood nervously fidgeted under the watchful gaze of their chaperone parents and four nuns *borrowed* from St. Bernedette's.

The speech, a prayer, harsh warning looks from his mother and then…*The Platters, Richie Valens, the Beach Boys and Buddy Holly!* God was indeed good, Frank thought, and RCA/Victor held His magic. The instant the player's needle gently scuffed the first record a surge of release swept through the young people in the room, and from that moment till last call at 10:00 p.m., there would only be the scuff of stocking-feet and the shallow timbre of adolescent speech, soundtracked by the songs of the fifties.

Frank couldn't remember exactly when he first spoke to Marie that evening, whether in passing or on one of his many visits to the punch bowl. Perhaps it had been just before that anxious, awkward first kiss. What he could remember *clearly*, however, was the overwhelming urge he had to run the moment their lips parted. He also remembered, at almost the same instant, the power in Marie's dark, wonderful eyes that held him there.

He had been talking with his friends about the next two months of summer glory, making great plans for their endless hours of freedom, when he turned to survey the dance floor for the hundredth time and bumped into little Marie Shamoun.

Marie was an attached member of the gang; attached meaning that she was not an official member, but was always hanging around with her older brother, and therefore connected. The gang itself consisted of Frank; the Bolarri twins, Cecil and Fred, who lived on 15th Street in an upstairs, front apartment with their widowed mother; Danny C. the son of Mr. C., a local grocer and small-time numbers runner for the South Side Gang; Paddy Lynch, who wound up in South Philly despite his obvious ethnic deviance; and Paul Shamoun who seemed to always have his little sister in tow.

The gang, in reality, was just a few guys who liked to hang out together. There was no cryptic significance to their association, no secret handshakes or special colors to wear. The fact was this particular half-dozen boys *(and one girl)* always found themselves in the same place doing the same things. They were neighbors and it was natural for them to be friends. So bumping into Marie was not unusual. To Frank as to the rest she was a part of their lives, like power lines in the neighborhood—anywhere he went she was always in his peripheral vision.

The fact of the matter was that Marie was not that much younger than Frank, only a year or so, and just out of the seventh grade like he was out of the eighth. So neither Frank, nor any of the gang, really cared if she hung around with them. In fact, sometimes having a girl along helped, like when they needed ice-cream money or a believable cover story for their parents.

"Sorry, Marie," he muttered, dabbing a paper napkin at the punch he had spilled when they collided. Yet when he had finished and was about to move away he hesitated. Marie, pale crimson spots coloring her blouse, was looking up at his face with the strangest expression he had ever seen.

"What?" he asked defensively, raising his free hand, palm up. Suddenly and without a word, Marie reached a delicate hand to his shoulder, stood on her tip-toes leaning forward and pressed her lips firmly against his.

It was strange what he remembered about that kiss. It stuck out in his mind more than any kiss since and it *still* haunted him. He remembered he hadn't closed his eyes like he always thought he would. All the movies he had ever seen had trained him to tilt his head and close his eyes in blissful surrender. But this one had happened so fast that he hadn't even had time to think.

He also hadn't caressed her or even touched her for that matter. He had just stood there, holding a paper cup half full of punch and a wadded up paper napkin staring at her. Only later would he recognize that image to be the sweetest, most beautiful face in the whole world. At that point, to his way of thinking there should have been more handling to this first kiss, or at least, hand*holding.*

The whole event had lasted about three seconds. In retrospect, it was one of the longest moments of his life and when she pulled away, he was changed forever.

It was strange to think of, even now. She had looked into him, past the point of his cumbersome adolescence, beyond the acne that was beginning to bloom, to that lonely part no one had ever seen, no one but him. It was as if he were suddenly naked and she a voyeur, watching him with open eyes. He shifted his weight, looking around in embarrassment for his friends.

"What's wrong?" she whispered, leaning with him as he took one small step back. Her hand was on his arm now and her eyes were on his face. Frank heard her words, but could not process her meaning. He was still looking around, just pulling his gaze from the astonished face of Cecil Bolarri, when he mumbled his best response.

"Huh?" he said flatly, returning his eyes to hers. And as he did, he was once again uncoupled from his reason, plunged into a void that his 14-year-old brain could not or would not navigate. Her eyes were black beyond believing, deeply rich and warm. He felt instantly adrift, untethered in a moist and mysterious night and too hot for his skin.

"Hey, what's going on here?" The sharp, nasal accusation of Danny C. sliced through the music and laughter like a sandlot homer, and heads began to turn before Frank could react.

"Did you see that?" joined the incredulous voice of Cecil Bolarri.

"Yeah, man did I ever! What's goin' on, Franky? Hey Pauly, your sister and Franky's been neck'n over here."

Paul Shamoun swiveled out of the twisting throng and sauntered over to his friend and sister wiping sweat from his forehead. "Yo, Marie, what's doin'? Franky, you kissin' my sister?" The crooked smile on his face gave an indication of the barely suppressed glee with which he inquired of his best friend.

Frank stumbled, looked around at the gathering crowd and then again at Marie. She was just looking at him, ignoring the crowd and her brother. "Well, yeah, uh…no! I mean, uh, Marie and I, uh…we were just…uh…"

"Oh man, he's got it bad," Fred Bolarii added, joining the tight circle.

"Yeah," Paddy Lynch echoed. "You's guys know my brother Sean, right? Well, he got hisself snagged by some *Eye*talian babe last summer, took him four months to get clear."

"Hey, shut up, Lynch, you Irish bug!" Shamoun snapped stepping between his little sister and Frank, who by now could've disappeared into the floor. "Geez Marie, don't let Franky kiss you, it's bad for the gang. 'Sides," he looked at his sister and then back at Frank, beginning to laugh, "you gotta let Franky grow up some more. A hot babe like you'll kill a guy like 'em," He walked back to the dance floor shaking his head and laughing.

Frank followed him with his eyes, hearing the chorus of laughter from his friends and then looked sheepishly back to where Marie had been standing, but she was gone.

It would be another two years before Frank had the nerve to speak to Marie. But all through those 24 months when he had avoided and pretended to ignore her, he never stopped hoping that she had not lost that moment. In the end, he found out much to his own surprise, that what had started in the basement of St. Bartholomew's church was still very much alive and that their next kiss, when it finally did come, was one that he initiated, closed eyes and all.

Six

"Hey, sweetness," the man smirked from behind thick, grease-smeared glasses. The woman, at whom he leered, rolled her eyes and brushed past him with a huff, twitching her polyester-clad bottom in raw defiance. "Jeez, Franky," the man wheezed, swiveling on his stool and following the somewhat large and misshapen rear as it retreated from his gaze. "Jeez, I sure would like to wrap my arms around that. 'Bout you, Franky? What'd that be like, eh?"

Johnny DeCalbrino took a long pull from his bottle of Iron City and eyed Vera Abide's sway hungrily. Johnny had been Frank's shift supervisor for seven years, and for each of those seven years, it was Johnny's delight to meet Frank at Tomaso's in South Philly and sit at the bar, watching the luxurious Ms. Abide while he dispensed Frank's weekly instructions and his thin, but necessary paycheck. This arrangement was unusual, but not unheard of.

Cabbing was a fugitive art filled with contradictions. Some companies, the large ones in particular, ran their crews with stringent and often military discipline. They fought for territory—the airport, the hotels, the clubs and fancy restaurants. The gypsies, one-, two- or sometimes three-man independents, often ran in packs, wheedling their way in at the airport curb, cooperating with each other by cutting off a "company car" and stealing a rich fare. It made a night's work somewhat more interesting, if not profitable. It also added a little excitement to the routine.

Frank was a kind of a gypsy. Johnny De's cab company had five drivers in three shifts. Frank drove second shift, "...*on account o' you being a family man,*" Johnny had said sardonically. But it suited him; he liked the time *and* the trade.

He also genuinely liked the independent drivers. They were, for the most part, men like him, who needed the cash and were forced to *hack*. However, there were a few veterans that loved the trade with an ardor only surpassed by their hatred for the bosses at the big companies.

"So, Johnny, how's the Mrs.?" Frank asked, putting a pretzel between his teeth to suppress his grin and turning to look at the sleet starting to fall through the neon glow. His heavyset boss turned his bulk as the swivel stool protested and rested his large arms on the bar.

"Not worth a damn," he snarled downing the rest of his beer and waving for another. "It ain't one night outa thirty I get any lov'n at home, and when I do, I pay for it the rest o' the week." For a moment he was quietly somber as the bartender brought a fresh beer and took the discarded bottle away. Then, as if he remembered the punchline of a joke, he began to shake with silent mirth, reaching a large arm out and grabbing Frank's shoulder and squeezing it hard. "Ah hell Franky, women's what we work for, ain't it? I don't know but that ya pay for it anyway. Whether it's Alice at home need'n some damn manicure the next day, or this piece here, wantin' twenty bucks and a ride back to work—it's all the same."

The big man smiled to himself as if he had solved life's greatest riddle and then he took a huge swallow of beer, emptying half the bottle's contents before he was done. When he put it down, he reached into his jacket pocket and pulled out the envelope that would contain Frank's weekly paycheck and a short, pencil-scrawled list of likely pick-up spots for the week. Looking away from Frank, he put the grime-smudged envelope down on the wooden bar and slid it over next to Frank's Coke. It was Johnny's ritual and Frank smiled again, too late for a pretzel.

For the same reason millions had fallen in love with the tuxedos and power of Copula's *Godfather* mystique, Johnny had fallen in love with the lowest rung of those verdant gangster operas. Somehow he saw in himself the undiscovered makings of a Mafia soldier and he apparently figured that if he couldn't actually perform the function, then he could have the appearance of a *wiseguy* at work. And this fiction, like the talk about Vera and his salacious looks was a posturing that added color to the otherwise gray, drab world he occupied. Frank knew it was a production, of course.

In fact, he happened to know that Alice, Johnny's wife, took charge of the big man without any trouble at all. It was well-known that Mr. DeCalbrino was not much of a hit man at home or anywhere else. Further, three years earlier at a gypsy Christmas party, the DeCalbrinos, after much wine and beer produced an emotional scene worthy of the stage, like Romeo and Juliet. After that evening, it had become an amusing and fond secret that the DeCalbrinos were silly for each other past all reason, like 16-year-olds wading into their first infatuation.

So in a way, Frank liked Johnny and saw his delusions as harmless, somewhat like his oldest boy's constant drama of cops-and-robbers. Still, he was always slightly uncomfortable reaching for the envelope, and noticing a newcomer to Tomaso's elbow her date and whisper frantically pointing at him. At this point, as if performing a scripted exit, Johnny always slammed his empty bottle down with a satisfied burp and made for the toilet. His parting words were cryptic and straight off the wide screen, "…nice job this time, Franky. Don't spend it all in one place."

SEVEN

"Shut up!"

The voice was harsh and shrill and shot forth from the back seat of the cab like an ice pick in Frank's ear. The six-year-old little boy that had been sitting up near the back of the front seat made a deflated sound and slumped back toward the far right of the back passing out of Frank's rear-view mirror.

Jeez, he thought, sneaking a look at the screwed up face of the child's guardian, what a witch. Turning onto Race Street and heading towards Penn's Landing, the cab began to roll over the rough, blue stones common to the historic districts, while at the same time, his doors and windows began to squeak in earnest protest.

"What a shit-wagon," the woman mumbled under her breath, as she pulled a lipstick from her bag and began to apply a thick coat of crimson to her distorted lips. Ignoring her, Frank focused his attention on the boy and offered an observation, which he felt, might be of interest.

"Hey guy, I don't know if you're aware of it, but the road we're driving on is built from stones which were once used as ballast in the bottoms of sailing ships." The boy, out of Frank's line of vision, did not speak and the woman ignored him. "Yeah, they're called Belgian Blocks and were used to balance the empty sailing ships when they came over from Europe hundreds of years ago. Once the ships got here, they dumped the stones and loaded on cargo to send back to Europe. I guess with piles and piles of these things laying around the folks here thought they might as well be useful."

"Fascinating," the woman deadpanned, staring at Frank in the rearview mirror. For a moment he didn't say anything, just navigated the narrow street. Occasionally he would look back and be caught in the menacing eyes of this hate-filled female. What could possibly make her so angry, Frank wondered?

Stopping abruptly, Frank leaned on his horn at a passing tourist bus that just barely missed his front fender. "Hey," he shouted out the window, waving his arm and roaring his cab close behind the bus. Gripping the wheel and taking a deep breath, he calmed himself and then once again looked in the rearview and locked gazes with the woman. For a moment, she didn't appear as angry, her eyes peering almost emptily toward the front not really seeing him. After a moment, he felt he should say something so he cleared his throat and attempted a brief comment.

"Is this your first time in Philly?" Glancing, he noticed the woman was peering out the window, the boy buried in the other corner, almost out of his sight.

After a long moment, she responded without looking up, "Yeah, first *and* last."

It was obvious this woman was not a person who wanted to talk. Frank shifted his attention to the boy, even adjusting his rear-view so he could see him better. In the shadows of the back seat, he appeared very small, perhaps six-years-old, with dark hair and sheepish black eyes. He wore a dress shirt and pants and carried what appeared to be a small stuffed dog. Frank remembered when they had hailed him the woman had been carrying a small bag, he thought a briefcase. Now he realized the bag was the boy's, some sort of over-night case.

A strangle hold had descended on the interior of the cab and any further communications seemed doomed to failure, but looking at that little guy in the corner goaded Frank into making at least an attempt to lighten the air.

"One of the great things about being in Philly is all the tourist stuff around here. You know, Independence Hall, Franklin's Print shop, stuff like that. They even have a great museum just for kids called 'The Please Touch Museum.' They do it up big at Christmas especially, my kids love it." There was no reaction from the back seat at all.

"Say, buddy, ya ever been to the Jersey State Aquarium?" The woman coughed an irritated sigh and directed her attention out her window. "It's over in Camden, just across the Franklin Bridge there. The Franklin's that monster blue thing up ahead on the left."

Nothing.

"I guarantee you they got fish you've never seen before. I mean really, they got sharks, stingrays, seals, octopus, baby squids, a whole tank of jelly fish…they got this enormous, round tank that you walk around and then you can go into a sort of depression in the glass wall that lets you be actually *surrounded* by the water." Turning the corner, he glanced in the rearview and saw the kid's face perking up.

"I remember takin' my kids last year, and we went into one of those glass depressions and there were these kind of funny, flat fish laying on top of the glass. But they weren't laying on their stomach, like you and I would; they were laying on one of their sides. You know how fish are kinda flat anyway, these guys just sort of settle to the bottom, lay over on one of their sides and blend in. What was really weird was, they had no eyes on the side that was laying on the bottom—both their eyes are on one side of their body, and they're both looking up. I'm tellin you, that was really weird."

The woman was staring out her window with an expression that betrayed something so dark, so personally enraging, that it grew out from her corner like smoke trying to suffocate him and the boy. She became like the buildings they passed; hollow and lifeless, casting shadows of loneliness across the road. The boy had edged out of his corner and had had the beginnings of a look of interest, but then his face took on a vague look of apprehension and he listlessly shrank back. He was staring past Frank, out the front windshield.

Turning back around he noticed a tall, thin man pacing on the sidewalk in front of *Philadelphia Fish*, his destination for the fare. As he pulled his car out of traffic and over to the curb the man abruptly stopped his pacing, drew his hands from his coat pockets and moved cautiously toward the car. In the back seat, he could hear the familiar sounds of leaving. Gliding to a stop near the curb he put the car in park and waited quietly as the woman exited quickly from the car and slammed the door behind her, leaving the boy with two short, viscous words, "Stay here!" The boy stayed in his corner, staring across the cab, as the woman strode up to the man and greeted him. Frank could tell the boy was frightened of the woman, but it was also apparent that he was embarrassed for her. As she left the car, though he could still sense some apprehension, Frank knew the boy was relieved.

The muffled throb of the engine provided a warm, comforting soundtrack to their silence. They both watched the thin man and the angry woman discuss whatever it was they were discussing and neither spoke, that is until Frank noticed a presence at his right shoulder. Turning slightly he noticed out of the corner of his eye the boy's stuffed dog being held up on the edge of the front seat, the boy's fingers curled tightly about the creature. With more light, Frank could see the years of affection etched into its tiny body.

"You're sure a good boy," Frank said softly, not turning around to look. After a moment Frank continued. "You don't look scared or anything, this being your first time in Philadelphia. I know I'd be a little nervous."

"I'm not scared," a small, pensive voice drifted from the shadows, "but Blue-Dog is…a little." It seemed this last comment was made in an attempt to correct any misconception that Frank my have developed concerning the dog.

"What's your doggie's name?"

"Blue-Dog," the quiet voice returned.

Looking more closely, Frank could see the faded, blue cotton batting which made up the animal's skin, its fur having long since been hugged away. It was a disparate and sad creature, but it had given itself to the boy, he thought, which was more than some had. Looking again out the front, he observed the thin man and the angry woman's conflict with detached resentment. The woman's face contorted, as she speared the thin man's shoulder with her index finger repeatedly, and the man's posture betrayed his defeat and overwhelming sadness. The melodrama before him was pathetic; it embarrassed him to be a spectator.

"So, is Blue-Dog coming to stay in Philly with you and your Dad?" Frank asked, guessing.

"I think so," the boy whispered. Near Frank's shoulder, the animal adjusted his perch, its black plastic eyes staring out the windshield, past the low beams. "Well," Frank sighed, "maybe I'll see you guys again. This city's not that big." The boy did not respond, there was no need.

Presently the light drizzle, which had begun earlier, worsened clouding the windshield and Frank reached up, turning the windshield wipers to intermittent. Whether it was the silent freezing drizzle that had begun to chill their skin, or the obnoxious screech of his windshield wiper blades, the man and woman abruptly broke off their debate and both turned and walked back to the cab.

Quickly, without ceremony, the back door was opened and the boy motioned out. As quietly as he had sat in his corner, he retrieved his dog and slid across the seat and out the open door. As he went across the back Frank watched in the rear view and caught his eyes for a brief second. He tried to smile, but the boy was as quickly gone and the woman back in the car, the door closed with a thump.

"The airport," the woman moaned, straightening her suit and brushing the mist off her shoulders and skirt, "and this time, hold the tour-guide crap." Frank didn't respond as he put the car in drive and pulled out into traffic. As he moved away from *Philadelphia Fish,* he noticed with some pleasure that the tall, thin man was kneeling on the sidewalk in front of the boy, holding him in an enveloping hug, Blue-Dog tightly clutched in tiny fingers unmoving on his shoulder.

There were worse endings.

EIGHT

His car screamed over the crest of the hill, brakes locked, past the blazing fire, through the torn and shattered vehicles, through the scattered pieces of unidentified cloth, paper and debris, and past the glaring headlights staring up into the night. As he flashed through the accident his car lurched over dismembered metal and the control he had had vanished in a maelstrom of spinning lights. His senses foundered as he clung to the wheel, whirling so rapidly that he all but blacked out in its grip. Words escaped his mouth; unintelligible sounds punctuated his faint cries for help.

He was quickly off the blacktop, careening down the shallow embankment toward the trees, sliding sideways and backwards. His teeth were clenched for the moment of impact, his eyes squeezed together as he dragged one last breath deep into his lungs.

But nothing happened.

No impact, no hollow tearing sound followed by lacerations from razor steel and shattered glass. No splintering wood or violent deceleration—no trauma at all. There was simply nothing. His car slid for another few hundred feet, and then came to a stop without hitting anything. The engine shuddered to a stop yet the radio played, strangely hollow in the silence of the moment, Streisand's voice like a ghost in the mist.

The headlights shown back down the road, illuminating the accident. Frank still held his breath, the shock of the spin slowing his thoughts. For a moment, he didn't know how long, he sat in his car with his eyes shut deceived by the motion of his own inner ear. When he did open his eyes, his head stopped spinning and he was quickly overwhelmed by nausea.

Before him the horror of the accident lay scattered across the road like broken and discarded toys. His car sat facing the scene backwards on the highway, as if he had skipped over the violence like a pebble glances off the water, and he had landed safely on the other side. For a moment, he watched the scene like some wide-screen movie waiting for the action to once again flare up. But the evidence of action on the road before him was of a previous nature. Any animation at all was revealed in orange-red flames smeared across the snowy grass shoulder, the unrestrained spinning of a suspended tire and the gentle cloud of freezing mist and oily smoke that drifted through groping beams of upturned headlights.

After a moment, he relaxed his grip on the wheel and exhaled, feeling his tension meter out with involuntary trembling. Inhaling sharply, he began to cry. Fumbling at his seat belt, he managed to unsnap its mechanism and forced the door open almost falling into the cold outside air.

Frank began to run toward the accident, stumbling rather like a drunk, rushing toward his own home when he sees it in flames. Is this what it feels like to be drunk, he wondered. His limbs were numb and unresponsive and his breath caught in his throat in short choking sobs. Tears were continually running from his eyes, blurring his vision, his head burst with pain until the images before him tilted into oblong frames, juggled and shaken with each step he took. He felt the whole scene before him in his stomach like a Dante's vision of hell.

Sloshing from the shoulder to the roadway itself, Frank forced himself forward, pushing stiffened legs and arms onward. Every motion he made felt forced and mechanical, like he were one of his son's creations, all steel and screws and pulleys made with thread.

The first car he arrived at was almost completely smashed. It lay near to the ground, crushed as if a giant's heel had come down upon it and left its structure no more than a few feet off the asphalt. It was completely engulfed in flames.

Shielding his eyes Frank edged around the blazing hulk, avoiding the debris that scattered the road in all directions. As he cleared the first vehicle, he saw the second one, turned on its roof with what was left of its forward section raised into the night sky like a defiant hand stretched upward in bloody contempt. The one intact headlamp, dangling from its entrails, shone upwards into the falling mist like a fantastic torch, like a lighthouse of the damned.

Moving forward, Frank's gate slowed and his stomach became sick. His head was whirling and his balance was not right. He did not want to look inside. An accident this bad; the films in driver's ed class flashed into his mind and the sudden horror made him retch. And yet, he had no choice.

Steadying himself, he walked toward the car, advancing to the forward section, which stood practically at eye-level. The engine compartment was all but obliterated, the shattered engine and drive components smoking in the cold mist, one forward wheel torn completely away. The air was rich with the pungent, sticky smell of gasoline and the closer he got to the car, the more the odor intensified. When he finally reached the vehicle he leaned cautiously over to look in the forward compartment and was stopped hard in his thoughts.

There were no reasonable words to describe what his eyes beheld. As his vision adjusted to the weird, unnatural light on the road, he saw that there was no windshield, no dashboard or instrument panel, no steering column for that matter. And there were no people…at least in one piece. The entire contents of the forward portion of the car to the front seat had been pulverized beyond recognition. If there had been anybody still in there, he wouldn't have known how to separate the elements one from the other. It seemed as he stared into the gutted car that the force of the impact must have been something out of a nightmare, oddly selective in its murderous intent, leaving portions of the car partially intact and yet annihilating the occupants.

It was at that moment that Frank heard the voice.

At first he thought he'd imagined the voice, it had been so small and weak. Then he heard it again, more forceful this time, alone and scared.

"*Daddy…*" it said sadly, like the whine of a cat marooned on a rooftop. "*Daddy?!*" it said again, this time with a hint of desperation.

"Hello?!" he shouted, and got down on his knees, for the voice was coming from the shadowy area where the back seat would have been. "Hello?" he shouted into the pitch-dark rear compartment, "I'm here!" The smell of spilled fuel was overpowering as he peered into the darkness. Glancing back over his shoulder at the flaming wreck he knew he couldn't wait for help, he had to get her out. A few more minutes and this one survivor, no matter how injured, would surely die.

Leaning down and reaching through the shattered side window, Frank felt quickly in all directions for any sign of the child who was calling but found nothing. It must be wedged in the far corner, he thought.

"Daddy?" the voice screeched, aware now that there was someone trying to help. "It hurts, Daddy, it hurts so bad!"

"I'm coming. I know it hurts, but I'm gonna get you out, okay?" he shouted, beginning to push his head and shoulders through the shattered side window and into the darkness.

"Okay," the voice whimpered, deep inside the crushed back seat. As Frank finally shoved his shoulders through the tight opening, a sharp pain lanced across his back accompanied by a sound like ripping paper. "Damn!" he cursed involuntarily, stopping to feel the warmth of his own blood oozing from the wound. It's all glass and metal in here, he thought.

"Daddy?! Are you all right? What happened?"

"I'm okay," he said, inching carefully forward across the car's roof, "I just got a little stuck getting in, but I'm okay now. How're you doing? You said you're hurting—where's it hurting?"

For a moment there was no response only the sound of struggling and then a sickly, dangerous-sounding moan. "Sweetie, are you all right? What's wrong?

What'd you do? Hello?!" Frank's heart was pounding now and he shoved himself forward hard, reaching out as far as he could until his fingers touched what felt like wet clothing. Suddenly the fabric moved under his hands and the little voice whispered in the dark.

"Daddy?" It was weak and barely audible, but now he could tell, it was female. "I can't get the seat belt undone and it's hurting me real bad!"

"I know," Frank said, running his hands over the dark figure in the car searching for the belt latch. "Just give me a second and…I'll get you…I'll get you loose from this…there!" he said, manhandling the latch on the belt until it snapped open and he pushed the distended, ruined straps away.

"You need to come to me now sweetie," Frank coaxed. From his awkward position, he was not quite able to get his arms around the tiny figure, she was so jammed into the corner. He was just able to feel her moving towards him in the dark.

"That's right, a little farther and you'll be out, just a little further…that's right." She was moving his way now; he could almost get his hands around her. "Just a little more, that's it…you're doing just fine. Keep coming…good girl…now, just let me have your hands…got you!" He grabbed her outstretched hands, pulling her across the ceiling of the car in close to his body. From there, he backed his way out, edging over the shattered sill and out onto the freezing pavement.

Once out of the car, he stood with the girl clutched in his arms. She's so small, he thought, leaning his cheek into her wet, matted hair. She might be six, maybe seven-years-old—she has dark-hair like Sally. For a second the likeness of his own daughter flashed before his eyes, her tiny hands and her sweet face. This can't be happening, he thought, tasting the blood from her hair mixing with his tears. She's so small, so young, she's just a little girl, she's…then it was gone and all that remained was a small, wounded creature, whom he didn't know, crying into his shirt. In that brief moment, his skin began to feel the bitter cold of the night and the stranger in his arms began to shiver in her blood-covered party dress.

God! Oh, God! His mind plunged and his heart leaped to his throat. I've got to get some help; I've got to get her to a hospital. Without thinking, he was running back to his car, past the burning wreck, through the debris and out onto the slush covered shoulder. She was light in his arms, barely there actually, but still his legs pumped against resistance as if he were in a dream being pursued, unable to quite fast enough, as if he were caught in quicksand.

Finally, at the car he leaned down and slid into the open driver's door with the girl still in his arms. She was shivering and moaning with her eyes tightly shut.

Please God, please help me! Tearing the microphone from its hook, he keyed it several times.

"*Central, Joh…Johnny!*" he shouted twisting his other arm under the girl to get to the ignition. "*Johnny, it's Frank. I'm at a wreck on the turnpike 'bout…'bout 20 miles east of the city. I need an ambulance…there's a little girl, she'…Johnny, Central this is Frank!*" Releasing the key, he listed to the static that answered and then repeated his message.

"*Johnny, this is Frank. I came on a wreck "bout 20 miles east on the turnpike and I got a little girl here whose hurt real bad. I need a freak'n ambulance, right now!*" Once again, static hissed back from the speaker.

NINE

"Now, Frank, you make sure you compliment her dress. You know how nervous she is," his wife fretted and fussed, moving around the kitchen like a hen marshaling the barnyard.

"I will," he said calmly, taking a sip of his coffee and smiling to himself.

"And her shoes. They're new, from Payless yesterday."

"I will."

"And her veil," she chirped.

"I *will!*"

"You know it was your mother's veil, Frank. Papa Teska said he wanted her to have it." She finished putting the breakfast dishes in the sink and turned toward her husband. "It was so cute, Frank. I wish you'd been here. He searched the attic yesterday for hours. I had to go look for him at lunchtime. He was sitting next to one of your Mamma's boxes with wet eyes, poor man." She stood for a moment, shaking her head and drying her hands. Then…

"Don't forget to say something nice about her hair, we must've spent an hour cutting it."

"Cutting it?" Frank stopped smiling. "What do mean, cutting it? Sally has the most beautiful, long…"

"Don't start with that, Francis Xavier, this is too important a day. It's the style. All the other girls have their hair shorter and Sally asked me if just this once could she *pleeeease* have hair like everyone else. I couldn't find you, so I made the decision."

Frank took another sip of coffee and stood from the kitchen table, grabbing his wife's arm as she whirled past him. "Hey," he said turning her toward him, "you know it's okay. I'll say the right thing."

"Frank, I know how much you love long hair and so does *she*. She worships you, you know? She's so scared you won't like it…"

"I'll love it," he said, pulling his wife into his arms. Leaning his mouth down to hers, he pulled a soft, brief kiss from her pursed lips. "You're cute."

"Frank, we're going to be late," she said, pushing lightly against his chest. "You always get this way about the kids."

"I can't help it," he grinned. "I'm Catholic."

"Oh!" and she squirmed from his arms and out the door. He turned to his coffee again and picked up the cup, hearing his wife's voice assembling the troops in the front room for inspection. In the back room he could hear his father coughing and then he heard the old man's door shut and his Sunday morning greeting.

"Frank?" Cough. "Where are you, son?"

"I'm in the kitchen, Papa," he called putting his empty cup in the sink and filling a fresh one for his father. In a moment the older man walked heavily into the kitchen, his black coat over his arm and his hat in his hand.

"Good morning, Frank," he said cheerfully, receiving the proffered cup in his free hand. "Big day today, eh?"

"Big day," Frank nodding feeling the nostalgia of the moment. His father looked like he always had on Sundays. He was shorter now, a little bent over and he was heavier, but he was still solid. And his suit, while a little out of date, was impeccable.

"I like your tie, Papa."

"Hmmm. That sweet wife of yours said it makes the suit look newer," he said frowning as he looked down at it. Then after a beat he grinned slyly. "Yet…she did say it was just right for me."

Looking at the crisp Yale stripes, alternating red and green against the old man's pressed shirt, Frank nodded in approval, even though he thought his wife had flattered his father with a younger man's tie. A minute after this exchange, his father's face still bore a grin and to his recollection it was one that in his youth had meant so many things whimsical and comic or born of mischief.

"You should have such a nice tie," his father remarked unable to resist tweaking his son. Frank smiled and looked down at his own muted paisley print. Then, like the slow diffusion of fog over water, Frank's mind cleared and recognized the style and pattern of his father's tie, acknowledging that it was indeed his own.

"Hey, that's my…"

"You *know* it's your tie."

Frank and his father laughed loudly, enjoying each other's circumstance and the intent of his father's prank. At that moment both heard a small voice call, "Papa?" and the two men turned at the same time, smiling toward the open kitchen door.

"How do I look, Papa?"

Framed in the doorway, his daughter looked for all the world like an iced pastry. She was wearing the snow-white dress he had seen his wife hemming the previous week with its lace borders and high, flattering waist. She had on her new white, patent leather shoes and her soft, dark curls were layered neatly around her face. Finally, like a crown, the delicate lace of his mother's freshly ironed, communion veil extended down to her shoulders. She was exquisite.

"Papa?"

Frank cleared his throat and looked over at his father who could offer no help. The older man had put down his coffee cup and was searching for a handkerchief to wipe his running eyes.

Blinking hard, Frank nodded, and motioned his daughter into his arms. In a moment they were together and her sweet fragrance filled his soul.

"You're the most beautiful thing I think I've ever seen," he whispered into her curls, "Father John's gonna faint." She squeezed his legs tightly and whispered a muffled, "Thanks, Papa." Then she was gone in a swirl of light and joy. The men did not speak for several seconds, but stood in the kitchen remembering their own secrets of communion.

His father stared past the years, into the tired, gray eyes of an old woman lying in bed receiving the host and the bitter wine from his shaking hands. It would be their last communion together, their last kiss, before a long lonely night and so the old man had begged from the priest a favor. It was a hard thing to do, to remember how to do—to hold onto why he was doing it, in the face of losing her. The priest stood by and gently led him through the ritual whispering instruction when necessary. The old man's hands shook badly, as he gave the cup to her lips, so much so that the priest worried he would spill, but the old woman reached out and steadied him. The priest whispered the blessing and she swallowed with difficulty, then lay down to die.

Frank blinked happy tears from his eyes and saw the next few hours. He saw the procession of the girls and boys down the center aisle of the church, all of them dressed in their finest. He felt their anxious hearts beating, saw their eyes flashing. He saw the kneeling figures at the rail, faces lifted expectantly toward the priest as he blessed them and then placed the host on their tongues for the *first* time. His mouth felt the blandness of the wafer as it melted, his nose the aroma of the incense and his eyes sparkled with the candles, the brass, the silver and the golden cross.

"The body of Christ…"

TEN

"*Dammit!*" Frank shouted hurling the microphone at the dashboard," *God dammed piece of shit!*" The tiny figure in Frank's arm cried out and he tightened his grip, pulling her closer into his chest as he twisted the key in the ignition and pumped the gas pedal.

"Come on, come on!" The car sputtered and coughed and the starter whined in protest. "Don't flood, for God's sake, don't flood now!" A muffled moan escaped the girl's lips, and he realized in his panic that he was squeezing her too tightly. "I'm sorry, I'm sorry," he offered tersely, then more softly, "I'm sorry, it's okay, it's okay, I'm sorry…" Relaxing his trembling arm, he gritted his teeth, slowly turning the ignition again and closing his eyes. This time after only a second the engine caught, roaring to life. Jerking the gearshift down, he gunned the engine, throwing mud and grass, he wallowed in the soft shoulder, sluggishly pulling him and the girl back to the highway. In only a few seconds, he was back on the road, accelerating past the atrocity of the accident onward toward Pleasenten and help.

Frank's mind was racing faster than his car, outpacing the speed of the light in his headlamps, like a deer leaping ahead of hounds in pursuit. Where was the hospital? What road should he take, which exit was right? Jeez, slow down a little, he thought glancing at the speedometer as it crested 80. Slow down, calm down. Suddenly his mind began to command his actions deliberately now, like a father, like his own father; composed and solid. And his body, slowly, reluctantly began to obey.

Her life depends on you getting to the hospital, not winding up in another accident. He nodded relaxing his foot off the accelerator and watching the speedometer drift downward. Your panic will not save her, only your action; your careful, sober action. Taking a deep breath and blowing the air out quickly, Frank cleared his head and remembered precisely where the new community hospital was in Pleasenten.

He remembered the mundane, red-brick buildings, squatting low near a setting of freshly planted hardwoods, the rounded banks and carpets of neatly cut grass interrupted by a clean expanse of white concrete with crisp yellow lines. He was discerning, in retrospect, backing away from the brightly lit emergency-room entrance, out the circular drive, past the red and white signs for the Liddy Dresher Memorial Hospital, back onto the tree-lined service road and then up onto the highway, retreating from exit 117, away from Pleasenten, fifteen miles in reverse to the cheerless gloom and obscure seclusion of this evil night's drive.

Yes, you have it now, his mind soothed. Calmly navigate the night, ignore the desire in you to panic, to scream, to cry. Reject the taste of her blood, the wet smell of her clothes and her hair. To deliver her safely, you must not be with her. You drive a cab, Frank. Yes, but she's not just a fare, she's more.

The drizzle, which had started earlier in the evening, began in earnest now and Frank could see it mixing with snow and beginning to freeze on the windshield and the roadway ahead, and he slowed the pace of his car in response. Fifteen miles, all I need is fifteen miles, he thought, feeling the sticky coldness of the tiny body nestled in close to him. The last thing I need is this!

"Daddy...?" the girl murmured into Frank's shirt.

"I'm not your Daddy, sweetheart, I'm just..." and she began coughing, almost choking. "It's okay, honey," he said, pulling her closer to him. "I'm here."

"Daddy..."

"Yes, honey..."

"It hurts so bad, I..."

"I know it hurts. We'll be at the hospital in just a few min..."

"Oh, not the hospital, no Daddy, no, no, no...!" The girl began to push away from him, crying loudly now, becoming hysterical. Frank adjusted his position and that of the girl, tightening his grip on the steering wheel.

"Honey, it's just so the doctor can..." but she wouldn't let him finish. She just kept crying and shaking her head, pushing against him. Soon she began to cough and choke, and the panic he had felt only moments before began to well up again, but this time in her.

Scanning the roadway ahead, he could see nothing but the thickening weather and the almost horizontal flight of the snow and sleet in his high beams. He should be able to see the lights of Pleasenten by now, but it seemed the night and the storm had cut them off from all comfort. His knuckles were white on the wheel and he closed his arm tighter around her putting his face near her ear.

"*You listen to me, little girl!*" His breath was hot in her ear and his words were quiet and powerful. "*I'm going to be with you the whole time, do you understand? I'm going to be holding you all the way. I've got my arm around you and I'm not going to let you go!*" He pressed her into him with each statement, leaning his lips closer to her ear while keeping his eyes on the road. "*I'm staying right with you and you're going to be fin...you're going to...I'm right here. I'm here."*

For several minutes he grasped her tiny frame to his. Through his shirt he could feel her words over and over again, "No, no, no!" And as she cried he began to understand what it was he was doing. He could hear it now, a distinct but distant thrumming, like a cello speaking to an empty hall.

Absorb her panic, her terror. You can't do anything about the pain, the loss of her family and you can't stop her from dying, but you can receive all of her fear, all of her horror.

He would, he *could* do it. He would contain her panic in his placid acceptance of this thing that was happening. It was in his power to spare her this, he thought, feeling the tiny body once again relax and her breathing begin to slow. And it would be all right, he realized. This was something he could do. He had been here before.

ELEVEN

Teresa fell into Frank's arms as he opened the front door, her near full-term awkwardness ungainly in his grasp. Frank caught her more than embraced her, carrying her from the threshold into the house. She was sobbing, blinded by her tears, muttering Frank's name over and over again.

In a just a few seconds her weeping brought Mary from the kitchen and his youngest boy and father from the back of the house. It was an odd scene; his sister so usually erect and formal collapsed in abject sorrow and in his arms. Frank looked to his wife for help and she moved toward them, wiping her hands on her apron.

"Oh, Teresa honey, what's wrong?" she asked, reaching both arms out to her sister-in-law. Mary and Frank looked at each other helplessly. Frank's father stood in the doorway of the back hall, his mouth slack, a dog-eared paperback he had been reading dangling by his leg. Little Stephen, who had wandered in behind his grandfather, watched his aunt for a moment with a confused expression then, as children will, clouded over in sympathetic emotion and tears began to pool in his eyes.

"*My baby,*" Teresa shrieked, as she broke from Frank and huddled into Mary's arms. "*My baby, my baby, my baby…*"

"What about the baby, honey," Mary asked, forcing Teresa's face up so she could look into her eyes. "What's wrong, Teresa? What's wrong with the baby?"

For a moment Teresa heaved a great sigh, straining to look Mary in the face. An incredible battle was raging inside his sister; Frank could see the strain. Her body, so roundly maternal seemed misshapen and contorted in anguish—she was losing this war, he observed, as she strained to answer the question put to her.

"*Teresa,*" Mary said firmly, looking deep into the panicked eyes of her sister-in-law. "*Teresa, tell me what's wrong? What's wrong with the baby?*" Mary's demand floated in the air like ether, numbing the room, thickening the air—suspending time. Frank's mind went to the image of his children when they were newborn, small and helpless. Even before.

He saw again the squirming shadow creatures inside Mary's womb, observed through the cunning sonographic device. He remembered the surprising rush of fluid and the slippery being that emerged, unmoving at first and then the tiny imperceptible gasp and the pitiful cry of new life. He remembered receiving the miniature person into his arms with a holy reverence he had never known before and he remembered how he had cried that very first morning of fatherhood. The emotions conflicted his mind, he recalled, but nothing to resemble what he was seeing now.

In that tragic, hateful second, as everyone waited for Teresa to form her answer the front door which had been left ajar, burst open and Teresa's husband came into the room.

Frank turned from his sluggish, drugged state at the opening of the front door and instinctively knew by his brother-in-law's expression that something was irrecoverably wrong. The husky affable Robert, so kind and innocent, so quick to laugh was now darkly serious, his brow furrowed and his mouth a tight, thin line. The whole of his face was panicked.

"Bob," Frank started, but the other man was oblivious to him, to everyone in the room in fact, except for his wife. At his entrance Teresa pushed away from Mary and straightened herself, smoothing her maternity dress over her abundant form and frantically began adjusting her hair and wiping the mascara from under her eyes. A brief agonizing smile flickered across Teresa's face as she made eye contact with her husband and went on preening. As she corrected her appearance, she began a stammering incoherent monologue on the eccentricities of pregnant women, all the while turning her very large stomach away from her husband's gaze.

Frank watched his sister in her pathetic dance and his heart shattered. It was as if the awful substance of what she carried within was leaking out and there was no place to hide. He and the rest could only watch the play unfold.

It was strange, he thought, watching his sister behave this way. All his life, he had always known her to be strong and forthright in her opinions, never afraid to speak the thoughts on her mind, even if they were trouble. He remembered the time when, as a 16-year-old, Teresa had been caught smoking outside St. Bernadette's after mass and taken by the hand to the priest by their mother. What he had seen that day would stick with him all the years that followed.

She had gone before Father Al, not with a look of contrition on her face but with her chin thrust forward and her eyes clear and defiant. He remembered how straight her back had been and how flushed her cheeks were as their mother had stood her before the priest angrily denouncing her behavior as sin or as his mother put it, "The willful destruction of the temple of God." And he would also never forget Teresa's answer to the priest's somber question, "Teresa, do you think the Lord would have you smoking Camel cigarettes?"

His sister looked at the crumpled soft-pack that the priest held before her, the evidence of her crime, and then with flashing eyes she responded with the words that would mark them at St. Bernadette's for years to come. Glaring at the priest, her head held high she responded in a calm, clear voice, "Probably not, Father. Why don't you tell me the brand *you* smoke and I'll switch."

It would be years before Frank would again recognize an atmospheric hesitation of that magnitude and then only in the electric pause before a deadly squall. On that day the clouds hovered above the ground, greenish gray and the hesitation raised the hair on his neck and the back of his hands. He had stood next to his sister all those years before, the hair also standing up on his neck, but it wasn't from static electricity. He had only to look at his mother to see the fury of the storm within her. Frank couldn't believe anyone could have the audacity to confront Father Al about his well-known, but covert occasional cigarette, least of all his older sister. But to see Teresa so blatantly confront her inquisitor with the hypocrisy of the situation was a decisive moment in Frank's life. It was also magical and not altogether unpleasant, despite the fact that their mother almost had a stroke on the spot.

From that day forward, his sister's words were feared, or at least respected, as was her unwavering confidence in her individuality and personhood. He knew that any hope he had held for dominating this older female was forever crushed in the vestry of St. Bartholomew's Catholic Church. So it was strange that now she played the fool, before him and the others, dancing around an obvious horror, pretending that what existed was in reality, not real.

In his mind, while watching her perform, he was suddenly struck with an image he had long forgotten. In fact, the picture in his mind was so potent, that he caught his breath audibly and his wife glanced at him as if expecting some profound insight about the drama before them. Perhaps it was, he thought.

If he remembered correctly, the incident had occurred on one of those cold, clear Saturdays so rare to Philadelphia winters that his mother had finally, after several tedious hours, shooed him out to play. Ordinarily, this was not a necessary chore for his mother, but on this day Frank had found himself without the usual pack of good-hearted "thieves" with which he so easily surrounded himself. And whether it was due to the influenza which had invaded 32nd through 15th Avenue, or because his pals had been spirited away by the promise of a hot dog and a soda at some big game, he did not know. He was only aware of the strange ache of loneliness lining his day like the fleece of his father's gloves. He despondently moped around the apartment, listlessly thumbing through last summer's *National Geographic* or lay on his bed reading for the thirteenth time the latest adventure of Captain America. As Frank remembered, it was his mother who finally came in with his coat and hat in her hands, summoning him to the great outdoors with more drill sergeant rhetoric than tender motherly charm. He took the hint and hastily vacated the slumberous warmth of their 28th Street front apartment, and went out to explore the mean streets of Philadelphia in a crystal blue day.

The event which had so stricken Frank, occurred later that morning when his wanderings brought him to the edge of the neighborhood along the rail lines, near the docks of the Delaware River. There, following a pair of rusting tracks past the motionless, snowbound barges, parked against the heavy piers, he found himself face to face with what appeared to be an abandoned boxcar.

In the cold light of that winter's morning, the car was a relief-cut braced against the sun-hardened snow and the blackened, pencil-thin trees that lined the tracks. Its partially opened door and rusted orange skin invited Frank in from the brisk January breeze into a dull, yet warm, retreat. Answering the frosted tugging of the wind with his back Frank decided abruptly to seek shelter. Yet as he neared the steel structure, examining its massive contour for the unusual or the dangerous, a sudden explosion of wings and feathers flashed before him and took his breath away.

The encounter was so sudden and unexpected, that he stepped back, tumbling over one of the many discarded wooden ties beside the tracks. Smarting from the fall he nevertheless quickly regained his feet and stood, mouth grimly set, watching as a large bird desperately flapped and fluttered on the tracks before him. After a few seconds he noticed that this bird wasn't just angry but was apparently injured, dragging around behind it one of its wings, as if it were broken. Instinctively, Frank thought he could help the wounded creature and he opened both arms up as it to contain the great thrashing mass and slowly began to herd the creature to stillness. Yet, every step he took seemed to push the tragic and desperate bird further away up the tracks. After fifteen minutes of this abortive rescue attempt, Frank shouted a frustrated oath at the creature and turned back toward the boxcar and its promise of shelter.

It was as he did this that he realized the bird he had assumed was wounded, who had waddled so pathetically away from him for the past quarter hour, trailing its shattered wing along on the ground, was neither wounded nor pathetic. The creature was cleverly acting a role of the wounded bird, attempting everything to draw him away from her fledglings which he soon spied in their nest just past the door of the box car. He had followed the ruse believing the bird's actions and appearance and ignoring the smaller, vulnerable babies she had neatly hidden. The frantic bird by the tracks had performed her dance of deception well, and he had been fooled. Now it turned out that his sister was attempting exactly the same fiction in his living room, in front of her husband. Hers was a dreadful promenade of illusion.

"Teresa," Bob abruptly, putting an end to her ramblings and commanding her gaze. "I know about the baby." Teresa hesitated and glanced up.

For a long agonizing moment the stricken couple looked at each other. Their mouths were opened, stretched into tormented grimaces, as if the words which must come forth were of such horror that their tongues rebelled at the prospect of their utterance. The aching intimacy of the display was so personal, so private, that Frank wanted to avert his eyes, but could not.

"The baby's dead," Bob said flatly, emotion gone from his voice. "It was our last sonogram today," he continued, as an aside to Frank, "we just found out."

Bob turned back and looked into his wife face, his arms opening to her. Finally, slowly, Teresa surrendered her internal war, capitulating to her husband's entreaty and collapsing on the living room floor, her large stomach pushing her legs away awkwardly, like a broken doll's. It was Bob who went to her, closing his strong arms over her, shielding her body with his own.

The news and the scene were so pitiful that Frank's heart broke, despite the contentious history that had existed between him and his sister. Heaving a great sigh and looking to the ceiling, he tried to form a controlled thought while his wife's words of comfort blended with the cries of his sister over the stoic silence of his father. Denial, anger—weren't there stages for dealing with something like this? But to him, at that moment, all of that was nonsense and the ceiling was interesting.

Cobwebs quivered in a corner by the rafters and he turned his gaze back to Bob, watching this father scooping together the remnants of his life.

God help them, he prayed. God help us all.

TWELVE

From that day, life became a blur of indistinct faces and outrageous tasks. The hospital was nightmarish, alien in its antiseptic efficiency. Teresa arrived at day-surgery, stolid and plaintive, her tears long exhausted. Going in, she made no notice of her family gathered; and though Bob nodded and attempted an encouraging smile, it was evident that the ordeal ahead was just short of perdition, a constructive melancholia from the pages of modern gothic fiction. He and Teresa were wending their way into hell, having only just arrived at the gates.

Hours later, Teresa and Bob's priest was requested and he left the waiting room with his small bag from which he would draw the elements of that last of all sacraments for Teresa's lost baby girl.

Frank's mind saw the priest beyond the pastel colored walls with their watercolor prints of sailing boats and summer days. He saw the somber-faced man tenderly kissing the vestment sash and placing it around his neck, saw him moving his hands mechanically in the sign of the cross and saw his mouth moving prayerfully in litany and canon.

His would be the hands, Frank thought, that would caress her tiny body, her soft rounded feet and her tightly curled and wrinkled fingers. His hands would anoint her softly fringed eyes and her slightly parted lips. His eyes would be favored above them all, to see the face of one who had only just departed; who had been born, not onto an Earthly shore but directly into Zion. His would be the task of waving a final farewell to one they all had expected to know and could not.

Following that terrible morning Frank wandered through the exercises of grief and mourning. He walked solemnly behind the tiny pink casket three days later. He helped at home with food and chairs and napkins and tissues. He sat quietly and listened to Teresa and Bob as they talked huddled on their sofa, with the door to the nursery closed. He helped Mary collect and return the baby gifts that Teresa could no longer touch. And he nodded with approval at the baby's name on her small bronze headstone a month after that.

"Sleep, Rachel," he wrote one day on the back of his pay envelope, sitting alone in his cab. "Sleep, little lamb, and do not worry or be afraid, sleep and God keep you from *our* pain and grief, from your mother's vacant eyes and your father's midnight weeping,

"Sleep and know no image of horror or anger or want, sleep and be at peace for we commit for a while to hold your portion of sorrow in our hearts. We

will keep it as an icon, as a golden image. We will nurture and feed it as a cherished gift and we will hold it close to our souls, for it is all we have left of you in
this place and that is a precious thing in our world. Far too precious, it seems,
than a thousand, thousand days in the sun."

THIRTEEN

"It's okay, honey, it's okay…"

"I'm sor…sorry. I'm so, so s…sick, Daddy. It…hur…hurts…and I'm s…sick!"

"It's okay, honey, I've done it a hundred times before; sometimes I get so sick *I* can't even make it to the bathroom. Believe me, I know how you feel."

My God, how could he know how *she* felt, he thought. Holding the wheel with his knee he reached his free hand down and tried to wipe the bloody vomit away from her mouth and nose. God, this is awful!

"You know," he continued, trying to keep his voice even, "when I throw-up it usually makes my tummy feel better—do you feel better?"

The girl nodded drunkenly, resting against his chest and moaning slightly. Her body did feel a little more relaxed.

"Daddy?" she whispered after a few minutes.

"Yes, honey…" Since he had picked her up she had persisted in believing that he was her father. In her present condition, he couldn't really tell her what had happened to her father. Truthfully, he didn't know for sure that what he had seen on the road had been her father. For all he knew she had been coming back from a party with relatives or friends.

"Daddy…"

"Yes, honey. I'm here." There was a beat in which the wind and road noise filled the car and nothing else.

"Am I going to die?" The question was so quiet and innocent, so blunt that for a moment he couldn't respond. His mind stuttered and he instinctively pressed the accelerator. What in the world could he say to that?

"Honey, what kind of question is that," he laughed. "You've just had a shock, that's all. You had a shock and the doctors need to have a look at you. You relax and try and rest now, okay?" He stalled.

He could feel her shake her head against him and a terrible stillness settled over the car. It wasn't working, she wasn't buying it. He needed to tell her something to comfort her, to take her mind away from this nightmare.

"Oh, come on sweetheart; don't worry, we're almost there, just hang on, just a few more minutes," he insisted, desperately pushing his thoughts to what she needed.

"Daddy, I'm sc…scared," she interrupted. "I'm so scared…I want to go home, I want to go to bed. I'll go right to bed, I promise, I will. Please, please, I want to go to home, I want to go to bed."

The sound of her words made him wince. His arm tightened around her and he responded gently, "We've got to go to the hospital first, hang in there sweetheart! Just a few more minutes and we'll be there. You've got to be a tough girl, be strong for Daddy, okay?"

"I can't, I can't," she cried into his shirt, and his heart began to crumble.

"But *I* know you can, honey," his eyes scanned the horizon looking for any sign of Pleasenten. "I've seen a great strength in you, little girl. Huge! You hang in there and after the doctors look you over we'll go home, and I'll snuggle you down in your own bed."

"Promise me, Daddy," she persisted. "Promise me I'm not going to die."

"We'll be there in a few minutes, you just go on back to sleep and I'll wake you when we get there…"

"No, promise me, Daddy, promise me." Frank's mind was strangling, drowning in an emotion he had never felt. What now? Don't leave me alone in this thing; tell me what to say to her.

The blackness of the night seemed at that moment darker and emptier then any night he could remember. The snow was thinning a little, but it was still thick on the road. Gripping the wheel and the girl, he seized his scattered and desperate thoughts, focusing them on one frantic silent prayer.

God, he trembled, you know what she needs now. She can't wait till Sunday, till Mass…she can't wait for the priest! She needs to know now, I need to know! Will she die? Can I get her to the hospital in time? God, please tell me! I know you're there, I know you can hear me…*tell me! Is she going to live?*"

His high beams were reaching into the blackness, sweeping across a glittering snowfield, revealing a highway wiped clean except for the occasional snow-coated mile marker. His cab wallowed, plowing forward sluggishly, his steering wheel loose and practically ineffective. Then, quietly at first, and then louder, beneath the wet hiss of his tires he could hear the voice of the cello again, but this time it boomed just one single, sustained note. Gripping her tighter and narrowing his eyes he strained to hear.

Ye…

He shuddered and looked furiously for any sign of the town or the hospital ahead. What the hell does that mean? *Yes? YES?* At that moment the girl convulsed and began to cry again. Desperately he pushed his car another hundred yards across the snow, gripping the tiny body closer to him. For a long, silent minute he strained against the darkness and waited, listening through the rush of the wind around his cab and the rhythmic thump of his wipers against the wet snow. But there was nothing else. The cello in the hall had gone silent.

Frank was driving his taxi in the snow and the time had finally come to speak the truth, the only truth he knew.

"Promise me, Daddy," the child continued, pressing her desperation into his mind, "Promise me…."

"Okay," he whispered after a beat, "You're going to live."

FOURTEEN

"In the name of the Father, and the Son, and of the Holy Spirit, Amen." Frank hesitated as he opened his eyes and looked at the indistinct outline of the priest through the screen.

He was adjusting himself slightly and leaning forward making the sign of the cross. Frank could see him faintly and he heard the words of welcome that he had cherished since childhood. Then…"Hi, Frank, what's going on?" the priest asked penetrating the gloom, "What's up?"

How many times had he heard that, Frank thought. Those short two words had been John's signature line since they were kids in the old neighborhood. He could still see his snaggle-tooth buddy, greeting him from across the street, a wry grin stretched his face.

But as Frank opened his mouth to tell his friend what had happened, what had been tearing his soul for the last two weeks, his fragile smile collapsed and the words vanished from his tongue. He just sat there and stared at his hands. After an eternity of silence he cleared his throat and apologized.

"Sorry, John," he whispered, "I'm having some real trouble."

"Obviously," the other man conceded quietly. Another awkward silence followed, lasting more than a few minutes. Finally the priest spoke. "Would it help if I talked for a minute, Frank?"

Frank looked past the shadowy figure before him and mumbled an affirmation not knowing if he really wanted to hear something or not. "I don't know, I guess…"

The wooden confessional creaked reluctantly with age following the priest's movements on his bench. In a moment he quietly moved into a story.

"A few years ago, I was working as a student counselor at St. Joseph's, you know—where do you think I ought to go to college, Father John?' 'My grades suck and I can't seem to make my parents understand that *I'm really trying,*' 'I hate my sister, brother, uncle, *whoever,* Father John. What should I do with my life?—that kind of stuff. Anyway it's like a rotation; in my order we each work at different tasks in the parish so that we can grow and learn."

"Anyway, they put me in this tiny little office…I'm mean *really tiny!* I think it had been some kind of janitor's closet or something, because there always seemed to be a faint smell of ammonia when I came in during the afternoons. Maybe it was just the regular cleaning stuff, whatever…so they put me in this tiny office, and I begin to see all these kids with their fairly predictable problems. Remember, I hear most of it in here, you know?"

Frank looked away from the screen now and sat back against the booth's cool, wooden wall. His mind was beginning to drift.

"So, here I am in this cramped little office, trying to pry up the window, *which has been painted shut*, trying to let in a little fresh, non-ammonia-smelling air when there comes this shy, little knock at my door. Well I'm right in the middle of jerking this window around, so I holler over my shoulder for whoever it is to come on in and grab a seat while I give this window one last yank. As you can imagine, when I jerked the window nothing happened except I wrenched my back. So I turn around, one hand on my back, one hand on the windowsill and try to see who it is, through the stars that are blazing behind my eyes.

After a minute I see this little girl I've never met before. She's really pale and skinny, with very black, thick hair and she's hiding behind the half-open door, peeking around the edge. I wave for her to come in and have a seat while I lower myself into my chair as gently as possible. As nicely as I can, *through gritted teeth,* I say hello and ask her what's up. For a moment all she does is stare at me. It's like she's doesn't know what to say or even why she came. So I ask again, 'what's up?' and tell her it really is okay, that she can trust me."

Frank sighed, beginning to rethink the wisdom of his idea to come to confession altogether. The priest, apparently sensing Frank's frustration, hurries his narrative.

"So anyway, she's in the chair, really scared, really pale, like she's going to be sick or something and just tight-lipped, not saying anything for maybe five minutes; then all of a sudden, she begins to spill everything and I mean everything. She tells me her name's Amy, that she just transferred to St. Joe's from city, that she's *not* Catholic, she's fourteen, she's never said anything to anyone about anybody before and…and…" His voice caught in his throat pulling Frank's drifting mind back to the vesper screen. For a few awful seconds a strange disquietude crept into the confessional, a silent dread Frank could not identify, but feared altogether. His instincts told him he didn't want to hear what was coming.

"And," the priest continued his voice still working past the subject, "…and she's been having sex with her Dad for just over a year now, and the night before last she found out that she's pregnant, about two months, and she wants me to tell her…wants *me* to promise her that her baby will go to heaven if she has an abortion, and…and that God will forgive *her* for having sex with her Dad! Can you imagine? She's worried about God forgiving *her*? Jesus, Frank! Jesus, Mary and Joseph!"

FIFTEEN

For a moment there seemed to be nothing to say. Frank sat unmoving, wanting to quietly slip out of the booth and at the same time wanting to scream. He did neither. Before long, the priest cleared his throat and spoke softly.

"So you see, Frank," he whispered, "there's nothing you can tell me that'll bother me too much any more. I think I've heard it all."

Frank's mind was reeling. The priest's story was a reflection of the world he was only just now seeing; a place where hopes struggled against the odds, and eventually, tragically, failed. Where in this world was the safe place the scripture talked about? More and more it seemed to Frank that the catechism of the church muddled and mucked around with spiritual things, but left physical realities in less than tender hands. From that point forward it didn't take much time for Frank to clear his plate.

"But that's exactly what I'm talking about, John," he blurted, sitting forward, no longer hesitant. "Look at this world, my God! Every time I turn around there seems to be more shit to deal with! I'm sorry, John, I'm *sorry*, but where's God supposed to be in all this? I mean, I don't see how this…this stuff just happens, and God's like, I mean, when do the prayers and sacraments and all this…this *bullshit* work?"

Catching himself up, Frank clenched his teeth and forced himself to relax a little, letting his breath out slowly, then inhaling quietly. After a few seconds, he finished his confession. "I'm in trouble here, John. I really don't know how to fake it anymore, how to be a good little Catholic and just trust the church, the Holy Father and…and…and I'm here to tell you I don't know if I believe anymore."

Through the screen, Frank could see his friend sitting quietly, stoic as always, even in the face of this betrayal. It was impossible. What could his friend say to bring Frank back from the brink. There was nothing Frank hadn't thought of or hoped for, no words he could truly hear in the place of this sudden vicious despair. His sin, so recently escaped from its secret place, lay before him more vulgar and more repulsive than he could have possibly imagined. Verbalizing his doubts in this way had shamed him more than he could bear, breaking him more swiftly than any judgment he could have invented. What's left for me now, he thought, feeling hot tears run on his face? Where can I go?

John began quietly, clearing his throat and shifting his weight. In all the years he had known John, Frank thought, sensing his friend's discomfort, he hadn't changed. He still needs a few minutes to get used to an idea.

"Doubt has a way of sneaking into life," the priest explained, "from trauma or infidelity. I don't know what it is in your life that's causing this, Frank, probably a lot of things. But I also know that what you're feeling is real, because I've been there."

"*You've* been there?" Frank mocked unintentionally. "When?"

Silence reigned for a few seconds, then quietly, "When you *and* I were much younger, Frank."

Neither man spoke for a time. The level ground that had been achieved was momentarily lost. Frank's pain, his anger was pushing them both beyond casual friendship, past accidental conversation. They were in a place where honesty became the fluid necessity of circulation. Truth was now the only valid currency.

"I know that there always seems to be something in us, in man, that encourages him to be accomplice in the murder of his own faith and hope. I'm seeing that in you, Frank, right now."

"So what do I do?" Frank asked directly.

"I don't know," the priest responded.

"You don't know," Frank countered, hopelessness filling his throat. "You're supposed to know, John, isn't that your job? Christ! Doesn't any of this mean anything any more? C'mon, *priest*, help me here!"

"The Bible says when you've done all you can do to stand, that *you* should stand," John responded, his disquietude evident. "I'm really not sure what that means. I know I probably should, I'm sorry.

For a moment there was only their breathing between them. The quick anger that had pounded behind Frank's eyes was back, irritating him again. This was not what he had hoped for. Then the priest spoke again.

"Jesus said the Kingdom of God is like a treasure in a field. The wise man is the one who sells everything he has to go buy the field. See Frank, Jesus was saying that the only way man would go for the Kingdom of God is if it's hidden. If it were obvious, we'd ignore it. Do you understand?"

"No, I don't," Frank said.

"Okay," the priest continued. "Scientists tell us we're all about 98 percent water and that if we are going to stay alive we need a constant supply of water into our bodies. But when water falls from the sky we don't even notice it, because it's natural. But Frank, it's also a *miracle*! The miracle of *sustained* life! Do you understand?

"John, I don't see the point…"

"We want God to be obvious. We want Him to show Himself in the midst of the horrors of this world—but when He is obvious, *like the rain,* we say it's only natural. And likewise, when He's not so obvious, we refuse to take the chance, to sell everything we have and buy the field.

"We all hope in God, Frank, but do we all really want Him? Do you see what I'm saying? From where we're sitting now, if there is a God, He might help us, but He also might not. Surely you see that's the way it has to be. We can't just expect that God's going to do something good for us just because He's God. Because if He *really is* God, He's not likely to be so controllable."

"Then why do we pray, huh? Why do we believe, hope? Teresa lost Rachel when she was *full-term!* And I'm praying like some *asshole,* pushing my puny belief through the roof of my cab hoping, *begging* some invisible hand to come down and change all this shit into something good! So you tell me, *priest,* tell me why we ask God for *impossible things?*"

"Because if He can make the rain, Frank, He can raise the dead."

"*Yeah, then why doesn't He?*"

The priest could feel his friend's desperation, his helplessness, his blind anger and inconsolable grief. After a moment he responded.

"Again, Frank, I don't know, I'm sorry. But my experience tells me that all the talk in the world won't fix this for you, Frank. I can give you absolution, can pray for you, *and I will*; but what you're dealing with goes way beyond some glib answer from divinity school. And it has nothing to do with hanging in there, with tenacity and trying harder. It's a gift from God.

"You see, Frank, the problem here is that you didn't come looking for the *Guidepost*® platitude of the week. You actually need answers. And the answers come from Him, not me. God's the only one that can help you, my friend."

This is comic, Frank thought. If a priest didn't know—couldn't know, then who could? All of a sudden, the profound anger which had pressed him for the last few weeks gave way and pain rushed out of him, splashing the distance between he and his friend, flooding the tiny chamber, overwhelming him. Gasping, he covered his face with his hands and collapsed onto the padded kneeler laying his head against the worn velvet rail.

"*Oh, God,*" he rasped, "*I'm lost...I'm lost and I'm so sorry! Help me, save me! I've sinned...against you, against me...I should love you...I should love...*" Frank choked again, trying to clear his throat. "*Jesus...God, have mercy on me; have mercy on me!*"

John, down from his bench now, and on his knees, pressed his hands and face against the screen, "And the Lamb in the center of the throne shall be their shepherd, and shall guide them to springs of the water of life; and He shall wipe away every tear from their eyes." The priest's words whispered through the partition, "*He will help you, my brother. He will save you to the uttermost and forgive. Unto you the peace and comfort of His love is given. This is your heritage: peace, joy, healings, miracles. Thrust into your hands is the Kingdom of Heaven!*"

Reaching trembling fingers through the lattice, the priest gently touched Frank's hair, "*Can a woman forget her nursing child or have no compassion on the son of her womb? Yes, even these may forget, but I will never forget you! Behold, I have inscribed you on the palms of My hands!*"

Raising his free hand John blessed his friend, his brother, covering for him the bane of guilt under the cloak of his own love.

"*The Father of mercies has reconciled us, you and me, Frank, to Himself. And He did it through the death of His own precious Son. He sent His Holy Spirit among us for the forgiveness of our sins, not just somebody else's!*

"*Frank, may God grant you pardon and peace, not just through His Church, but by His own hand.*"

Kneeling as he was, his face and right hand against the partition, his other hand raised in blessing, he observed the bowed head before him and saw once again the dark curls of a twelve-year-old buddy, an altar boy like he had been, who loved the sound of church bells more than Fats Domino and the taste of communion wafers more than anything.

The priest cleared his throat, deliberately tracing the sign of the cross as he spoke softly, gently in the language of their childhood.

"*Ego te absolvo ab imnibus censuris, et peccatis, in nomine Patris, et Filii, et Spiritus Sancti. Amen*"

"Go in peace, Frank, your sins are forgiven."

SIXTEEN

"Help me, help me!"

"Let's go people. Move your ass, Quentin!"

"She's coughing blood, she can hardly breath, she…"

"We've got her, mister. Jana! Take her feet…*let go of her, mister!*"

"She's really hurt, she's….

"*Get out of the way, Jesus!*"

"You her father?"

"No, I was just driving home and…"

"All right, easy now, easy…"

"*Get him out of here!*"

"Move, move…"

"*We need help in here! Steve?*"

"I'm on it!"

"Okay, ready? Move her on three…One, two, three."

"Let's get her clothes off, come on."

"Looks like a party dress, probably a birthday or something…"

"Oh that's a *lovely* thought…"

"*Damn!*"

"What's your name?"

"Frank, Frank Teska."

"You see the accident, Frank?

"No, I came just after, I think the parents are dead, I…"

"Let's go folks…"

"You *think* the parents are dead? Is there anyone who knows for sure? Do we have confirmation?"

"I couldn't stay, she was hurt, I…"

"Did anybody see the accident? Where are the parents? Anyone see this…"

"Cops just got here, Phil, says there wasn't much left of the family."

"Some party, eh?"

"Yeah, happy birthday."

"*Goddammit!*"

"Call Russell down here, stat! Jeez, what a mess!"

"Mister, was she moving around, did she speak to you…"

"She said her stomach was hurting, she vomited blood on me…"

"Did you pull her out of the car or did she get out herself?"

"She was trying to get out, crawling, but the car was really torn up…"

"Belly's distended, she's probably bleeding. Okay, people let's not panic!"

"*Somebody call Russell?*"

"Yeah, we called him—man, did he sound pissed! No tellin' what he was doing."

"I don't care if he was smokin' cigars with Castro, he's gotta be here."

"Said he'd be here in 15…"

"Is she going to live? Is she going to live?"

"*Jana, move that guy out of here!*"

"Start an I-V of Ringer's, draw some blood and get her on a monitor…"

"Jesus, where's all this blood coming from?"

"Talk to me! Is all this coming from her?"

"*Not* from her—minor lacerations to the face, six inch abrasion on her right arm…"

"Contusions manifesting on her pelvis, thighs, hips, abdomen—gotta be seat belt trauma."

"Nothing on the head, no puncture wounds, no major lacerations, no other signs of trauma."

"Has anybody seen her move?

"Yes, I did. Positive reflexes, she was jerking around pretty good—positive Babinsky"

"Shallow respiration, she might be obstructed."

"Where do you want me, Phil?"

"Intubation."

"No apparent head trauma, pupils are equal and reactive."

"She's taching at 130, systolic's 90…"

"Do we have an airway yet?"

"No problem, I'm in. She's got good breath sounds…pulse ox, 95 percent…"

"Belly's distended, Phil…"

"Portable X-ray stat! I'm going to go ahead and lavage her belly…

"*Jesus…*"

"Come on…peritoneal lavage!"

"Lavage kit…"

"I'm cutting…catheter and syringe…"

"Has anyone gotten any blood?"

"Just got a line in now, doctor, pushing plasma."

"Systolic 84, taching at 140."

"OK, fine. I want CBC, lytes, type and cross, PT, PTT…*shit!* I've just got 20cc right here, she's bleeding out. Where's x-ray? Where the hell's Russell?"

"Just talked to him, he's less than 10 minutes out. X-ray's coming in."

"She's not going to last 10 minutes. Let's get another line going and call the lab, get some blood down here *right* now!"

"Blood pressures still dropping, doctor. Systolic at 70."

"Second line's in…"

"Are those IV's wide open?"

Yes, doctor."

"Notify the OR, get a team ready for Dr. Russell, possible laparotomy."

"Yes, doctor."

"Systolic 60, heart rate 150, tachycardia…"

"Man this thing's not going down like this, *goddammit!* Not on my shift, *not on my shift!*"

"Come on sweetheart, *come on.*"

"Surgery's ready when you are, doctor."

"There she goes, pressures off the machine."

"Get me a manual pressure."

"BP's 40 palp, she's crashing! Heart rate's…."

"*Damn, damn, dam…come on folks, I need ideas, talk to me…*"

"Heart rate's dropping, doctor…"

""*Shit!* Not tonight, not tonight."

"Pulse is thready, doctor."

"We're losing her…"

"She's asystole!"

"OK, flatline. Let's start CPR!"

"Somebody get on her chest."

"Give me an amp of Atropine and an amp of Epi."

"Can anyone feel a pulse?"

"Nothing, doctor."

"Stay on her chest. Where's the hell's Russell?"

"I'm right here, Phil. What do we have?"

"Six-year old female, high impact MVA, unconscious at presentation, hypotensive, tachycardic—*stay on those compressions, goddammit!*

"Take a breath, Phil."

"No evident chest or spinal cord injury, positive belly lavage, blood pressure cratered, two lines open, she's been CPR for two, almost three minutes…"

"Have you called Care Flight?"

"No, I called you!"

"X-rays?"

"Not yet."

"Hmmm...

"...two, three, four, five, *breath!* One, two, three..."

"Probably a lacerated liver. Looks pretty bad, Phil."

"Doctor, surgery's on the phone..."

"...four, *breath!* One, two..."

"Who's cellphone is that?"

"Doctor, what do I tell surgery?"

"Pulse?"

"No, tell him I can't make it Saturday night, maybe Tuesday but I'll call..."

"It's thready, pressure's 35 palp..."

"Give me another amp of Epi, *Jesus, Quentin, watch what the fuck you're doing!*"

"...*breath!* One..."

"Time?"

"Seven minutes, doctor."

"She's not going to make it, Phil. Give her another minute or so and then call it, we can't go too far with this thing."

"Phil?"

"Continue chest compression. Do we have a pulse at all?"

"No pulse."

"*Jana, kill that damn alarm!*"

"Should I cancel the OR, doctor?"

"*No...*"

"Yes nurse, cancel the OR."

"Right away, doctor Russell."

"*Dr. Russell, we need to go in, we need*"

"One, two, three..."

"Jana, you can let the OR go."

"Yes, Doctor Russell."

"Are we getting anything?"

"Nothing, doctor, she's not responding."

"*Come on, sweetheart, come on...*"

"Do you want the paddles, doctor?"

"That won't be necessary, nurse."

"*Dammit, come on!*"

"Giver her another second here…"
"No pulse, doctor. She's flatlined now for about 3 minutes plus…"
"Does anybody mind if we call it?"
"Paddles, charge to 110…"
"Cancel that. Step out, Phil. Quentin, you can stop compressions."
"Jesus!"
"Jesus is right…"
"Call it?"
"Time of death, 03:43 a.m."
"Dammit!"
"Where's the next of kin, who brought her in?"
"He did."
"Who?"
"Him—over there in the corner."
"Great."

SEVENTEEN

Wiping his eyes with his sleeve, Frank shook himself and stood. She was so small, he thought, looking at the excess sheet draping her tiny form, he could barely discern her presence on the table. As he stood in the cubical, his mind clouded for so long began to clear and a sigh escaped his lips. There was still blood on his hands, he thought, he needed to wash.

To his left, situated against the wall was a scrub sink. Taking the two steps over he pulled the hot and cold wings forward and let the water run hard into the basin. He liked that sound, he noticed, it was somehow very soothing at that moment. Funny, he thought, that's the first time he ever noticed.

Placing his hands under the water, he allowed the warm torrent to tear the clotted blood from his skin and swirl it down the drain. The tiny, whirling storm in the basin stayed in his eyes. The fury, he thought, was dead and gone. The storm had at last faded to a whisper and the whisper had died.

Looking up from the sink, he caught his reflection in the metal towel dispenser. Like a funhouse mirror the surface tore his image apart, stretching and scattering the familiar patterns into fantasy shapes. At the same moment beyond his distorted image he noticed the rest of the room peering around his shoulders, quiet and softened by the metal, a mass of unintelligible contours and muddled splashes of color and shadow, a lifeless stranger with cold hands.

For a second he stared numbly at the image, contemplating the comfortable warmth of the water rushing upon his skin and the stillness of the room. Then, without warning, in the center of the cluttered image two familiar objects began to emerge, plaintive and tender in a sea of white, tragically small and defenseless. Turning sadly, he looked upon Sarah's feet protruding from the sheet and he walked away from the sink leaving the water to run.

Her feet were both exceptional he observed, cut from alabaster stems, clean and luminous and perfect. One foot was turned slightly on its side as if frozen in a moment of perfect repose; cast, he thought in the casual ambivalence of sleep. Reaching one hand out he tentatively touched their dry surfaces feeling nothing but stillness and indifference. Then he embraced them, letting the agony go.

His hands, wet from the sink, bathed the gentle slope of her instep as his lips stammered incoherent pleas. His wet hands brushed the pallid complexion of her skin, brightening the blood that clung to them. In large slow drops her blood, now like Madeira, slid from the soles of her feet to the tile floor, wine from the press.

"*Oh, God, Jesus God,*" he shouted into his hands, "*please, God, please spare her…save her, God. This should not happen; not this, not to this little girl. God, no!*

Outside, his muffled words spread from the curtained room and stumbled down the quiet hallway, falling into the nurses' station. Heads lifted momentarily, eyebrows raised. Questioning looks went from the staff to the charge nurse to the resident at his chart. As the muffled pleas continued nurses and aids renewed their scribbling and the incessant clicking of their keyboards. The charge nurse shook her head and took another drink from her diet Coke, leaning nearer the doctor with a conspiratorial grimace. The young resident flashed irritation and excused himself. He had yet to change his bloody scrubs and he needed some sleep.

"*Help her, God! Save her, save her!*"

He did not beg or plead; he hurled his prayers at heaven. They were demands, rightful claims upon a power that he knew was available, an intervention that must come.

"*No, this cannot stand!*" There were no landmarks near, no friendly gates or warmth of kinship there. He was alone and his pockets were empty. "*No, no, no! This cannot stand, will not stand!*" Water dripped from his hands onto her feet and his nose began to run.

Death had stolen her, he choked, right from the palms of his hands. There had not even been much of a struggle. It was just an ebbing, a surrender too simple and passive for his understanding. She vanished quietly from the room, ghosting into the ether. Where was God? He strangled. Where was the miracle?

"*Send the rain, God! Send the rain!*" In his mind, he saw the faces of his children, his wife, his father, his priest and they were all changed. The passion in his breast was enraged and in that split second, the last vestiges of doubt within him were incinerated and his faith released. Strangely, explosively, in a voice strangled with emotion, guttural, almost incoherent in its intensity, he called out the child by name.

And at that very moment, beyond his streaming eyes and trembling hands, past the storm in his emotion, he heard the words that would stay with him forever.

"Mister," she asked weakly from the bed. "Are you alright?"

And Frank, wiping his face with his hands looked up into the girl's confused expression…astonished.

AFTERWORD

Beginning this work was easy, concluding it was not. How does one put into a book the various conditions of man's heart and soul as he passes from this earthly life to what lies beyond? How can words on a page frame the moment between mortality and immortality, between care and past care? It is more daunting because I, as an observer, am trapped in the very eventuality that I am examining. No objectivity here. And yet, from my vantage point the passing away of this life holds an enduring fascination. Since it is inevitable that I one day see beyond the farthest horizon, I strain my eyes now to gain even a glimpse of that, as yet, *undiscovered country*.

In addition, most of us pass from this life to the next crabbing about injustice, ignoble in our self-pity, artists with paint, brush and palette knife before an empty canvas, content to natter about the gas bill instead of capturing sunsets. Hopefully, after experiencing this work, we will see life's terminus in such a way that for the few short years we have left on this planet we will be reminded to be part of the dance.

This last tale develops a fiction through which the reader sees a man of common experience plunged into a vortex of terrifying circumstances with an unbearable conclusion. Frank, my Taximan, is propelled along a perilous track to spiritual intimacy with God, staggering as the Word penetrates his parochial understanding, finally crushed with the power of divine revelation and miraculous intervention. Frank is like *everyman* when encountering God authentically after experiencing the religious fumbling of so-called spiritual men. Like all of us, he is driven forward not by the hope of eventual reward but by the assurance of immediate and terrible consequences. And when confronted with a *real* God he is understandably shocked, having never met him before.

Frank is forced against his will to see his personal bankruptcy when presented with a situation in which all of his pity and all of his effort and all of his anger are useless to effect change. Each of us has encountered or will encounter these moments though perhaps not as horrifically as the Taximan. And each of us, in turn, have made or will make decisions that embrace our weakness, hear the voice of God and either retreat into self-pity and excuses, or act. Life is funny that way, an intricately designed machine through which God mangles our self-reliance and establishes His Kingdom, whether we're a part of it or not.

Another idea I wanted to examine in this last piece was the distinction between our strident wishes for the resurrection of our own bodies *(while putting off our suffering)* and the true resurrection from the dead promised in Scripture. After much prayer and contemplation, the conclusion that I reached was a strange and unexpected mixture of both.

Resurrection, it turns out, *is* both. Biblical resurrection is not the resurrection *from* the body, but resurrection *of* the body. The former idea is that of Aristotelian origin, whose thesis is one in which perfection is a state obtained when all flesh or its attributes are finally put off and we are, in the end, nothing but spirit. The Bible, Old and New Testaments, describe another resurrection. What is clearly evident by the testimony of Scripture is that God created the physical world and pronounced it good. And as Christ remarked, upon his appearance to the disciples having already risen from the dead, "Touch me, handle me; I am not spirit as you suppose, but flesh."

We must embrace our flesh but in the manner of Christ Jesus. We are the vessels of God, His habitation, and we must cherish this state, looking forward to its fullness and all the possibilities that that implies.

If Christ be flesh, oh God, then make me flesh!

Finally, any observations that I have made through this collection concerning death are more than just recognition of the surface tension that exists upon a fluid barrier between two lives. While it was important to recognize the intersection of the temporal and eternal spheres that death represents—the portal of eternity if you will—it was likewise important for me to show the unexpected form that this most predictable event often takes. No matter how prepared we think we are, death always seems to surprise.

"The day which we fear as our last is but the birthday of eternity."

—*Seneca*

978-0-595-36736-8
0-595-36736-4

Printed in the United States
42731LVS00004B/284